THE HOUSE

Young Adult Titles Also by Christina Lauren

Sublime

THE HOUSE

christina lauren

SIMON & SCHUSTER BFYR

NEW YORK LONDON TORONTO SYDNEY NEW DELHI

SIMON & SCHUSTER BFYR

An imprint of Simon & Schuster Children's Publishing Division
1230 Avenue of the Americas, New York, New York 10020

SIMON & SCHUSTER BFYR is a trademark of Simon & Schuster, Inc.
For information about special discounts for bulk purchases,
please contact Simon & Schuster Special Sales at 1-866-506-1949
or business@simonandschuster.com.
The Simon & Schuster Speakers Bureau can bring authors to your live event.
For more information or to book an event, contact the Simon & Schuster Speakers Bureau at 1-866-248-3049 or visit our website at www.simonspeakers.com.
Also available in a SIMON & SCHUSTER BFYR paperback edition
Jacket design by Lizzy Bromley
Interior design by Hilary Zarycky
The text for this book is set in Granjon.
Manufactured in the United States of America
2 4 6 8 10 9 7 5 3 1
Library of Congress Cataloging-in-Publication Data
Lauren, Christina.
The House / Christina Lauren. — 1st edition.
pages cm
Summary: Told in their separate voices, Gavin, a loner outcast, and Delilah, back in small-town Kansas after years at a Massachusetts boarding school, reconnect their senior year, but as their relationship deepens, it is clear that the eerie house Gavin dwells in will do anything to keep the two apart.
ISBN 978-1-4814-1371-8 (hardcover) — ISBN 978-1-4814-1372-5 (paperback) — ISBN 978-1-4814-1373-2 (eBook)
[1. Supernatural—Fiction. 2. Haunted houses—Fiction. 3. Dating (Social customs)—Fiction. 4. High schools—Fiction. 5. Schools—Fiction. 6. Kansas—Fiction. 7. Horror stories.] I. Title.
PZ7.L372745Bre 2015
[Fic]—dc23   2014037641

FIRST EDITION

For Erin, who loves the scary and the swoon

ACKNOWLEDGMENTS

We've written fifteen books together. FIFTEEN. Of these books, thirteen are adult romance; one is still up in the air, and though Young Adult was our first love, this book you're holding right now—*The House*—is only our second book for teens. It's been a story in our hearts for nearly four years now, and we hope it's found a home in yours as well.

Publishing is a strange and mysterious world where creativity meets practicality; books need to be categorized and labeled and shelved correctly (for what it's worth, if there's a Kissing Books shelf, we'd like to be put on that, please). We are endlessly lucky to be surrounded by people who encourage us to write the stories in our heads, whatever they may be.

First on that list is the ninja agent. But Holly Root isn't just an agent; she's a magician, a sage, a closet piglet, and a champion. Thank you for a thousand things, Holly, but most frequently for agreeing that another kissing scene is *always* a good idea, and for showing us that it's possible to juggle *all the things* and still kick ass at every single one of them.

Thank you to our amazing editor, Zareen Jaffery. Romance + monster houses = a rare combination. It was a blast to be able to tackle this, and your editorial touch brought it to life.

Simon & Schuster is the perfect home for us, and everyone there deserves a corner office, two recesses a day, and thirty-seven high fives. Thanks to Justin Chanda, Katy Hershberger, Chrissy Noh, Julia Maguire, and Mekisha Telfer. A world of love to Lizzy Bromley for giving us the most beautiful covers.

Erin Billings Service, thank you for your honesty, for reading every word we write, and for your enthusiasm when you have to read those same words over and over and over again. Thank you for also not blocking our e-mail. *heartkite*

Thanks to Lauren Suero for being the most awesome—and best dressed—assistant ever. Heather Carrier, we would be nothing but badly drawn stick figures and Comic Sans without you. Don't ever leave us.

To have writers you adore and respect read your words and love them means the world to us, so thank you to Ransom Riggs and Alexandra Bracken—Ransom is spoken for (and we adore his wife), but we're definitely going to marry Alex someday. It's a total deal; instead of one ring you get two. That's just math, Alex. Ransom, you get cake. And hugs. And typos in our e-mails because you left us with the giddy shakes.

We couldn't write acknowledgments to any YA book without thanking Nathan Bransford and Tahereh Mafi. Along the way you've both given us advice, support, and encouragement when we needed it. You're real, and positive, and wise—we owe so much of what we have to what you've been willing to share.

Our families put up with a lot of mumbling-in-slippers, crazy travel schedules, overflowing bookshelves, and oh-right-it's-dinner-times. Thank you for loving us anyway. We'll try to do better for the next few books, but it's probably best to not hold your breath.

We still remember when we would have sold our souls to write books for a living, and so we've saved the most important for last: Thank you to our readers. Writing these stories for you is a dream. Thank you for your trust and your endless enthusiasm, and for following us when we wanted to stretch our legs and do something a little different. We hope we make you proud.

Lo, I hope we're still ridiculous and screaming from the front row of concerts we're too old for even when we're eighty. Thank you for being my left quote.

C, I love you so much I'd sell my soul in any direction for you.

CHAPTER ONE

HER

PLACES WITH BOYS ALWAYS SEEM SO DIRTY.
As soon as Delilah had the thought, she hated
herself for it because it was exactly what her mother
would think. Girls were just as dirty after all, with thick,
sticky makeup and every flavor of perfume clouding the
locker rooms. The public high school seemed to have a dim
film layered over the lockers and floor, walls and windows. It
was the first day back after the winter, so Delilah assumed that
everything had been cleaned vigorously over the break, but
maybe the fog of girl and boy hormones mixing together had
permanently dulled every surface.

All around, students pressed past her and lockers
slammed near her head, and she struggled to appear unaf-
fected by the public-school chaos. Delilah looked down to
the piece of paper clutched in her hand. Before she'd even
been dressed and fed this morning, her mother had already
begun highlighting all of the important information for her:

locker number, locker combination, class schedule, teacher names.

"I should have printed a map for you," Belinda Blue had said as the highlighter squeaked across the page. Delilah had looked away to the neat rows on the carpet left by the vacuum cleaner, had waved politely to her father as he'd walked into the kitchen wearing his standard outfit of tan pants, a short-sleeved white collar shirt, and a red tie. Even though he wasn't going to work and maybe didn't even have a job interview today, she couldn't fault him for dressing the part. She, too, was still more comfortable in clothes that resembled her private-school uniform than she was with having this new freedom to wear whatever she wanted.

"Mom, it's only two main buildings. I can handle it. Saint Ben's had seven."

Morton City High was smaller than Saint Benedict's Academy in pretty much every way possible, from the size of the classrooms and number of buildings, to the minds of the student body. Whereas—perhaps unexpectedly—imagination had been embraced and nurtured in her beautiful Catholic school, there had always been a single way of thinking in her small Kansas hometown, a tendency to embrace normal and disregard anything else in hopes that it might simply go away.

It was what had happened to Delilah six years ago, after all. Her parents had tolerated her strangeness with shared looks of exasperation and long-suffering sighs, but then had shipped her off to Massachusetts as soon as an excuse presented itself.

"Still, you're used to calm. This school is so big and *loud*."

Delilah smiled. When her mother said "loud" she really meant "full of boys." "I'm pretty sure I'll make it out alive."

Her mother had given her the look Delilah had seen countless times over winter break—the look that said, *I'm sorry you can't finish your senior year in a fancy school. Please don't tell anyone your father lost his job and your nonna's money is all tied up in her nursing care.*

The look also said, *Be careful of the boys. They have* thoughts.

Delilah had thoughts too. She had a lot of them, about boys and their arms and smiles and how their throats looked when they swallowed. She had infrequent contact with these things, having been sequestered away for the past several years at an all-girls boarding school, but she certainly had *thoughts* about them. Unfortunately, the schedule in her hand didn't mention a thing about boys, and instead read: English, Phys Ed, Biology, Organic Chemistry, World Studies, AP French, AP Calculus.

She felt her enthusiasm wilt a little before the day had even started. Who wants to have PE so early in the day? She'd be a sweaty mop and would never factor into any *thoughts* anyway.

Delilah successfully negotiated her locker combination, stowed some books, and headed to English. The only empty seat in the room—Room 104, Mr. Harrington, highlighted in yellow, *thank you, Mother*—was of course in the middle, up front. Delilah was a bull's-eye for the teacher and for the fellow students. But even if she sat in the back of the room, it wouldn't have made a difference: She was a target anyway.

Delilah Blue was back from the fancy East Coast boarding school.

Delilah Blue had come home to go slumming.

Although she spent some of each summer back in Morton, being at school here was different. Delilah had forgotten how many teenagers could come out of the woodwork, and all around her they were yelling, throwing notes, whispering across aisles. Was this how they always behaved while waiting for the teacher? *When your time is yours, use it to create something,* Father John had always told them. *A picture, some words, anything. Don't rot your brain with gossip.*

Having seen only her best friend, Dhaval, with any sort of regularity—and maybe a handful of her classmates around town during breaks—Delilah's memories were an old stack of pictures of her eleven-year-old peers. She struggled to place the faces she remembered from six years ago with the reality of the faces now.

Rebecca Lewis, her best friend from kindergarten. Kelsey Stiles, her archnemesis in third grade. Both were looking at Delilah as if she'd kicked a puppy before class. Rebecca probably glared at her because Delilah had left Morton so successfully. Kelsey probably glared at Delilah for having the gall to come back.

Not everyone had been hostile when they recognized

Delilah; some girls had greeted her in front of the school with hugs and high-pitched welcomes, and Delilah knew that she had a completely blank slate there. She could be anyone she wanted to be. She didn't have to be the girl whose nervous parents sent her away when she was only eleven for getting into a fistfight defending her unrequited first crush.

Delilah took her seat next to Tanner Jones, the only person to ever have beaten her at tetherball in sixth grade, her last year of public school.

"Hi, Delilah," he said, eyes on her legs and then chest and then mouth. Six years ago he'd been looking at her pigtails and skinned knees.

She smiled to hide her surprise. Delilah hadn't expected the first boy to speak to her to also have *thoughts*. "Hi, Tanner."

"I heard you had to move back because your dad lost his job at the plant."

She kept her smile and stayed quiet, thinking of her mother's innocent-at-best, naive-at-worst hope that people would assume Delilah came home for a single semester for educational purposes, and not because Nonna's well of money had dried up. Clearly the town knew better.

Your business is only yours until you share it, Father John had always told them.

Just as Mr. Harrington was closing the classroom door, a boy slipped in, mumbling an apology and staring with determination at the floor.

Delilah's breath grew trapped in her throat, and the old protective fire flickered to life between her ribs.

He was the same, but not. His shirt was black, jeans were black, and shaggy black hair fell into his eyes. He was so tall he must have been pulled like taffy. When he looked up at Delilah as he passed, the same eyes she remembered from all those years ago—dark and stormy and shadowed with bluish circles—seemed to flicker to life for a moment.

Just long enough for her to lose her breath.

He looked like he knew every one of her secrets. Who would have guessed that after six years Gavin Timothy would still seem so perfectly dangerous?

Apparently, Delilah was still smitten.

CHAPTER TWO

HIM

I T WASN'T UNHEARD OF FOR GIRLS TO WATCH HIM, but usually it meant one of two things. Either they were terrified that Gavin might pull a knife from his shoe (which had never happened), or they were building up the courage to ask him out, with hopes of bringing him home to terrify their parents into buying them a car (which had happened twice).

Delilah Blue was back in Morton and was watching Gavin in a singularly different way. She looked like a wolf stalking a rabbit.

He spun a pencil on his notebook and blinked up, looking right into her eyes and causing her to whip around in her seat, sitting ramrod straight. Her caramel hair was braided and secured tightly with a red elastic band, swinging into position at the middle of her back just below her shoulder blades. Her foot tapped impatiently under her desk. For the remainder of class, she was obviously attentive, maybe overly so. But what she was attending to was definitely not at the front of the room. If she were a cat, she would have her ears turned back, facing *him*. Gavin was sure of it.

He could still remember the way she'd looked the last time he'd seen her: scraped knuckles, bloody nose, and an expression of protectiveness so feral it made his stomach twist. He'd never even had a chance to say thank you.

The end-of-period bell rang, and Delilah jumped, looking frantically for the source. Did they not have bells at her fancy private school? Because yes, Gavin knew enough about Delilah to know exactly where she'd been. But why she was back was an entirely different question.

Just as she appeared to spot the bell, perched above the whiteboard, the door flew open and Dhaval Reddy swept into the room, pulling her up and wrapping his arms around her.

"My girl is back!" Dhaval sang loudly to no one in particular. As everyone gathered their things, Gavin felt the room settle: Delilah's return had been approved by the in crowd.

Gavin collected his books and papers and slipped past her, but not before he felt her hand reach out and touch his, or before he saw the tiny drawing on her notebook: a dagger dripping blood.

CHAPTER THREE

HER

HEEDING FATHER JOHN'S ADVICE, DELILAH always understood that the best way to keep a secret was simply to not tell anyone. And over the years, she had accumulated hundreds of secrets. Like the time Nonna took her to Saks in Manhattan and Delilah walked in on two people having sex in the bathroom. Or the time she snuck Joshua Barker into her dorm room and kissed him for ten minutes before making him slink back out across the dark, dewy lawn.

Those were secrets she planned to eventually share as currency, in the girlfriend version of "I'll show you mine if you show me yours." But there were other secrets too—ones she might never share because she knew they made her weird. Secrets like her strange appreciation of gore: depictions of fifteenth-century torture devices, paintings of people dying at the hand of swords or arrows. The idea of reanimation, zombies, exorcism. Books on the Black Plague. It wasn't that she particularly treasured the idea of dying, or of other people dying; it was the visceral reaction to the creepy, the spectacularly scary, the otherworldliness of horror. Delilah loved the catch of breath when she was afraid, the feel of goose bumps dancing up her arms.

Back at Saint Ben's, she used to wander the cold stone hallways of the Fine Arts Building at night, barefoot, without a flashlight. With every light extinguished, the halls would be pitch-black, stones heavy and silent. Not even a draft could slip in and ruffle the heavy drapes or rattle a painting on the wall.

Delilah knew every turn by heart. Everything was perfectly still, empty but for the girl slipping between shadows, looking for a sign that things happened in the school after dark. Searching for some long-forgotten history that would come alive only when the students were all safely tucked in their beds.

She'd been caught once, two weeks before she was jerked back home for good. Father John had found her tiptoeing down the hall between Sister Judith's ceramics classroom and the auditorium. In that small stretch was an old jeweled chest from the eighteenth century, an elaborate work of art and wealth that simply sat, so trusting, in the middle of an ordinary hallway. The chest was big enough to hold a small child or, Delilah preferred, a very patient hellhound.

"Hunting for ghosts?" Father John had asked from behind her, making Delilah jump.

Once her heartbeat slowed, she admitted, "Yes, sir."

She'd expected a lecture, maybe one of his bits of wisdom. But instead he'd smiled knowingly at her, nodded, and said simply, "Back to your room, then."

Her parents had no idea of these fascinations; Delilah had worked hard to keep this side hidden. It hadn't been that hard, living more than a thousand miles away for the past six years, and also given who her parents were: Her mother had cardigans in every shade of pastel and had worn the same brand of sensible penny loafers for as long as Delilah could remember. Her mother's books all had bare, muscled chests on the covers, and her hobby was collecting tiny ceramic animals, which were a form of creepy that Delilah had never really appreciated.

Her father, before he lost his job, had been a workaholic, and when he was home he was generally planted in front of the television, where he would be grousing about something or another. To Delilah, he was an inanimate object in a dad suit: Since she'd been home, Delilah had the sense that she wouldn't have known her father better even if she'd lived at home these past six years.

Though Delilah had longed for a sibling, none had ever appeared, and she'd had to settle for her partner-in-single-childom, Dhaval Reddy, whose parents were as obsessive and attentive as her own were disinterested. But while Dhaval's rebellion would turn out to be his loud and exuberant manner in a gently spiritual household, Delilah's quirky obsession would always remain silent: She had hundreds and hundreds of drawings of severed heads, fists curled cruelly around still-beating hearts, and dark, endless tunnels squirreled away beneath the loose floorboard in her closet.

It was the same dark fascination that drew her to Gavin Timothy.

Dhaval was with her when the obsession started. They were nine and had been at the theater watching *Wallace and Gromit: The Curse of the Were-Rabbit*. Delilah had insisted they sneak into *Corpse Bride* after and had made him sit through two consecutive shows. Her life in the tiny square mile of Morton felt small and easy, oppressively ordinary. The idea that another world like this could exist—one that wasn't beige or boring or *safe*—was like a siren song.

The next day at school was the first time Delilah really noticed Gavin. He was tall and hunched, with hair so dark and shaggy it would have covered his entire face if Miss Claremont hadn't made him at least tuck it behind his ears. His eyes even then were ringed with darkness below and long black lashes above. He had no blush to his cheeks, but bloodred lips and arms so long and skinny they seemed to be made from string.

Gavin had always been her classmate, but she'd never really noticed him before that day. For as much as he looked *other*—like he'd stepped straight out of the movie from the day before—he'd mastered the ability to vanish in a crowd.

She was sent away right at the strange, obsessive peak of her fascination—after she'd watched him for two years, after she'd decided to ask him to the first girl-boy dance at school. But at recess, instead of finding him reading under a tree like usual, she'd found him limply ricocheting between two bullies on the playground. Delilah had kicked Ethan Pinorelli in the shin, punched James Towne in the jaw, received a reflexive shove to the face, and promptly been expelled.

Horrified, her parents had sent her to live and attend private school near Delilah's eccentric grandmother. But far from the strict Catholic school Delilah's parents had hoped for, Saint Ben's was the key that had unlocked Delilah's imagination.

The distance might have also muted her crush over the years, but Delilah found she could hardly stop watching Gavin now.

"What are you staring at?" Dhaval asked, nudging her shoulder and bringing her out of her thoughts.

She swallowed a bite of apple and lifted her chin toward where now-teenage Gavin sat beneath a tree, reading alone.

Dhaval snorted. "You've been locked up too long in the school full of girls if you think that's the best you can do."

Shaking her head, Delilah insisted, "No, *look* at him."

"I'm looking."

"He's so tall now . . . and *long*." Gavin had always been that way, long and gangly with joints that seemed to be too big for the parts they connected. Now his skyscraper legs fit his huge feet, and his arms were a perfect match for the torso that kept going and going. Gavin was all grown up, and looking like *he* had a million secrets: He was Delilah's form of kryptonite.

Beside her, Dhaval hummed in neutral agreement.

"And he's not that skinny anymore," she added. "He's actually kind of muscular." Even Delilah heard the way her voice shaped that word—"muscular"—like it was a little dirty.

"If you say so."

"And . . ." Delilah trailed off. What could she say? *I've been sort of obsessively fascinated with him since we were nine, and I'm shocked to find out he's even better than I expected?*

"Didn't you slip a note in his locker?" Dhaval asked. "Before you were shipped off to Saint Ben's?"

Delilah nodded, laughing. Apparently, her fascination with Gavin Timothy wasn't as secret as she'd thought.

"What did it say again?" he asked.

"It said, 'I don't want you to hide. I like you.'"

Beside her, Dhaval burst into laughter. "That's so cheesy, Dee. Also, it's still true."

She chewed her fingernail, unable to look away from the shadow of a boy beneath a tree. "I wonder if he ever got it."

"He did," Dhaval said through a bite of sandwich. "Then someone—I don't remember who—took it from him and made a big deal out of it."

"What do you mean, 'made a big deal out of it'?"

Dhaval waved his hand dismissively. "Like, read it in

front of a group of kids on the playground, made kissy noises, whatever."

"What did Gavin do?"

"I think he laughed along for a minute and then asked for the note back."

Delilah smiled a little. Gavin wanted the note, at least. Sadly, it might be the most romantic thing that had ever happened to her and she was only hearing about it six years later.

She had a thousand questions about life in Morton since she'd left for boarding school. One day Delilah was a sixth grader at Morton Middle School. The next afternoon she was on a plane to Massachusetts. Coming back for a week here, two weeks there was never enough time for her to get back into the rhythm of the small town. Just when she was catching up, it was time to leave. Other than Dhaval, who would have been her friends? Who would have been her first kiss? Who was dating whom?

But now most of her questions were about Gavin. Did he have a girlfriend? Did he still play the piano? And, of course, had Dhaval ever seen a parent, or any grown-up really, near him? It was the biggest mystery of Delilah's childhood: Gavin had been the one kid without anyone at Back to School Night, or school plays, or even waiting for him at the curb at the end of the day.

Her fascination had always been a mixture of preteen longing and bearlike protectiveness.

"Are you glad to be back?" Dhaval asked, oblivious to her train of thought.

Delilah shrugged. For as nice as it was to see Dhaval and ogle Gavin again, the answer was easily "no." She'd been unceremoniously shipped away to Saint Benedict's, but it had become her home far more than the square two-bedroom cookie-cutter stucco house on Sycamore Street ever had. Delilah missed her old school, her friends, and her increasingly senile grandmother, in whose home she spent most of the past several years, as her parents had started to assume that Delilah would rather stay in Massachusetts than come home for a week over spring break, or a week around Thanksgiving or, eventually, for the entire summer. But Nonna was in a nursing home now, entirely lost to dementia, and without Nonna, Delilah's parents couldn't afford to keep her in school fifteen hundred miles away.

"Okay, don't answer that," Dhaval said, after she had been silent for way too long. "*I'm* happy to have you back. We need some quirk around here, Dee."

"I'm happy to see you, too," she said, leaning into her oldest friend. "And I'm happy to see Gavin all grown up."

"I bet you are. You little demon."

Delilah gave Dhaval a wicked grin. But then the bell rang loudly, startling her and signaling the end of the lunch break. When Delilah looked back to the tree, Gavin was already gone. She packed up the remnants of her lunch and followed Dhaval back inside.

By the end of the day, with only tiny glimpses of Gavin after lunch, Delilah's curiosity got the better of her. *What does he do after school? Does he meet up with friends? Does he have a job?* The questions grew into a maddening itch inside her mind, and it reminded her of how it felt to lie in bed at Saint Ben's, trying—but failing—to resist sneaking into the Fine Arts Building.

She followed at a safe distance as he walked away from school, paying the necessary amount of attention to the gardens, her phone, anything to look absorbed in her stroll and definitely not like a stalker, following a boy seventeen blocks home.

It wasn't that weird, was it? How many times had her girl-friends snuck off grounds to walk past the dorms of the boys at Saint Joseph's or had Nonna told her about walking past Grandpa's house when they were kids, just to get a peek inside his living room? It had sounded so innocent when Nonna said it; couldn't this be the same?

She didn't even have to follow Gavin, really. She suspected he still lived in the same house, the one they all called the Patchwork House for how it seemed like every part of it came together in a different color and style and shape.

It was on a generous lot, nestled between rows of identical houses but encircled by a tall fence obscuring most of it from view and long since covered in exuberant, violet morning glory that bloomed every day of the year. From the glimpses she'd caught from the sidewalk while trick-or-treating—the only time she'd been allowed to get that close, and the only time the iron gates out front remained open—she knew the front room was all modern glass, the side parlor lined with wood shingles and a cozy bay window. There was a turret on the third floor and a portion with Victorian paint and elaborate embellishments carved out of wood.

Kids used to say the house was haunted, but it never looked that way to Delilah. It was stunning, *thriving*, like something out of an old story, or an ancient black-and-white movie. Teenagers had always bragged about egging the house on Halloween, but to her knowledge, no one had ever really done it. The house—like most strange things in Morton, including Gavin—was just different enough to make the town residents want to pretend it wasn't there at all.

He turned a corner in the distance, and Delilah hung back, stepping behind the trunk of a large elm to watch. She waited for him to approach the fence, and she told herself that as soon as he reached for the latch at the gate, she would turn and walk home.

But it never happened.

Gavin crossed from one side of the street to the other, and the iron gate began to move, creaking open without being touched. The doors swung apart just far enough for him to slip through before closing again with a clang. She never saw him turn, never even saw him touch the gate at all.

Delilah didn't know what to make of this and stood

stock-still, frozen in place behind the old tree. Why would anyone need an automatic gate that wasn't for a driveway? Had there been some sort of remote in his pocket? But Gavin's hands hadn't been in his pockets. His thumbs had been causally tucked beneath the straps of his backpack. If there was a remote, he hadn't used it.

She crossed the road and stood next to the imposing fence that surrounded the Patchwork House. Peeking through the thick vine there, she saw the same thing happen with the front door: It swung open long before Gavin reached it. And here, too, there wasn't another person on the other side, just empty darkness to greet him.

She'd planned on going home, but now, walking away from what she'd seen felt impossible. Without giving herself time to think on it, she reached out with the toe of her shoe to check the footing, summoning every bit of courage she had before scrambling up the sturdy vines, lifting her body over the edge, and falling hard onto the lawn on the other side.

After she caught her breath, she took in the view. And what a view it was.

The house looming in front of her bore little resemblance to the house in her memories. In fact, it looked as if someone had taken *that* house and tacked on two or three others, all of varying styles and from different eras. It was all different colors—deep burgundy, goldenrod, forest green, and cornflower blue—and looked as if it had never borne the brunt of any windstorm, rain, or dust. Upstairs, two stained-glass windows gleamed in the late-afternoon sun, looking just like eyes watching over the street below. One half of the front lawn was emerald green, glistening and lush. Oddly, the other was just as dead as the first was alive, yellowed and brittle. Around the back, apples bloomed ruby red on the trees. In fact, every tree in the yard was plump with spring . . . in the middle of January.

Delilah blinked hard into the light, feeling as though she'd been ripped from her own ordinary existence and dropped into another world, one rich and ripe and bursting with color.

She looked back over her shoulder, convinced she must have fallen through some sort of rabbit hole and she would find herself fast asleep and dreaming on the other side. Did things like this house even exist in real life?

She turned to the sound of his voice from inside, yelling hello, and the *thunk* of his backpack as it hit the floor. Delilah crept to the nearest side window, peering in. A fire burned with gusto in a deep stone fireplace, and she felt a dizzying wave of relief that someone was there to welcome Gavin home. Maybe cook him some soup, bake him some bread for dinner.

But just as his long figure slipped into her view, the curtains in front of her closed with such violence that for a moment Delilah imagined the entire house had shaken.

CHAPTER FOUR

HIM

GAVIN HEARD A YELP, THE SOUND OF SOME-
thing scratching outside, and ran to the window,
fighting with Curtain. "Just let me see!" he shouted,
somehow knowing what had just happened.

He saw only the bottom of Delilah's shoes as she hurled
herself over the side fence. Thin coils of vine reached for her
feet. He pounded at the window, and the tendrils shrank back,
limp and contrite.

He hadn't confronted her earlier, when he knew she was
following him, because he didn't imagine even fearless Delilah
would have the guts to climb the fence. Before he could think
better of it, he was out the door, pushing through Gate and
chasing her down the street. "Delilah!"

She froze, turning to face him with a blush that could have
set his mouth on fire. "I'm sorry! I just..." She blinked, shrugging as if she'd lost her words. "I just wanted to know if you
still lived here."

"I do," he answered, confusion giving way to another feeling entirely when she met his eyes. Hers were green, and she had a dusting of freckles across her nose. He *should* have been focused on the fact that Delilah absolutely did not belong there. He should feel protectiveness for House welling inside him instead of the odd urge to pull Delilah closer. Nobody had ever dared scale the fence that surrounded House before, and certainly no one had dared to get this close in years. This was completely new territory for Gavin, talking to another person while House silently vibrated behind him.

He doubted Delilah could feel it from where she stood, but *he* could.

But with her so close, Gavin had to work to keep his attention from her mouth: It was soft and pink, with a top lip as full as the bottom. It was a mouth made for trouble, lips to be caught between teeth. Over the past six years, and with only tiny glimpses of her from afar when she was home over school breaks, he'd imagined how she might be growing up and, recently, that involved some interest in what it might feel like to finally kiss Delilah Blue. Standing here on the sidewalk in front of his house, he was closer to her than he'd ever been.

"Don't follow me home," he said as gently as he could. "Please, Delilah, don't ever follow me home again."

"I was curious," she admitted, adding, "Then with the gate . . . I just wanted to know you were okay." Her jaw had set with a familiar twist of protectiveness.

"Why wouldn't I be?" Gavin asked, eyes not quite meeting hers.

Delilah shifted her weight to peek at House behind him, as if the question alone might send it rising up from its foundation. "People talk about this place," she said.

"People talk about you," he replied.

"People don't think *I'm* haunted."

"Bet you wouldn't be insulted even if they did." He hadn't missed the things she doodled in the margins of her English book.

"No, I wouldn't." They stood at an impasse for a moment before she added, "Is it haunted?"

"Do you think it is?" he asked.

"I don't know," she said, and he could tell that she really didn't. "I might not know exactly *why* it looks the way it does, but I'm not *blind*, Gavin. *Look* at it."

He didn't need to turn and look at his house; he knew it better than anyone in the world. "I like that you wanted to make sure I'm okay, Delilah. I promise I am. Please, don't do this again." That wasn't at all what he wanted to say, but he knew it was for the best. Delilah couldn't come this close again, and she definitely couldn't come inside.

Her eyes narrowed, and for a minute she looked fierce and determined. He couldn't stop the smile that spread across his face. For a heartbeat, he hoped she would shove him, because it looked like she wanted to, and he'd always wanted to know how such a forceful touch would feel. Delilah looked at him a beat longer and then turned and walked away.

Gavin didn't know what to expect from Delilah the next day. He'd always known the rumors about his house, how it was haunted, or the site of the gristly murder of his entire family or—his personal favorite—the unofficial headquarters for all of Kansas's satanic rituals. He didn't know if anyone actually believed any of the stories, but even if they didn't, the terrible possibilities kept people away from the place.

Except Delilah. She'd followed him, not turning from the gate like everyone else. And even when Gavin had caught up to her on the sidewalk, she'd looked more embarrassed to have been caught than terrified from having been grabbed by a plant on his fence. She didn't seem to be scared at all. Did he want her to be?

Gavin had never been particularly good at reading people, and he gave up pretty early on, after inviting a friend over on the weekend and watching him run away screaming that the house was full of ghosts. Gavin had endured questions and looks and taunting for a week afterward, but it stopped abruptly after Delilah beat up the two worst bullies on the playground. She was promptly shipped off to Catholic school eight states away. Gavin had been tall and stringy at eleven, all daddy-longlegs limbs with too-long hair and pale skin, odd even to the kindest eye. But after Delilah—the prettiest and toughest girl at school—had stood up for him, the bullying had stopped. People ignored him, sure, but at least they left him alone. He'd wished he had a way to thank her.

So that night, after she'd walked off and left Gavin a little stunned on the sidewalk, he went back inside and found the dusty box in the back of Closet, where he'd stored his old papers and drawings. Buried in the crumpled mess was the note from six years ago, written in the scrawling hand of the wild and protective Delilah.

I don't want you to hide. I like you.

Gavin read it over and over, trying to puzzle out what it meant to be liked, and if—even then—she meant it a certain way.

He didn't sleep well and was up before dawn, eating breakfast in the backyard, where it was quieter and he could think in relative peace. He had plenty of thoughts about girls, about their lips and their necks and their hands and all kinds of other parts. But he had never had such fascination with a *mind* before, because as tiny as she was, Delilah was ferocious. What a pair they must make standing beside each other. Her fire so huge it spilled out of her and onto the pavement. His entire world so small she couldn't even see it with him looming over her.

As much as Gavin liked Delilah's face, he liked sitting behind her in English even more. She didn't dare turn and look at him the next morning, but he could feel every bit of her attention focused behind her, toward him.

She was so wispy, such a slip of a girl. Gavin imagined laying her on her side on the grass and playing notes up and down her skin.

"Mr. Timothy?"

His eyes blinked to focus, and he realized Mr. Harrington was staring at him. "Yes, sir?"

"We're covering Poe this week, Gavin. And I've asked you which of his works you chose to read and discuss with us. Unless, of course, you were hoping to be able to read and discuss Miss Blue's thoughts instead?"

Gavin felt a smile spread across his face. "I should be so lucky. But no, I'm happy to discuss 'The Oval Portrait.'"

Finally Delilah had an excuse to turn around and look at him. Her eyes were wide and burning with curiosity. She wouldn't follow him home again—he was pretty sure she would listen to what he'd said the day before—but she wasn't nearly done with him either.

CHAPTER FIVE

HER

DELILAH STRODE ACROSS THE LAWN, IGNOR-
ing the weight of a dozen pairs of eyes on her back as
she bravely walked over to the loner beneath the tree.

I should be so lucky.

Ever since English class and Gavin's scandalous comment,
her mind had been filling with a hundred different interpre-
tations of what he'd said. Her heart rate seemed to accelerate
with every step until she felt like, once she reached him, she
might crack open and spill everywhere.

Gavin sat on the grass, leaning against his oak tree, reading.

"What did you mean 'you should be so lucky'?" Delilah
blurted, and then cringed. She'd wanted to walk over, start out
with something friendly. A greeting, maybe. *Hi. Let's start over
again after yesterday. First question: How is it possible you're even
cuter now after all these years?*

Instead she'd cracked and spilled after all.

He looked up slowly from his book, as if he couldn't break

his attention away until he'd finished his sentence. And then he smiled. "Hi, Delilah."

"Hi," she said, shifting on her feet while she waited for an answer. Finally, she asked again, "What did you mean?"

He patted the grass next to him. "I wasn't speaking in code. I just think you're fun to try to puzzle out."

"*I'm* the puzzle?"

"To me, you are."

Reluctantly, she sat down and tried to force her blush back into her veins. "Why didn't you want me to see your house yesterday?"

He considered his answer for a few breaths before admitting, "Because I know all the rumors. I guess it makes me uncomfortable to imagine you there."

Delilah felt a heavy wave of defeat. Was it because of how the rest of the town talked? Did he think she was saying those things too? Or was it that he simply didn't want her there, which was . . . a different thing altogether.

"I'd never talk about your house, you know," she said.

His long thumb traced the spine of the book he'd been reading, and she shivered, imagining what it would feel like for that same finger to move up and down *her* spine. "I know, Delilah," he said, but he didn't look up.

Was this it, then? This was going to be the extent of their relationship: She stared at him for almost a solid hour her first day back at public school, followed him home, and then humiliated herself again today. She pushed up from the ground, ready to stand.

Gavin wrapped his fingers all the way around her forearm, with plenty of finger left to spare. "Don't go yet. I still need to hear at least a couple of stories about the horrors of Catholic school."

"'Horrors?'" she asked, sitting back down. Nothing horrific came to mind. Only unending detentions in the corner and bored, undersexed teenage girls causing drama where there wasn't much need for it.

"Exorcisms," he suggested, pursing his lips thoughtfully. "Abusive nuns. Haunted dorms. Give me something good, Delilah."

She inhaled and held her breath, staring at him. He was too good to be true, saying just what she needed him to say to show her she wasn't wrong about him. "How about the wild tangle of lesbian orgies?"

His eyes widened playfully. "I'm all ears."

"Well, in that case you're going to be disappointed. No abusive nuns either, or exorcisms, at least none that I witnessed. But everyone was sneaking in booze and drugs and boys."

"Boys?" His eyebrows inched up slowly.

Delilah laughed, loving that this was the most shocking contraband. In truth, she didn't have much experience with boys. She'd kissed a few, snuck one into her room to see what making out felt like in a *bed*, but never more than that.

Holding up his hands, he qualified, "No, I mean obviously boys are much less illegal than drugs, but presumably harder to sneak in?"

"Not necessarily. I mean, *you* would be hard to dress up as a girl and sneak inside, even in the dark. You're about seventy feet tall. But most boys our age can pass a little easier for female."

He snorted. "Now it's settled. You have to go back to Catholic school just so we can see if you can sneak me in."

"Sneak you in where?" she asked, voice low and meaningful. "*My* room?"

But she'd gotten carried away, forgotten herself and how new this delicate friendship was. His smile wilted slightly. "Maybe just into the building to start."

"Sorry. I seem to always act crazy around you. I'm not usually like this. I swear."

"What are you usually like, then?"

She considered this. "Bored. Looking for someone to ask me about exorcisms and hauntings."

He looked past her, contemplating the school in the distance. "I'm not quite sure what to do with you, Delilah Blue. You seem intent on making me your friend."

"Because I like you," she said plainly.

"Still?" he asked, smile stuttering back to life.

"I think I like you differently now than when we were eleven. Though not necessarily. Maybe I liked you this way then, too."

But he didn't press, didn't ask what she was hoping he would ask: *What way? Tell me how you like me, Delilah.* Instead, he shrugged as if it all made sense and told her he was always happy to have another friend.

"How could I forget that all you ever wanted to do was watch scary movies?" Dhaval groaned. He looked like he was on the verge of an enormous pout. "We could go over to Seneca Park and sip some booze from my flask and talk about boys."

"I don't drink," Delilah reminded him. "And are we openly talking about boys in public now?"

He shrugged. Delilah had always known Dhaval was gay. It may not have been an actual conversation they'd had, but they hadn't really needed to. Two summers ago, Dhaval told her he'd kissed Aiden Miller on the last day of school, behind the bleachers. Delilah was only mad that his first kiss happened before hers. She cared as much about who Dhaval chose to kiss as she did for what shoes he chose to wear: It mattered only that neither hurt him.

"My parents give me one night out a month," he told her. "*One.* I don't care if you drink. *I'll* drink and you can tell me all about the wild Catholic-school parties."

Delilah snorted. "Why does everyone think it's like that?"

"Isn't it?" His face relaxed into a grin. "You had a single room last semester. Don't break my heart and tell me you never snuck a guy in."

She gave Dhaval a stern look. "I want to see a movie. I don't want to head over to the big city and drink in a park."

"Not all of us were lucky enough to attend boarding school outside of Boston," Dhaval said, in the worst Boston accent Delilah had ever heard. "Maybe trips to Wichita parks are the highlight of our week around here."

She slipped her arm through Dhaval's and led him to his car. "Slasher flick. My treat. I promise you'll have fun."

The Morton Theater was run-down and exactly how Delilah remembered it. Had anything changed? Her bedroom was still an almost blinding purple, and she slept on the same, tiny brass daybed. Her parents seemed to be wearing the same clothes, styling their hair just the same. The crack in the sidewalk out in front of the house was still there. It felt as if time had stopped while she was away and the only person who'd kept growing, and growing was Gavin.

Delilah paid for the tickets and dragged a reluctant Dhaval in behind her. "Popcorn?"

"No," he said sulkily.

"Candy?"

The promise of sweets seemed to penetrate his foul mood. But as they moved closer in line for food, Delilah looked up and saw Gavin just beside the concession stand. Every time she saw him she couldn't believe that he was real. He didn't look like anyone she had ever seen. He was so wonderfully, perfectly odd.

"Did you know he worked here?" Dhaval hissed in her ear. "Is that why we're here, you *fiend?*"

Gavin looked up and offered a tiny smile, a little wave.

"No!" Delilah hissed back. "These are the details you need to share with a friend who's been gone for *six* school years!" She tried to return Gavin's smile but was sure it came out wobbly. His eyes lit with amusement as he watched the whispered exchange.

"I had no idea," Dhaval whispered. "I never come to the damn movies, remember? I can't ogle hot boys in the dark!"

Delilah straightened her shoulders and walked up to where Gavin leaned against the vacuum broom he was holding. He took his time looking her over, from the top of her shoes to her mouth, her cheeks, and finally her eyes. "Hi, Delilah."

She felt completely naked somehow. "I didn't know you worked here."

He shrugged. "We spent most of our last conversation pondering how to break me into your old school. We hadn't covered my employment status yet."

"True." Delilah thought there might be a swarm of sparrows in her chest. Why did he have to look at her so intensely? If he wanted to know her every thought, she would just tell him. "I didn't realize movie theaters were still using those." Delilah pointed to the roller vacuum. And then she smiled because he'd smiled, and it was slow and kind of flirtatious.

"Yes. Theaters are still using them." His smile turned a little secretive, and it added a tiny bite to his words.

"Right. Obviously." The next words flew from her mouth. "Can you put the vacuum broom away and come watch the movie with us?"

Something clouded his eyes, but it didn't feel wholly unfriendly. Conflict, maybe, or confusion. "Sorry, I need to stay out here." He stood straight up and nodded to where Dhaval waited a ways behind her. "But you two enjoy the show."

"I'm sure we will," Dhaval drawled, moving to Delilah as soon as Gavin had turned around a corner and hissing, "Girl, you have it bad."

She groaned, feeling defeated, but it came out sounding a little breathless. "I know. I act so abnormal around him."

"I'll admit, he's not *that* bad-looking. I guess I just never noticed before," he said. "There's something about him."

"'Not bad-looking'? Dhaval, that boy is sex on a stick."

Two nicely groomed dark eyebrows inched upward. "Delilah Blue, what do you know about sex on a stick?"

"Nothing," she said, grinning. "I don't need to have ridden a roller coaster to know what one is, do I?"

A laugh burst from Dhaval and filled the nearly empty theater. "That school back East did something to you."

Delilah and Dhaval sat in the fourth row, with their feet up on the seats in front of them. Every time someone got stabbed,

Dhaval shrieked and Delilah groaned. The gore was overdone. The fake blood too thick, too scarlet. Real blood, in such quantity, was deep and rich, like the heart of a rose.

A dark figure appeared in Delilah's peripheral vision just before Gavin moved into view. Even though he tried to make himself as small as possible as he made the rounds with a tiny flashlight—presumably checking to ensure that no one was causing trouble or having sex in the theater—he cut a long, crooked silhouette when he passed in front of the screen.

Dhaval immediately dropped his feet from where they rested on the seat in front of him, but Delilah kept hers in place. She hoped Gavin would stop, tell her to put her feet down and give her a playfully stern look. Maybe he would even lean over and touch her leg. Maybe he would sit down with them after all.

"Delilah, please put your feet down," he said, but he didn't give her a second glance before he moved on.

She watched him walk back up the aisle on the other side. "Well. That was anticlimactic."

Dhaval laughed and put his feet back up. "You can only be a flirt if he notices you."

"He notices me," she insisted. On-screen the killer was breaking another man's fingers one by one, and for a moment Delilah was distracted.

But then she broke her attention away and looked at Dhaval. "Have you ever seen Gavin with his parents?"

Dhaval closed one eye, thinking. "Mom used to know his mom. She says she's kind of a hermit now, never comes out of the house. There *was* something freshman year, about Social Services coming to the school to talk to him and his teachers. Some random teacher said his parents didn't come in for a mandatory meeting or something, that they'd *never* seen them. It was all anyone could talk about—that Gavin Timothy didn't have parents, that Gavin Timothy had killed his parents and was living alone in that crazy house." Dhaval shook his head and reached for another handful of popcorn. "Ridiculous. Anyway, after a few days it just went away. I guess she showed up eventually."

A new routine grew out of the lunch hour. Dhaval walked Delilah to the edge of the lawn and then thought of some reason or another why he needed to go hang out with his friends near the basketball courts, when there wasn't a single bone in his body that had any natural inclination for the sport. Delilah would walk the rest of the way over to where Gavin sat, reading beneath the tree.

And over time, Gavin stopped reading during her approach and would instead watch her walk from the lawn's edge to where his feet rested, practically miles from his smile. Her journey would feel like it was happening in stop-action; with his eyes on her like that, she would turn into the most awkward girl alive.

Looking at Gavin on a hazy Tuesday afternoon, Delilah felt like she was behind in the race to shed her childhood skin. He was tall, with stretching, growing muscles. The hair on his arms was dark. She could see a hint of chest hair beneath the collar of his shirt. Chest hair! She was so scrawny. She barely had boobs.

It seemed like Gavin finally couldn't take it any longer. "Delilah?"

"Mmm?"

He wiped a hand over his face. "Are you . . . staring at my chest?"

Delilah nodded, moving her eyes up his neck to his face. "Yeah. Why?"

"Well . . . shouldn't it be the other way around?"

Oh. Delilah almost choked on her tongue.

"I mean—" he started, backtracking.

But Delilah didn't want him to take it back. "Aren't girls supposed to mature faster than boys?" she asked, interrupting him. "I feel like I'm sitting next to a *man*. I'm not even done blossoming." She considered this and looked down at her own chest. "God, I hope."

"'Blossoming'?" Gavin asked, with a slow-growing grin. "I can't believe you aren't more embarrassed to say that out loud."

"And," she continued, ignoring him, "I think you won the puberty race."

"The what now?"

"Look at all these high school kids around us; they look

tiny compared to you." Gavin looked away from her face when she said this and out to the distance, where their classmates went about their business of socializing and eating and shooting hoops. "You have *chest hair*."

It was his turn to look down at his shirt. He admitted, "Some."

"And I have demi-boobs."

Half of a smile flirted with his lips, and when he blinked down to her chest, Delilah thought the skin on her neck and cheeks might ignite. "Your boobs are fine," he said after a lengthy inspection.

"Fine. Yes. Thank you. Be gone, feeble insecurities. My boobs are *fine*."

"More than fine. Stunning. Perfection, even. Better?" He was outright laughing now.

"A little."

"And puberty race? Really?" He was attempting teasing and skeptical, but he really just looked proud.

Laughing, she mumbled, "Shut up, Gavin."

He split open a thick collection of short stories, sly eyes slanting a smirk in her direction. "Do I get a trophy?"

"Yes. Made of chest hair."

But Wednesday afternoon he didn't watch her walk to him; instead he watched Dhaval walk away. "Why doesn't Dhaval ever come over here with you?"

"Because he knows I want to be here with you, alone."

Gavin swallowed awkwardly, as if this weren't plainly obvious, as if they hadn't spent their last lunch together talking about puberty and breasts and his body beneath his shirt. He looked past her to the school building. "Do you think *he* wants to be your boyfriend?"

"Dhaval?" She laughed. "He's about as straight as a rainbow."

Gavin's face scrunched up slightly with confusion. "Rainbows aren't . . . *Oh.*" He looked up to where Dhaval walked in the distance. "I had no idea."

"Then you have the world's worst gaydar. He practically comes out every time he opens his mouth."

Gavin was too lost in contemplating this to smile at Delilah. Instead he sat very still, thinking very hard, for what felt like far too long.

"What are you thinking about?"

"Do his parents know?"

"That Dhaval is gay? I doubt it."

He pulled his lower lip between his teeth and blinked his eyes to Delilah. "How does that work? You share a house with someone and don't know something so important."

Delilah shrugged, feeling like the context of the conversation was eluding her. "I don't think he wants his parents to know yet. He just wants everyone *else* to know."

"What would your parents have done," he asked, "if

you *had* snuck in drugs or had a wild lesbian orgy at Saint Benedict's?"

Delilah shivered, unable to stomach the idea of being romantic with any of her former classmates. "Ugh, no."

Finally, this made him laugh. "I'm not asking you what girl you would have been with. I mean, what would your parents have done?"

"Flipped out. Completely."

"What does that mean? What do they do when they flip out?"

Delilah wanted to ask him, for about the millionth time, what his parents were like. Didn't they flip out on him? Wasn't he keeping at least some secrets from them? She wondered if this was where the game of "I'll show you mine if you show me yours" came in. She didn't particularly like talking about her family—there wasn't anything interesting to say, really, and it always made her a little sad that her parents were so unaffectionate and awkward, particularly when compared to Nonna's exuberant love—but if opening up showed Gavin that his family couldn't possibly be any weirder than hers, she was willing to try.

So with a shrug she said, "My parents are . . . hard to describe."

"How so?"

"I don't actually know them very well."

He seemed to digest this for a few breaths. "Because you were gone a lot, you mean?"

"That, and I think they aren't very good at talking, or

connecting to other people. They have this little marriage bubble, and I'm their kid, but to them it means I'm a joint project. Like building a birdhouse together is the same as raising a daughter and redecorating the kitchen."

"That's . . . too bad."

"Don't get me wrong. They care that I'm raised right and want me to be safe. They just aren't very warm. They don't ever ask whether I've done my homework, but they have very strong opinions about boys and dating and sex and even *thoughts*."

"You can't have *thoughts*?"

"I should try not to, is what my mother says. There's no use thinking about things I can't do yet anyway. My dad is just . . . a dad. He works; he eats; he watches TV. He works; he eats; he watches TV."

"No sleeping in there?" Gavin asked with a small smile.

"Maybe a little. My mom is sort of charm-free. Nonna always called her 'Belinda Bluenose.' I finally had to look it up to realize she was calling my mother uptight. And it's true. I think my mother would fall over dead if she ever thought I masturbated."

Gavin had been listening intently to all of this, but when Delilah said this last bit, he ran a hand over his face and coughed out a laugh. "Good God, Delilah. You're going to kill me."

"What? How?" she asked, suddenly distracted by a line of black words that peeked out from beneath the cuff of Gavin's sleeve. She wondered what thoughts and ideas he found so important he would draw them in ink across his skin.

He shook his head, and instead of answering, he asked, "Have you never had a boyfriend?"

"Um, no. Were you listening to the flipping-out bit? I've kissed a few boys, but each of those stories is in my collection of secrets."

"Not anymore."

She deflated, having broken her one cardinal rule. "I didn't tell you the details."

"Hey," he said, touching her arm. "I promise I won't tell anyone you *kissed a boy*."

Her eyes narrowed and she noted the brightness in his eyes. "You're making fun of me."

Gavin laughed. "I am. Completely."

In Massachusetts, the local Trader Joe's was a beacon of color, with bright signs suspended out front and fresh produce practically spilling from the shelves. Morton's only grocery store was beige and as commonplace and average as everything else in town. Economy Grocer was a long rectangular building wedged between a run-down used bookstore and a small Payless ShoeSource.

Engrossed in one of her paperbacks, Belinda had placed the car keys in Delilah's hand and sent her off to fetch onion powder. Delilah thrilled at any chance to drive on her own. Driving alone meant the chance to listen to loud music of her choosing.

Delilah wasn't sure which cosmic force to thank when she

pulled into the cracked parking lot of Economy Grocer just in time to see Gavin Timothy's lanky frame disappear between the automatic doors. Keys and purse in hand, she hopped out of the car and made her way into the supermarket.

Standing at least a full head taller than everyone else, Gavin was instantly visible down the middle aisle, where he reached to pluck a box of ice cream from the frozen-food case.

"Hello there, Gavin Timothy," she said, stopping a few feet away.

He straightened and looked at her over his shoulder. "Delilah Blue." As usual, Gavin was dressed in black from head to toe, his jeans practically painted on and his T-shirt doing really, *really* nice things for his arms and the flat lines of his stomach. But it was his smile that had her taking a step back and stumbling into a display of Hershey's Syrup.

"I'm fine," she said before he could ask, righting herself almost immediately.

"Good," he said, his smile widening, approaching indecent levels. Closing the freezer door, he turned to face her, motioning to the box of Drumsticks in his hands. "I was leaving work and craving ice cream."

Together they turned and walked side by side up the aisle. "I hope you have one in there for me," Delilah said, bumping his arm with her shoulder.

"I'm not sure what watching you eat one of these would do to me," he said, and Delilah almost dropped her keys and Gavin shook his head next to her. "I probably shouldn't have said that."

"I think we need to figure out which of us is going to be the scandalous one here, because I'm not sure this friendship can handle two."

Friendship, she reminded herself. *Friendship*.

"Just giving you a run for your money," he said, following her around the corner to the spice aisle. A woman of about sixty was reading the back of a box of cake mix and glanced up, frowning in judgment as she inspected the messy-haired shadow at Delilah's side.

Delilah scanned a row of spice bottles. "That one," she said, pointing to the top shelf.

"Here?" he said, finding it easily and handing it to her.

"Thank you. Why do they put things so high? I need a stepladder to reach it."

"Or maybe you need a grocery escort from now on."

Her heart turned into a thousand fevered bird wings. "So what are you doing with the rest of your night?"

"Eating ice cream and thinking wholesome thoughts," he said. "And I have a history test to study for. You?"

"Watching my dad watch TV? I don't know." She looked up at him. "Not much going on, really."

Gavin looked like he might say something more, but they'd reached the checkout.

"Hey, Dave," Gavin said, setting his box on the tiny conveyor belt before shoving both his hands in the pockets of his jeans. A middle-aged man with hair that thinned on top and grayed at the sides looked up at him in confusion.

"Hi," he said slowly, watching Gavin through narrowed eyes like he was trying to place him. "Do I know you from somewhere, kid?"

Gavin blinked to Delilah and then back to the man. "Never mind," he said slowly, pulling a five from his jeans and handing it to him.

Dave rang up the onion powder wearing a similar haze of confusion, his gaze repeatedly darting back to Gavin like he was sure there was something there to puzzle out.

With change in hand, Delilah and Gavin headed toward the entrance together. "That was so weird," Gavin said.

"You do know him, then?" Delilah asked.

"He's only delivered our groceries every week for, I don't know, the past seven or eight years? How could he not know who I was?"

Delilah followed his gaze to where the man was ringing up the next customer. There was no way to meet Gavin and not remember him, and there was absolutely no way to forget his house.

Ten lunches together and two weekends in between interrupted her time with Gavin. Saturday was the most dreaded day of the week. On Fridays, she'd doodle skulls and torches and severed hands discreetly in class just to distract her from the impending doom of the weekend. Two days at home with her parents: torture.

She wasn't one to snap. Granted, she wasn't the most patient when it came to Gavin. She had no idea why, but early on she'd decided *he* was what she wanted. She wanted those lips to be hers and that forever-long torso, too. She was possessive of his quiet, husky laugh and wanted to know that the fingers he used to play the piano or sketch in his notebook were the same he would use to touch her jaw or her lips or her waist. Until he said no, she was going to be near him as much as possible. He seemed comfortable with her, would ask her questions and reply. But he never shared many details about himself.

"You didn't bring lunch today," he said, biting into a mottled red-green apple. He reached into his lunch bag and pulled out a second. "Here, I brought you one."

"How did you know I wasn't going to bring lunch?"

"I didn't," he said, taking another gigantic bite. It pushed his cheek out, and she could see his sharp canine tooth as he moved the bite farther back in his mouth. "But these apples are really good, and I thought you might want one."

"Is it from your apple tree?"

He froze, swallowing roughly before he'd finished chewing. "Yes."

"So, it's January and your apple tree has fruit?"

"It's not uncommon for apples to bloom in January," he said robotically.

"It's uncommon for Pippin apples." She knew, staring down at the apple. She'd seen his blossoming, fruit-filled tree and she'd looked up what kind it was, and now he knew she had.

She stared down at the apple in her hand and then rubbed it against her shirt, shining it. She could almost feel him struggling to think of some way to change the subject. Giving up and letting him off the hook, she said, "Do you like when I come here at lunch?"

"Of course." He dropped his ravaged apple core into his empty lunch sack.

"Do you like me the way I like you?"

He scratched his cheek, ducked to meet her eyes, and finally asked, "What way do you like me, Delilah?"

She looked up at him. He knew how she liked him. She'd made herself completely transparent. Why was he so intent on making her say it? When she saw his dark eyes widen slightly, she understood: Gavin didn't totally believe that she could feel that way.

"I want you to ask me out on a date."

CHAPTER SIX

HIM

GAVIN STARED AT THE GIRL IN FRONT OF HIM, processing what she'd just said. A date, with food and maybe milk shakes, hands coming together, palms pressed tightly later. Maybe even lips and teeth touching later, too, and her quiet girl sounds muted by his mouth.

He'd never been very good at the romantic negotiations. The heavy, insinuating looks from girls when they moved to stand close to him. The cloying awkwardness of a girl trying to speak to him and becoming more and more self-conscious as he politely waited for her to finish saying whatever it was she wanted to say. Thankfully, most girls would eventually decide it was easier to pretend he wasn't even there. But Delilah was a battering ram.

It was partly what drew him to her, but only partly. Her complete fearlessness felt calming and trustworthy, but her lips, and skin, and the hint of her breasts beneath her sweater didn't hurt either.

"What are you thinking?"

"Nothing," he lied.

"Liar. I just told you I wanted you to ask me out. Whether you're intrigued or horrified, you have to be thinking about *something*."

He didn't bother denying it; he just smiled and looked at her face some more. She was so beautiful. Her skin was unreal, tiny freckles but otherwise smooth and clean with just the right amount of color blooming across her cheeks as she watched him. He could draw those eyes, he thought. Charcoal, maybe smudged with the edge of his little finger. Delilah's eyes were wide-set, almost strangely almond shaped, and a turbulent gray-green like the crashing surf of Hallway Painting, waves pummeling stone and sand.

He would draw her later. He'd take the sketch downstairs, sit with Piano, listen to a song that he imagined would make drawn Delilah come to life, and he would pull her close to him, dance her across the floor. She would feel him, so real with her hands tugging his hair and her teeth pulling at the collar of his shirt like an impatient kitten, purring into his neck.

"Gavin?"

The real Delilah was waiting for an answer. How could they date when they didn't even inhabit the same world? She, a mystery in her crisp shirt and pleated skirt, so unable to give up the prim uniform of Catholic school. He, with his tangle of hair, black shirt, jeans in the final throes of coherence.

"I'm not sure I'm really your type."

Her smile curved her mouth into something edible. "I think you are."

"I think you might be dangerous." His left eyebrow quirked up, teasing her.

She laughed then, all husky and soft, and the sound burrowed into him, warming him from bones to skin. "I don't think so, Gavin."

"What would we do on a date, anyway?"

Her smile straightened, and she looked so earnest he would believe her if she told him the ground had turned invisible. "We could get milk shakes."

His brows lifted.

"And maybe after we walked around for a while drinking our milk shakes, you'd hold my hand."

He laughed. "Slow down, now."

"And we'd talk. *You'd* talk."

His expression fell a little.

"I hear it's required on dates," Delilah added. "It's what I do every day with you. It's your turn soon."

"Talking really isn't my strength."

"I know," she assured him.

"Then why would you want to go on a date with me where we have milk shakes and eventual hand-holding and awkward conversation?"

"Because," she said, licking her lips into a sweet, shining

red-apple kiss, "I've basically been at a convent for six years, and I've had a crush on you since we were nine. When I get you to say more than two words at a time, I feel like I've won something major."

"Like a trophy made of chest hair?" he teased.

"Like a *war*."

His skin pebbled in gooseflesh when she said that, not because it scared him but because it thrilled him to hear it from this tiny girl who drew pictures of bleeding crosses and eyeless skulls.

"What do you want from me, Delilah?"

"I want to be the only girl you look at." No pretenses; she always said things like this, as if it cost her nothing to bare herself.

"You already are."

"I'd like to be your *girlfriend*, Gavin Timothy."

"Girlfriend? Or girl friend?" He felt the need to offer her plenty of chances to take it back.

"One word. 'Girlfriend.' 'Sweetheart.' Whatever you call it. That's what I want with you."

"Sweetheart?" he repeated, teasing. "My best gal?"

Shrugging, she whispered, "Yeah."

He looked to the side, considering what that would mean. "You would have to know about me."

"Obviously. I haven't hung out with you under this tree for the last few weeks so I can know you less well."

Looking back at her, he said, "It's not like I have a weird kink like a foot fetish. I mean, I'm different."

"Again," she said, smiling, "obviously."

"I live in . . . a house." His words came out heavy as marble.

Her eyes narrowed as she considered him and he realized with a small laugh what he'd just said. Huffing out a breath, he dug both hands into his hair. "No. Right. Everyone lives in a house of some sort. It's just that my house is different."

"You mean because of the patchwork?" she asked, eyebrows lifted hopefully.

"No." But then he understood her meaning, the way House came together on the outside. He was so used to seeing it that way and knowing each individual part just as that— individual—that he'd stopped noticing how it appeared so heavily seamed, so awkwardly plugged together. "Yes, actually. I mean, the reason it looks like that is the same reason you wear those little skirts and I wear jeans and boots."

"Like, every room is decorated a different way," she said, smiling that she seemed to be following. Except she wasn't. The rooms weren't *decorated* a certain way; they *were* a certain way.

"No, Delilah. The house, and everything inside it, is unique. Everything has its own style, because everything in the house is alive."

Delilah laughed, clearly disbelieving. "Okay, Gavin. Sure."

Blinking away, Gavin took a deep breath and considered

his options. He could laugh it off, too, pretend that he was making a joke. But that would mean nothing else between him and Delilah could move forward. He wouldn't really be able to be himself with her the way he suspected he would want to be . . . or maybe already did.

Or, he could try to make her believe.

"I realize how this sounds," he started. "But I wouldn't lie to you, or tell you this to mock you somehow." Gavin looked back at her, his eyes tripping on a strand of hair blown across her face, stuck to her lip. Without thinking, he gently urged it away with a long finger. "I've always been a bit of an outsider, you know, but given how I was raised, how could it have gone differently? My first day of kindergarten, there wasn't a parent walking me there but a tricycle that squeaked down the street next to me. Not with me on it. *Next* to me. It sat outside my classroom until I was ready to go home and then walked me all the way back. I hadn't even known what school was until the moment I saw the other kids playing and understood I was supposed to go too. But even then, when I was five, I knew not to tell anyone. I knew to put my hand on the handle so it would look like I was leading it and not the other way around."

Delilah looked like she might silently blink herself into a faint.

"And when I got home that day," he continued, "there was a snack on the kitchen table and a new Lego set—a present, okay? For getting through my first day. Until I was in the third grade, something from the house would take me to school. The tricycle or a wagon or even a small toy that grew warm in my hand, like it was reassuring me. The house has a way of slipping into things that are inanimate. It takes care of me. It always has."

She seemed to try to make a few sounds before anything came out. "Slipping into . . . *what*?"

"I don't know what it is, really," he admitted, and when he looked at her incredulous expression, he wanted to tell her how many times he'd tried to puzzle it out, too. Was it spirits? Some sort of spell? Was it just . . . magic? In any case, it was his reality, his family, his life. "Things inside House can come alive in a way that I don't think things anywhere else can. When an object is inside House . . . it can be alive."

Still, Delilah stared blankly at him, repeating, "'*Can* be'?"

"I mean, it doesn't hijack onto my clothes," he said with a little laugh that wasn't returned. "Though, I think the energy, or whatever it is, can leave, too, through power lines, or through roots in the soil. I've tried to figure it out because obviously nothing there can really explain it to me."

He realized he'd said too much. Delilah had leaned away a little, eyes wide. Growing slightly panicked, Gavin told her, "I'm telling you this because I really like you. And I trust that you won't . . . won't tell me I'm crazy." He ducked low to meet her eyes, weary. "Say something," he urged, after at least another half a minute had passed.

"But it *sounds* crazy," she whispered.

A part of her *had* to believe it was true. Had she not felt the vine grasping her ankle? What would the human mind do to deceive itself?

"It's crazy, yes. But the world is full of things that are crazy and wild and unbelievable." When she didn't say more, he added, "You of all people know this, Delilah. It's why you love the idea of demon possession and things coming back to life. Is it so hard to imagine that objects might have life in them, too?"

Delilah looked as if she had been punched in the chest. "How do you know those things about me?"

He tried not to roll his eyes. "Anyone who pays attention knows that about you."

"No one knows *that*."

Gavin raised an eyebrow. "I'm paying attention in a way others aren't."

"So let's say you're telling the truth and you aren't crazy. How does it work?" she asked. "Like, does everything . . . talk?"

He shook his head, his skin tingling faintly with the surrealism of the moment. "The things inside are alive, but nothing can speak because nothing has a mouth. Except the television, I suppose. But every single thing is alive. The rooms, the furniture, the paintings."

"The curtains," she breathed, playing with her lip.

"Yes, the curtains."

"And the vines." Delilah looked all around and down at her feet as if she expected something to have reached up and ensnared her ankle. "Is this why your parents never leave the house?"

He paused, wondering again whether he should lie. He started to, but the words got stuck in his throat, and instead the bare truth came out in a whisper. "I don't have parents. I've been in the house for as long as I can remember."

Delilah couldn't process this, it appeared. She blinked a few more times and stared at him with her lips slightly parted. Gavin focused instead on her eyes.

"Where are they?" she asked, voice tight as if her throat was holding back more emotion.

He licked his lips, unable to look at her when he admitted, "I don't know."

"So they . . . just left?"

"Yeah. I don't have any memories of my dad, but my mom . . . I know she was here at some point—there's a picture—but . . . she left. She left me."

"But you have food and—"

"I have everything I need," he told her, because he did. Groceries were delivered each week, the account prepaid by someone—he'd never really thought to check by whom. When he was younger they were left at the front steps, but now Gavin always answered the door. That's how he'd known Dave from the grocery store. Dave had been stopping by every week for years. How in the hell hadn't he recognized Gavin? Beyond that, there wasn't a single physical thing he needed that he didn't have. Somehow House provided all of it.

"Aren't you lonely?" she asked.

He shook his head.

"How . . . ?" she started and then stopped. "How is that even possible?"

With a smile, he explained. "It's all I've really known, you know, so it doesn't seem that impossible to me. I have some friends here at school. I have friends online. Things in the house move. . . . They take care of me. They always have. *They* would never leave." He took a moment to look around the school yard. "It's a bit like having a really big family, but no one speaks."

Her jaw set, determined, when she said, "Then show me."

The wind blew around them, picking up leaves and spinning them in the air.

"Okay." He grinned because he suddenly loved everything about this conversation. It felt like he was exhaling a burning lungful of air after holding it in his entire life. And this girl, this gorgeous, crazy girl wasn't running away screaming.

She caught his smile, her eyes narrowing in suspicion. "You're really not messing with me?"

"I swear I'm not."

"Why are you laughing?"

"Because, Delilah," he said, running an index finger along

his eyebrow, "I never expected the pretty girl who wrote me a note in the sixth grade to ask to be my girlfriend six years later, hear all this, and not run screaming."

"Did you want to be my boyfriend?" she asked, eyebrows pulled close together. She looked preemptively mad, as if she were preparing for a fight.

For a war.

As if he could have said no. He nodded slowly. It seemed predestined, he realized, that this girl would walk back into this dirty, rumbling school with an unending tangle of words and innocence trailing behind her. And that the first thing she would want was him.

CHAPTER SEVEN

HER

S O HE WAS HERS. SHE GRINNED SO FIERCELY SHE felt like she might growl. That crazy hair, the dark, playful eyes. The lips—she couldn't even imagine. That neck and those shoulders, ropy arms and torso that went on forever.

She'd consider the rest later.

"I think you might be a little unbalanced," he said, watching her reaction with a smile.

Delilah shrugged. "Probably." She moved closer, closer than she'd ever been to him, and reached up to put her hands flat on his chest.

Gavin sucked in a giant breath, startling her, and squeezed his eyes shut so tight his face contorted as if she'd hurt him. But when she tried to pull away, he stopped her with his palms covering the backs of her hands.

Had he been touched before? "Haven't you had girlfriends?"

He opened his eyes. "A couple. But I didn't want them for long, and none of them made me feel this way."

"What way?"

"Relieved. Maybe a little terrified."

She dropped her hands this time before he could stop her. "I *terrify* you?"

"Yes."

"That's . . . not good, is it?"

"For me it is," he said, and followed it with a little one-shouldered shrug. "I'm just overwhelmed by you. I finally *have* you. I don't want to mess this up."

She considered his expression. He looked almost desperately hopeful.

Gavin walked her home, away from the scrabbly bushes surrounding school to the neat lawns of her neighborhood. Tiny pastel houses were set back an equal distance from the street and only an arm's length away from each neighbor.

Delilah didn't think these houses would look very interesting to Gavin, having grown up in a sprawling, living mansion, but even so, he looked around her neighborhood with barely concealed hunger. "What time do your parents get home?"

"My mom gets home around four. She does hair down at the Supercuts. My dad used to be a manager at the plant."

"What does he do now?"

Delilah shrugged, surprised that Gavin didn't already know this. The rest of the town seemed to. Looking at the dark windows of her house, she wondered if one or both of her parents were watching her from the living room. What would they think, seeing her talking to this tall, slim shadow on the sidewalk? She found she didn't really care and was more surprised it hadn't occurred to her sooner. Her parents had lots of opinions, but most of them seemed to be about unimportant things. Delilah wondered where Gavin would land on their spectrum of relevant worries. Knowing them, they wouldn't think to look out the window to see who had walked her home, but they had noticed this morning that her skirt was an inch shorter than the one she wore yesterday.

"Is your dad home?" Gavin asked, prompting.

"He might be. He's looking for work. I guess there isn't a lot in this town for managers right now."

Gavin nodded as if this made sense, but Delilah had to wonder what he knew of parents being out of work and what it cost to run a household. He worked in a movie theater for a few hours a week. How much money could he really have? She could hardly ask that. Who did he talk to about careers and school? What did he do if he got stuck on his math homework?

"You should go in," he prompted, lifting his chin toward the porch. Her mom now stood there, waving.

"I know. But I don't want to."

"You're not going to go in there and freak out on me, are you?"

She looked up at him, stretched to kiss his cheek but made it only to his jaw. "See you tomorrow."

CHAPTER EIGHT

HIM

GAVIN LAY ON BED THAT NIGHT, LONG LEGS stretched nearly to the footboard. He was getting too old for this room, but he'd been here since he was seven and had finally decided to move out of the nursery. Here, blue wallpaper lined the walls and model airplanes hung from wire, twisting errantly from the ceiling above.

He'd gone through an aviator phase when he was twelve, right after watching a documentary about the Wright Brothers on Television. He could still remember how he'd talked about the program for weeks and how content House seemed to just listen. He'd jabbered endlessly about wing warping and gliders, and it had seemed to understand, the flowers in Parlor Painting nodding encouragingly each time he paused to take a breath.

He remembered how boxes of books on aeronautics and aerospace engineering had magically appeared on the porch—silently ordered, silently delivered—how encyclopedias had found their way onto Table near Bed. He'd pored through volume after volume, read countless biographies, even found plans on building models to scale. But no maps. Not a single atlas or globe to be found. It was the first inkling Gavin had that although House provided him with everything he'd ever thought to want or need, it might be trying to keep him from the one thing he'd never really paid much attention to in the first place: the outside world.

As he usually did when these sorts of thoughts occurred to him, Gavin shuffled it to the back of his mind, along with all other equally unpleasant things. This was the only life he'd ever known, after all. And hadn't he always been happy? Or at the very least, content? He'd always reasoned that everyone lived their lives in one type of box or another; his was just a bit more oddly shaped than the rest.

And now Delilah wanted to come here.

Gavin had no idea what to make of this, having never been wanted so sincerely—and so fiercely—before in his life. Other girls had been curious, maybe using him to explore their own borders of what felt safe and what felt dangerous, but with Delilah it always seemed clear that if either of them was to be handled carefully, it wasn't him. She was like a fire-cracker standing too close to a match: all potential energy, still wrapped up so neatly. He wanted to watch her explode.

Hell, he was the match. He wanted to *make* her explode.

He squeezed his eyes shut and let out a frustrated sigh, saying, "You're too small," to Bed.

Almost as soon as the words were out, a great metallic groan rang through the room. Bed trembled, springs creaked, and the scraping of metal against metal rattled all around him.

Gavin waited calmly as Bed stretched beneath him, growing more than a foot beyond its original length and several feet wider. Sometimes he wondered if House realized he'd grown at all, or if everything inside still imagined him as the tiny boy they'd raised.

"Better," he said. "Thanks."

Gavin looked around then, eyeing the sky-colored paper, the childish clouds on the ceiling. He couldn't let Delilah see this.

"I think maybe a redecoration is in order." He paused, wondering what would be an acceptable substitute. How did seventeen-year-old boys decorate their rooms, anyway? "More black," he finished, satisfied that this would at least be a step in the right direction.

The room cooled, and House rumbled deep within its foundation, a gentle admonishment.

But Gavin ignored this, heaving himself off Bed and crossing the room. He peered out to where the sun hung low in the sky, its golden fingers just visible behind the rooftops of houses in the distance.

The yard sprawled out beneath him, a kaleidoscope of blossoms still visible beneath the thin layer of frost. Delilah had known about the apples, but Gavin wondered what she would think when she saw roses blooming in January or a garden full of vegetables still thriving in the throes of winter.

She'd seemed completely unruffled by his secret earlier, at school, but it was one thing to accept the idea of a house living and breathing and growing all around you and quite another to actually *see* it. How would she react to Ferns that picked themselves up, settling beneath whichever Window had the best view of the sun? Or Lamp, who followed him from room to room because there weren't actual light switches on any of the walls? Or Hall Table, who was one of the few pieces of furniture that never moved during the day but creaked as it prowled through the halls in the middle of the night?

She wanted to come here to see the sideshow that was his life. A part of him worried she'd see the fire burning that nobody ever tended, or Grandfather Clock that told him exactly what he was late for, and she would run out the gate and never speak to him again.

But another, darker part of him worried that she wouldn't. That perhaps Delilah Blue was every bit as brave as she appeared, and would stay. And it was this possibility that frightened him more than all the others combined, because Gavin was fairly certain that once Delilah walked through the front door, he'd never want her to leave.

Gavin took the long way to school, still not sure what he would say the next time Delilah asked to go home with him. He trudged through the slush as he considered this. She would, he knew. It was just a question of whether he'd even get one word out before she asked again.

She was waiting near the front entrance, her bag in a forgotten heap at her feet. Gavin spotted her long before she spotted him, his gaze moving from her braided hair down to legs that peeked from beneath the bloom of her pleated skirt.

Gavin didn't know a lot about girls, but he knew enough. He knew that when most girls wore things like that, they hoped to drive boys crazy. But it didn't take a genius to know that by wearing what she considered to be a boring uniform, Delilah was completely clueless about what she was doing to him, or to any other boy for that matter. She just didn't think much about clothes. But the innocent slip of leg below the knee, all wrapped in knitted tights and boots, was enough to make him wonder about the parts of her he couldn't see.

She blinked over to him just as he crossed the street. Delilah's eyes widened, a smile lighting up her face, and the twist in his stomach was back, even tighter than before.

"Hi, Delilah," he said, trying to swallow the crack in his voice.

"Hi, Gavin," she said back, gray-green eyes moving over every one of his features. "Finish your paper on Poe?"

"I did. You?"

Delilah pivoted and began walking toward the school. "I did, but it took forever."

"Why? You probably already covered Poe in freshman year at Saint Benedict's." They climbed the steps, and Gavin held open the door, breathing in her apple-blossom scent as she passed.

"I still had to do a lot of research."

He looked over at her, wondering about her mysterious little smile. "I'm sure you just forgot some of the smaller details."

"Or maybe there are just too many distractions in my English class," she said.

Gavin considered this, taking in her teasing expression. "Well, Mr. Harrington is very distracting," he said with a small grin.

"We could be distracted at your house," she said in a whisper. "I'm sure you'd make an excellent tutor."

He swallowed and blinked away, but just as easily as he'd turned awkward, Delilah laughed, reaching out to take his hand in hers. She lifted the edge of his sleeve and stared down at the black ink there, the words he'd written just this morning:

She takes your voice and leaves you howling at the moon.

"What is that?"

He tugged his sleeve down and blinked behind her, to where several students watched their interaction with interest. "It's from a song I love."

They stopped when they reached Delilah's locker. "Are

you sure about this?" he asked finally. "The house is a lot to take in." He looked around them again, then back at her. "Being with me is a lot to take in, as well."

Her eyes flamed, and she stretched up on her toes, her lips almost touching the shell of his ear. The halls were a whirlwind of activity, but none of it seemed to matter to either of them.

"I'm sure."

CHAPTER NINE

HER

G AVIN OPENED THE HEAVY DOOR AND STEPPED through, looking around as if making sure everything was as it should be. With a small smile, he waved her in, nodding to let her know it was okay.

The entire walk there, Delilah had been high on anticipation and the thrill of seeing inside Gavin's secret world. But on the porch, she was suddenly terrified of being gripped by the arms of a chair or tripped by the leg of a table. Was everything inside ... wild? She imagined for a panicked heartbeat the feeling she'd had as a child, staring at the illustrations in *Jumanji*: vines growing on the ceilings, rhinos storming through the house, enormous bees dive-bombing from overhead.

"Come on," he murmured, smiling in reassurance.

One tentative look past Gavin at the inside of the house showed her that it was actually very houselike.

She walked through the rooms, trailing her fingertips along each surface until it occurred to her that she might be molesting everything she touched. The furniture was pristine and beautiful, the floors—whether wood, or tile, or soft carpet—lacked any trace of dust or grime. Thick wall-papered walls were decorated with the occasional painting with life inside them—seaside scenes with gulls calling out from behind the frames, the smell of oranges as she passed a painting of a fruit tree. But other than these sounds and smells, the house was completely silent.

Gavin watched with a mixture of apprehension and amusement, his eyes wide and bottom lip snared between his teeth. He followed, studying her as she took it all in.

"That's where I sit and read," he said as she ran her hand over a leather couch in the living room.

"I wouldn't sit there." He laughed as she eyed a particularly severe-looking chair at the head of the table in the dining room. "This room has a bit of attitude."

She expected some reaction from the space, something like a hum or a shiver, but everything was well and truly still, except for the paintings, which she'd actually forgotten. Now standing in the quiet calm of the kitchen, Delilah wondered if this house was anything special after all.

"I can't tell that the house is . . . different."

Gavin smiled as he turned and opened the refrigerator, grabbing two bottles of juice. "If you say so."

"Do you think it will be weird to live somewhere else? Like when you go to college?"

She'd said these things innocently, but the house jerked to life, shaking once so violently and with a terrible groan that Delilah screamed and instinctively sprinted for the door.

The handle was locked, and she stood there, madly rattling the knob until Gavin came up behind her, wrapped his hand around hers, and gently pried her fingers away.

"It's okay, Delilah." He curled his hand around her shaking fist and pressed their hands to her stomach. "It's okay."

The house had gone still, the rooms no longer shaking or cold. Delilah could feel Gavin's breath against her ear. She slumped back against him, calming. "It just surprised me."

"I'm sorry," he whispered in her hair. Somehow, though, it felt like he was speaking to the house as well as her.

When Delilah turned to look at him, her attention was drawn over his shoulder, at the light that continued to swing over the kitchen table, at the walls that now seemed to pulse and breathe as if before everything had been holding its breath, suspended.

"It was just behaving before," he said with a small smile. "I've been talking about you for a long time, so everyone is excited. I think we're all a little unsure how to act."

"No, I'm sorry," she said, her voice cracking. "I didn't mean to upset anyone by asking that."

She was shaking and wild-eyed when Gavin pulled her in to his chest, wrapping his endless arms around her. She pressed her face against his breastbone, listened to the steady pound of his heartbeat, and for a moment she felt like she was being held by him inside another body, a bigger and much more powerful one. She felt an odd tickling at her thoughts, like shadow fingers pressing in from her temples.

Blinking hard, Delilah shook her head and felt a wild pulse of anger over the violating sensation. In a tiny gust, the feeling was gone.

Gavin ran a long finger up her spine, bringing her immediately back into the moment with him. She'd been spooked by the shaking of the house. That was all.

"Let's go outside, to the shed," he said, and Delilah felt his lips move against her hair as he spoke. She wondered what stories his mouth might write across her skin and where he would put them.

"Are you scared?" he asked, very quietly.

Delilah shook her head. She wasn't scared, *exactly*. But it was strange to reconcile always *wanting* the weird and strange and having it groan and shake all around you. It was wonderful to finally see something like this with her own eyes, but she hated to admit that it was also a little frightening to feel the presence of the house press up against her, so close, nearly in her own thoughts. The house was huge and real, and Gavin lived *inside* it. There must be slivers of her boringly normal parents inside *her* somewhere, but Delilah wasn't sure she'd ever be able to wrap her brain around that.

"I just don't want to do anything wrong," she said.

The quiet rumble of his laugh rose up from where her cheek rested against him and came out in an exhale over the top of her head. "You couldn't. I think the house is worried about the same thing. Haven't you ever heard the phrase 'it's more scared of you than you are of it?' Come on."

Gavin led her into the backyard, which was huge and green and ripe with lush trees. Ruby apples hung from heavy branches. Tangerine, cherry, plum, and peach trees were thick with fruit and planted to create a small, delicious forest beside a shed.

Here the lawn was also perfect, soft and springy under her shoes. "What's wrong with the front lawn?" she asked, remembering.

Gavin laughed. "The twins. I think Dead Lawn does it to piss off Alive. But that's just a guess."

Of course it was, Delilah thought. There wasn't exactly any way for him to ask, or for them to answer.

"I have about a million questions."

"I'm surprised you only have that many." He led her farther back, into one of the small sheds, saying, "Come in here. She's cool."

She wanted to ask how on earth he knew the shed was a she or the lawns were twins or the house was worried for Delilah's reaction, but when she saw the shed, she understood. The walls were softly curved, the wood smelling faintly of fruit tree blossoms. Gavin stepped aside after opening the door, letting her walk in ahead of him.

Delilah wasn't sure what she expected, but it certainly wasn't this. A shed, to her mind, was meant to be dusty and a place where old garden tools go to be forgotten and grow crusty with spiderwebs. This shed was nothing like that. The floors were shiny and pristine, the two small windows crystal-gleaming. Two walls were lined with shelves stacked high with jarred fruit, vegetables, and sauces. Another wall had a sink, a small stove, and several drawers with polished brass knobs. A blue sofa was tucked beneath the larger window and a stack of books rested nearby on the floor. Without having to ask, Delilah knew that Gavin spent a lot of time out here.

"Who made the jars of food?"

"Shed," he answered, confused.

Delilah looked up in time to catch his curious smile. "How is that even possible?"

He opened one of the drawers near the stove and pulled out a couple of random utensils: a peeler, a slotted spoon, a beautiful knife with an ivory handle. "She uses utensils." Delilah wanted to know *how*, but before she could ask, he said, "Do you want to take some fruit home?"

The space grew noticeably warmer, and Delilah felt her eyes widen, looking instinctively to the window in search of an aggressive ray of sun.

"It's warm because she wants you to take some."

Nodding politely, Delilah took the jars of peaches and plums when Gavin handed them over.

"These, too," he said, tucking a jar of tiny pickles between her forearm and ribs. Delilah looked down at them, half expecting them to wiggle a little hello from behind the glass, but they were as still as any other collection of pickles. "They're my favorites."

"Is this place your favorite place to be?"

"It's one of them."

"What are some others?"

"Kitchen. My room." He shrugged and then added, "I love playing Piano, but Dining Room is a nightmare sometimes."

She lifted her eyebrows in silent question.

"He's a bit of a hermit and keeps it really cold so that I don't like being in there."

He led her back outside, and Delilah felt as if she'd stepped off a boat: a little wobbly, her stomach flipping at the sturdiness of the earth beneath her feet.

"You okay?" Gavin's hand came around her upper arm, warm, long fingers curling deliciously over her skin. The sensation of falling heightened until she swayed, leaning in to him and wondering if a part of her did it intentionally, because once his arms were fully around her, she felt perfect. Cocooned and stable, but—unfortunately—desperate for a kiss.

They lay down on a patch of grass beneath a cherry tree. The sun shone through in tiny bursts, and Delilah managed to position her head to avoid getting a sunbeam in the eye. It also meant that her head rested against Gavin's shoulder.

"You can ask me more questions," he said. "I'm sure you're a little overwhelmed."

She nodded, and she knew he felt it because he leaned a little closer to her. The feeling that took over was how Delilah imagined it would be if someone flushed hot water through her veins.

"Does the house possess things? Is that how everything works?"

"I'm not sure what it does, really, but that's probably as good a description as any. The utensils move. The stove turns on. I feel like it's the shed making it all, but maybe it's more than one thing in there. The house sort of feels like one . . . *thing*, with just a lot of moving parts."

She reached down, tugged at his elbow so he'd move his hand closer and let her hold it. "Are you happy here?"

"Yeah," he said. "I mean, it's all I've really known. I know that my home life is different, to say the least."

She knew she should ask about the yard, or the house, or how he learned to walk, talk, or interact with other humans. Instead, she asked, "Have you ever had a girlfriend over before?"

He laughed. "No. You're the first."

"Have you ever had your heart broken?"

His voice was wary. "That's not a question about the house."

"Answer it anyway." She looked up at him, admired his sharp jaw and the dark stubble forming just beneath his skin. She wondered if he would ever let her draw something on him. Bloodred swirls and jagged, slate-gray lines, or words, like he did. Some runes, maybe, to scare anyone else away from ever touching him the way she wanted to. "If I'm your girlfriend, I get to ask things like that."

"Fair enough," he said with a little smile. "And no, I haven't. Not the way you mean. I had it broken a lot when I was little, just from being ignored or rejected or teased. I don't think it could be broken now."

Her heart broke a little at that. "That's pretty terrible."

"It's not." His fingers squeezed her, and inside her chest, her ribs seemed to mimic the gesture, coming together tightly. "I haven't been lonely. House is very affectionate. Objects as family is my reality, and I'm a pretty happy person. Like I said, I have people I chat with online who just know me as a username and don't have any clue that I'm the Monster House version of raised-by-wolves. Of course, now I have you."

She grinned. "Yes. You do."

"But I'm just saying that a person probably couldn't break my heart. But maybe House could."

The branches from the tree had started stretching down, and now they touched his other arm, the one she didn't feel pressed along the length of hers. He whispered a "thanks" as he pulled a cherry off with a careful tug, popped it in his mouth, and turned to throw the pit across the yard. The branch smacked him lightly on the shoulder.

"What? You wanted to take it?" The tree ran a leaf across

his cheek and then retreated. An obvious "yes." It was then that Delilah realized how Gavin must have learned to walk and talk and all the other things he would have needed: House had taught him. If it could do something as delicate as feed him a cherry, reprimand him for tossing a pit into the grass, and then caress his cheek, it could certainly care for and nurture him.

Gavin was loved.

From where she lay, Delilah watched the interaction with wide-eyed fascination.

"I don't know what to ask," she said finally. "I think it's amazing."

A warm breeze blew through the yard and carried with it the smell of spring and warmth and the best kind of summer day, in the middle of the winter.

They left not too much later. Delilah was absorbed with everything around them, but still so self-conscious in front of it, wondering how much it could hear, or see. Wondering, too, if it saw through her directly to her not-so-innocent intentions where Gavin was concerned. She'd spent a good fraction of the time they were there imagining where they would kiss when they spent time together at his house.

He didn't say anything when they left; he gave a small pat to the trunk of the cherry tree before leading Delilah out the back gate and onto the street. Back on the ordinary sidewalk, she didn't think she would ever see the world the same way again. How many homes were like this? How many trees had the same consciousness as the ones in Gavin's yard?

Just as she pondered this, his pocket buzzed. She looked up at his face in surprise as he seemed to hesitate for a moment before digging into his pocket.

"You have a cell phone?"

"Yeah. Of course." The way he looked at her, she felt as though she'd grown an eyeball on her forehead.

"Did you buy it?"

Gavin held up a finger, asking her to wait as he answered. He didn't answer like she would, with a "hello," or a "hi," or a "This is Gavin." He just said, "I'll be back by nine." And then hung up.

"You have a curfew?"

"Of course I do," he said, laughing.

"But if the house knows where you are all the time, why would you need to tell it when you'll be back?"

"It can't always *see* me unless I've taken something with me that's . . . possessed." He laughed when he said this, giving her a little apologetic smile. "Or unless it follows me in the grass, or in a wire, which . . ." He paused. "I'm not sure it's ever done that. It's weird to find the language for all of this. I mean, sometimes I know when House is worried, and it leaves a small object at the door for me to carry. Like on days I have a big exam. Or when I had my job interview and it knew I was nervous." He smiled down at her. "But usually when I leave, I'm just . . . by myself."

Delilah nodded, thinking about what he'd said and how much freedom he really had, in a weird way.

And nine o'clock felt like an eternity. Delilah looked at her watch. Did she really have five more hours with him? A blur of images flew through her thoughts like a stack of photos being flipped through his long, knobby fingers. Hands held, lips to palm, mouth moving up her wrist, kissing her chin, her lips, her eyelids. The smooth glide of his tongue on hers and a quiet exhale from her mouth into his.

But no, she didn't have five hours. She was lucky if she had two, because her own curfew was sunset, and the sky was already sagging: the dim gray-blue of abbreviated winter days.

Gavin slipped the phone back in his pocket and gazed at her. His eyes were so dark and shiny, like her favorite black marbles when she was little. She used to pretend she found them while on safari in Africa, hunting for magical roots and fruit.

"I work because it's nice to have some independence, but also there's always money in the jar."

Delilah blinked into focus. "What?"

He smiled, as if catching her daydreaming about his eyes and the adventures he saw for them behind the dark, dark irises. "In the pantry. There's a jar of money; it's always full. I don't know how, but I never run out." When she still didn't respond, he reminded her with a patient smile, "It's how I got a cell phone."

"Is the *jar* alive?"

"I assume so." He shrugged, shoulders pointing to the clouds and then relaxing again. "I don't have much of a relationship with it other than to get some money when I need it."

"Sounds pretty typically teenager," she said, and grinned.

His smile stuttered and then twisted into a full curve, lighting up his entire face. Delilah thought she'd lose her mind or melt into the sidewalk if he smiled at her like that much longer.

"I haven't been called 'typical' before."

"I guess you're not, except with the money jar."

"Have you?" he asked.

"Sure, lots of times. Maybe not with that word, but with others—like sweet, or quiet, or well behaved."

"Well, you're not."

"I'm not well behaved?" She fought another smile. Delilah liked the idea that he thought she had something wild in her, trapped in a steel box beneath her heart. If he would only kiss her, maybe it would all come tearing out and claw at him.

"I suspect you're not that, either, but I meant you're not typical," he said. He reached forward, took a strand of her hair and wrapped it around his finger, sliding to the end and tugging gently. "Not even a little. And when you look at me like that, I want to lick your lips until the sun is gone."

A thousand horses galloped in her chest. "You could, you know."

He ignored this, saying very quietly, "No one has ever looked at me the way you do."

She believed him. She'd never seen anyone the way she saw him, either. "Why won't you kiss me?"

"I'm afraid I won't be able to stop, and you'll miss *your* curfew."

She thought of her father's angry face and her mother's worried one as they both hovered in the kitchen, as close to the clock as they could get. "It might be worth it."

He pulled his bottom lip between his teeth as he seemed to consider a kiss. Soft red flesh turned white where he pressed down with a sharp canine. He was too much for her. He was the most sensual person she had ever met. Delilah closed her eyes.

"I think about kissing you a lot," he whispered.

She inhaled sharply, squeezing her eyes shut more firmly. Wanting him to stop and hoping he never would.

"And other things. Like how it would feel if you bit my shoulder. Or whether I could bite you back and if you'd like it."

Delilah thought she would, *knew* she would. That unknown dark and dangerous thing about him was what pulled her in, but what kept her feeling more and more and more infatuated with Gavin was the reality: He would say every thought he had and wasn't embarrassed that he was different and a little dark.

She considered opening her eyes and seeing what he looked like when he said these things to her, but before she had a chance, she felt the brush of his lips across hers, fingers wrapping around her waist, and a small, sharp bite to her bottom lip. The pain made her gasp and then immediately want another taste.

"Tell me tomorrow if you liked that."

When she finally managed to open her eyes, Gavin was a small black dot in the distance as he disappeared down the sidewalk.

Chapter Ten

Him

GAVIN TOLD HIS ROOM WHAT HE COULD about his afternoon with Delilah without turning into a lovesick poet. How she had a thousand smiles, how she was smart and unafraid even though when she stood close to him, she was positively tiny. All around him, the room grew warm.

"I'm exhausted, though. Talking to her wipes me out. It's like she just looks at me and it pulls every thought I have from my brain. I couldn't keep a secret from her if I tried."

The room cooled.

"She's already been here, Room. She knows about all of you, so you're not even a secret anymore. Plus, she thinks you're all wonderful."

The edges of Blanket lifted up, wrapping Gavin in its embrace. Who knew that the objects inside House could be collectively sensitive, so possessive, so meddling?

"Do you watch me when I'm out there?" He'd always

wondered this, and the conversation with Delilah tripped that same curiosity again. When he was little, something from House would always accompany him on walks or to school. But as he grew older, he had the sense that House wanted him to feel like he could be independent, even if he was never really alone.

He suspected House did watch over him most of the time, though he never completely understood *how*. Through a network of trees or wires buzzing dully in the sky? He'd never bothered asking, because he'd never really cared before.

But now he needed to know whether he could be alone with Delilah if he wanted.

"Do you, House? Do you watch me all the time?"

The room didn't warm or cool. The blanket neither tightened nor loosened. No answer.

"That's what I thought," he said quietly.

CHAPTER ELEVEN

HER

"STOP TOUCHING YOUR LIP, DELILAH," HER MOTHER said and then smiled stiffly, trying to take the bite off. "Your chin will break out just below. You have dirt and oils on your fingers and will give yourself pimples."

"Okay," Delilah mumbled into her plate. Flavorless vegetables, bland chicken, undercooked rice. She looked up at her ceiling and wished for a brief pulse that the lamp would sway in some happy dinnertime rhythm. The silence in her house was intimidating. She missed the chaos of mealtimes at her old school, with forks clanging and drinks spilling and hundreds of girls speaking in excited whispers. She wondered what dinners were like at Gavin's house and whether she could kiss Gavin at his dinner table.

She wished she'd asked him for his phone number so she could call him after dinner from beneath her blankets and tell him that she had liked his kiss.

"Delilah Blue, I said stop touching your lip."

· · ·

Delilah's dreams were twisted and wonderfully terrifying that night. Each time she woke with a start, she remembered a dream where she'd died from the most innocent household accident—she left the stove on all day and the house exploded—and she'd fall back asleep and have another one, this time about dropping the hair dryer in the full tub or falling down the stairs and landing on a knife in her hand.

Somehow, Delilah must have gone to bed with a butter knife clutched in her fist. She dropped it to the floor with a dull clang and felt her muscles shake and pull as she stretched herself fully awake. Delilah's head hurt, a dull ache in her temples that echoed of fingers pressing into her skull. She found Tylenol in the cupboard in the bathroom and lay back down, falling asleep until the sun was barely starting to brighten the sky.

Getting up on such dark mornings allowed Delilah to pretend she'd never slept and had been out all night, dancing wildly. In the shower she pretended that it was three in the morning and she was washing off sweat accumulated from crashing into other soaked bodies on the dance floor, and not just the innocent layer of sleep and wild dreams.

She put on whatever clothes were folded at the top of each drawer, suspecting that Gavin didn't even really notice what she wore. To be fair, though, if he showed up at school in khakis and a polo shirt she would have a heart attack. So maybe her clothes mattered too. Delilah smoothed her hands down over her crisp red skirt and white sweater. So plain. She had traded one uniform for another. Trying to fit her personality in her clothing had always just felt like so much *work*.

In the mirror, she let her hands run over her hips—narrow and girlish—and up over her chest—barely there. She felt stunted from private school, as if her body needed the added chemistry of boys to become a woman and was years behind everyone else. She liked the long, sinewy lines of Gavin's body beneath his T-shirt. She liked the way the veins on his arms stood out when he heaved his backpack over his shoulder and how his biceps peeked out from his sleeves like thick ropes. He looked strong and scrappy and like he'd just as soon wrestle her onto the grass as he would slip his hand into hers.

Breakfast—more bland. Walk to school—too long. But the sight of Gavin waiting for her at the edge of the school property made something wiggle inside her chest and her stomach turn to fire.

"So did you?" he asked, before she was close, certainly before she was close enough to be sure of what he'd said.

"What?" she called.

"Did you like it?"

She answered by walking faster and then pressing against him, arms around his neck and pulling him down

down

down

down to her mouth, where she could offer her lip again.

"I liked it too much," she said, after he'd bitten her and she'd sucked on his lip and pulled his hair and heard the sound he made that set off fireworks in each of her toes.

"Too much how?"

"I couldn't stop thinking about it. Mom yelled at me for touching my lip."

Gavin's eyebrows inched toward his hairline. "Really? Yelled?"

"Well, no. She doesn't yell. But she nagged me all through dinner in this voice that sounds pleasant but isn't."

"Because you touched your lip all through dinner?"

Delilah nodded. "So you're obligated to do it over and over and over now."

The school bell clanged in the background, and Gavin wrapped his arm around her shoulders, steering her toward the building. "Did you have bells at the other school?"

She gazed up at him, wondering if the topic of kissing was finished. "No. We were expected to be responsible for our time." She heard how the words came out rote and programmed, straight from the Saint Benedict's handbook.

"That's it, then. Public-school kids aren't trusted to be responsible."

She stared at the pavement as it passed beneath their feet. She noticed that he had on new black shoes and watched them instead of wishing he would obsess about kissing as much as she did.

"Though I like to think that I'm not *typical*," he said. She heard a twist in his voice, like he was smiling out the words. "I like to fulfill my obligations. Kissing or otherwise. But especially kissing."

Delilah knew her grin was ridiculous, and ahead in the distance, Dhaval caught her eye. His reaction—raised brow, arms crossed—told her that he saw the wild smile and would keep at her the entire day until she spilled every detail about the boy at her side. Gavin slowed his steps and finally released her, kissing the side of her head and promising he would find her later. When he walked away, shoulders square and broad, hair as black as the shadows under the tree, she felt a little hollow, like maybe he'd taken one of her ribs with him when he left.

The grass spread brown and muddy, forming a dim smudge across the front of the school. Dhaval sat at the top of the steps beside Cornelia Stinton, a girl Delilah knew only from Dhaval's lesson on social hierarchy Delilah's first day back at school. Cornelia seemed nice enough. She'd moved from Wichita the year after Delilah left for private school, and therefore was one of few girls in school who didn't seem personally offended that Delilah had ever left.

"Come here, girl." Dhaval patted the concrete next to him. "Spill."

Delilah sat beside him, waving politely to Cornelia, who seemed to sit a little too close to Dhaval and watch him with more interest than she maybe would have if she knew he was more interested in boys than girls.

"What's today's adventure?" he asked, bumping Delilah's shoulder with his.

"Discussion of unreliable narrators in fiction, archery in phys ed, and—"

"And more kissing your new boy toy?"

Delilah gave him a meaningful glare and didn't bother to answer.

"Girl, you work fast," he said. "You always get what you want?"

She snorted. "Definitely not."

"Are you dating Gavin?" Cornelia asked, leaning past Dhaval so she could give Delilah full view of her wide blue eyes. Cornelia was pretty in the way that girls often were at seventeen: prettier beneath all of the things she put on her face.

Maybe Cornelia was pretending she hadn't seen Delilah and Gavin on the lawn just now. Maybe she really hadn't seen them. So Delilah nodded and watched Gavin disappear inside the side door, wishing he didn't sit behind her in English so she would be able to stare at his shoulder and remember how it felt to rest her head against it.

"He was a little too weird for me," Cornelia said, leaning back into position and sounding sharply bored. "I'm glad that's over."

Delilah understood the dismissively territorial behavior: By casting off Gavin, Cornelia was allowing Delilah to have him. Dhaval made a skeptical noise in his throat. "You had it bad for him, Corr."

Cornelia smacked him. "I did not."

"Liar," Dhaval drawled.

"Well, he seems just weird enough for me." Delilah stood, telling Dhaval she would see him later, and walked into the building.

Students pressed into her as they walked past, hot and heavy all around. Everyone seemed so carefully disheveled, as if their hair had been mussed into the perfect disarray, their clothes selected to be ideally mismatched. Delilah looked down at her skirt, her sweater, her plain brown shoes.

She leaned against her locker, feeling the press of bodies behind her like a riptide. She could join it, get pulled along to class. Or she could pretend to bury her feet in the sand and wait for her world to stop spinning.

Delilah wasn't all that familiar with jealousy. She'd had what could only barely be considered a boyfriend for a few weeks last year. She'd kissed a couple others. But she'd always let them go with as friendly a smile as she could manage, and tried not to tell them they just didn't have the right twist for her tastes.

Giant footsteps echoed toward her, and she didn't even realize she'd been alone in the empty hall until the second, late bell rang and the toes of black sneakers moved into her line of vision.

"Why are you still out here? I thought you were the queen of time management." Gavin bent to meet her eyes. There was a tightness in his face, something pulling the edges taut and worried. *Where is the mystery?* she wondered. It wasn't as if he hadn't seen her sitting down next to Cornelia. It was exactly why he hadn't joined her there, she realized.

"Did you kiss her?"

"Who?" He studied her for a beat before his eyes widened in understanding. "Cornelia?"

"Yes."

Gavin nodded, and Delilah blinked down to the ink on his forearm. "Did you take her home?"

In her peripheral vision, she saw him smile, shake his head. "I told you, you were the first. Delilah, are you jealous?" He seemed to find the whole thing fascinating.

"A bit."

"Of *Cornelia*?"

She looked away, fighting a smile. She liked the way he seemed unable to conceive of such a thing. "Yes."

"Well, I promise you, I was only a tool used to completely freak out her parents."

"But you dated her."

"Of course I did. Why not?"

It wasn't exactly what she wanted to hear, but Delilah

appreciated his honesty. "Did you bite her bottom lip?"

His smile faded as fast as a lit match put under water, but his eyes smoldered with a hunger that made Delilah's fingertips tingle. "No. Never wanted to do *that* with her."

She took his hand and pulled him toward Room 104, Mr. Harrington's English class.

CHAPTER TWELVE

HIM

ER HAND WAS ALMOST CONSTANTLY IN THE air during class. Gavin watched Delilah's skinny arm wave back and forth, as she volunteered to answer her seventh question in forty minutes. *She'll speak enough for both of us*, he thought. He imagined them in a quick montage of scenarios—at the grocery store, buying a car, walking through the park together—and wondered how that would work over time, if he would start to feel more a part of her world, or if she would always just grab his hand and pull him along in her determined, tiny wake.

For once he was thinking of a relationship in the abstract unit of time, not in a finite unit as small as classes or kisses. He'd never really thought about how to integrate a person into his life long-term, and Gavin's thoughts immediately turned to her question yesterday: *Do you think it will be weird to live somewhere else?*

He'd never actually considered the alternative. He'd always assumed he'd be in the house forever.

Their shoes crunched on the dried leaves as they walked across the lawn to their favorite tree.

Gavin looked at her profile and, as always, wondered what she was thinking. "Why do you talk in class so much?"

As soon as the words were out, he heard how critical they sounded. It was the kind of thing he would have said to another girl like Cornelia, or Tabitha, and she would have said, *Gavin, that's super-rude.* He would mumble an apology and wonder why they didn't just give him the benefit of the doubt. It's not like they were dealing with Dhaval Reddy—Mr. Social—or Tanner Jones—Mr. Jock. They had chosen the weird guy for a reason and then expected him to act typical.

But apparently Delilah didn't expect this. She shrugged, completely unfazed by his tone. "My school—my *old* school—was pretty strict about participation. It just became part of the routine. This school just lets you sit there and not say anything."

And thank God for that, he thought. "Do you miss Saint Benedict's?"

She chewed her lip while she considered this. "Yes and no."

Briefly he pondered which part was yes and which was no, but he put himself in her situation and figured if she was comparing this mess of a school to a fancy East Coast academy, she probably missed most things. Hopefully, the one thing she didn't miss was that *he* wouldn't have been at Saint Ben's.

She sat on the grass and opened her lunch bag, popping

a grape in her mouth. She chewed, thinking, and Gavin sat beside her, slanting his body toward hers, kissing the side of her head before opening his own lunch.

"There are a lot more students here," she said. "People care more about what they're wearing, but in a really silly way. Like, they want to look messy and take a lot of time to do it. We didn't care as much about that, and when given the option of free dress, we all just wore whatever we slept in."

Gavin's thoughts slipped away to something dark and silky and very, very tiny. He ran his hand up her arm, to her neck, to pull her in for a kiss.

"Not like that," she said, smiling against his lips.

He tried to see House the way she might have the day before. It had stayed so still for her initially—almost as if it were holding its collective breath—but he'd been so absorbed in Delilah's reaction he hadn't given it much thought. And her reaction had been completely unexpected. He'd been sincere when he said he'd never had a girl over before, but he had to imagine that if he had, they would have kept their arms tucked closer to their bodies than Delilah. She'd reached out, touched Walls and Couch, even Stiff Chair.

As always, Delilah was fearless. Maybe even foolhardy.

Gavin pulled up short, staring at the soft pastel wallpaper of Hallway and wondering where that thought had come from. If he trusted House, why shouldn't she? Why should she come in with trepidation? Was there something about House to fear?

With this burst of thoughts, he walked faster down the hall to the upstairs bathroom—the only functional bathroom in House and also the only room Gavin had never thought was alive. It was his sanctuary, and the one place in House he realized he felt safe thinking whatever he wanted.

See? That bothered him too. His thoughts were his own everywhere, weren't they? In any room he entered he could think about anything he wanted, whether it was Delilah naked and waiting for him on his bed, or any number of flittering images that entered his mind—seeing himself in college, laughing with a family, sailing in the middle of the ocean—and were gone as quickly as they'd appeared, and no person or object would even know. His thoughts were his and had always been. Hadn't they?

For the first time in his life Gavin truly wondered if his reality were accurate. Every object in House could move, could feel, could think. But each lacked muscles, flowing blood, and a brain to process it all. Why *wouldn't* House be able to hear his thoughts? What else could House do that he had never considered?

Before Gavin could trip his way down the tangle of worries and thoughts that led to the dreaded question—*where did I come from?*—he heard the sound of a small fist against the front door.

He wasn't expecting a package or a grocery delivery, and nobody ever, *ever* just dropped by. The knock came again.

"Gavin?"

Through the thick oak of the door, Delilah's voice sounded tinny and frail, when in reality and despite her size, her voice was low and scratchy, as if she'd grown up screaming everything and had only recently decided to tone it down. Gavin opened the front door and grinned. "What brings you here, Miss Blue?"

She shrugged, slipping past him as if she owned the place and dropping her bag on the floor. "My hot boyfriend."

Gavin looked around the room in mock surprise. "He's here too?"

The corners of her eyes turned up as she smiled. "Yes! Could you get him for me? He's short and burly and never stops talking. Just my type."

Gavin bent to kiss her forehead. "Sorry it took so long. I wasn't expecting anyone. It took me a second to realize someone was at the door. People don't *stop by* here."

"And now you can't say that ever again." She brushed her fingers across his chest as she walked past him and into the dining room. Delilah ran a hand over the top of Piano, and then with fingers from both hands pressed lightly into a few keys, playing a middle C chord.

"Oh boy," Gavin mumbled under his breath. As predicted, Piano held the notes far longer than Delilah's fingers lingered, the sound of C, E, and G in harmony filling the cavernous room.

"Wow, it has good reverb. Or whatever it's called on a piano," she said, starting to walk deeper into the room.

"Piano is . . . ," Gavin started and then trailed off, knowing what was coming anyway.

"Is what?"

But as soon as she asked, Piano played another chord, C-sharp major. And then, after a pause, another, D major. Piano made its way through the majors: E-flat, E, F, F-sharp, G, A-flat, A, B-flat, and finally ended with a lingering, *pointed* B.

Delilah, who had turned back when the notes began, stood frozen, staring down at the keys. "I don't actually play the piano. Is it expecting me to do that, too?"

"It's teaching you." And on cue, Piano played the C-sharp major chord again and then paused. The room cooled impatiently as Delilah's hesitation endured. Gavin could remember this exact routine over and over from when he was six. He hadn't been allowed upstairs that night until he'd mastered every chord through the majors.

"Does it *know* I don't play?"

Gavin laughed. "I think it assumes you don't, because you didn't put the right fingers down."

Delilah pressed her fingers down on the keys—her index, middle, and pinky—but no sound came out of the instrument.

"Wrong fingers," Gavin offered. He wished there'd been

someone there to give him that prompt. That had been the longest part of learning to play: where to put his fingers, how to move them along the scales.

"Cripes, Gavin, is this like Pitfall!? I have to finish this thing before I can see the rest of the house?"

He stared at her, confused. "Pitfall?"

She looked over her shoulder at him and grimaced. "Sorry. It's a video game. My dad has an old Atari. Turns out before he turned into a cardboard-cutout dad, he was a geek."

With a wry smile, Gavin stepped closer and correctly positioned her fingers. "Who knew?" He'd never even seen her father, but from what she'd said about him—very little, to be honest—Gavin had a hard time imagining he'd ever done anything besides silently eat dinner and watch the news.

Beneath his hands, her fingers were warm and long for her height, as if she were a puppy and would soon see a growth spurt. Gavin liked all of the ways otherwise-small Delilah was surprisingly big. He realized his fingers were running up and down her arm and stepped back to let her learn.

"Stay close like that," she said quietly, still staring down at the keys.

He returned to her, aligning his front against her back, and she leaned her head against his chest as she let Piano teach her. She laughed every now and then, made goofy sounds when she messed up or little shouts of victory every time Piano moved on to a new chord. It seemed like she was having fun, and the lights brightened and the room warmed to perfect, and Oven began baking something so the entire house smelled like warm sugar and chocolate. Gavin kissed her hair and wondered if House had the ability to freeze time and hold this moment in reverb for an entire week.

His heart seemed to grow three sizes too big for his body when Delilah looked over her shoulder at him, lips all ripe fruit and teasing and her smile a little dangerous. He was pretty sure he didn't want to have sex inside House, but in the moment, he could probably be convinced.

But instead of stretching and kissing him, she asked, "Do you know how to dance?"

He shook his head, both relieved and disappointed.

"That's okay," she said, turning in his arms. "I do."

CHAPTER THIRTEEN

HER

MUSIC FILLED THE ROOMS, BOUNCED OFF the walls and seemed to fill every dark corner. The piano didn't stop playing for hours as Gavin spun her around the floor, his hands on her waist, his fingers pressing into the exposed skin just above her skirt.

Delilah liked the way that Gavin held her almost too tightly. He was never really careful with her, not the way her family seemed to be or her friends were, back at her old school, considering every word before they said it, treating one another as if they were made of blown glass.

She wondered if Gavin had ever laughed this much, and she watched as he fell into one of the dining room chairs, eyes bright, cheeks flushed and rosy. His perfect bow of a mouth curved up into a mischievous smile, close enough to kiss whenever she wanted.

"You do know how to dance," he said, reaching up to push his mess of dark hair from his eyes.

"I've never really been allowed to dance before," she said, breathless. "Not unless you count Saturday square dancing at Saint Benedicts."

"You didn't have dances with other schools?" he asked, incredulous.

"Well, okay," she said after a moment. "We had a few. But the boys at Saint Joseph's were even worse off than us. Imagine being sixteen and the only real chance you had to interact with girls your age was supervised by a bunch of crotchety old nuns."

"Sounds like a recipe for a lot of awkward groping," he agreed. Gavin settled back into the chair, stretching his long legs and black Converses in front of him. A small serving tray rolled along the floor with a pitcher of lemonade and two glasses sitting neatly on top. The ice sloshed noisily inside as the table rolled to a stop at his side.

Delilah was positive she would never get used to this. Outside, snow had begun to fall, dusting everything in white. Every once in a while the trees would quake from the tops of the leaves to the lowest branches, shaking off any flakes that had accumulated there. Delilah laughed when she saw this, thinking of the way Nonna's old shepherd would do the same thing after a bath.

"How could any other house ever compare?" she asked innocently.

Gavin opened his mouth to speak but was cut off by

a sudden and resounding clang from the piano, as if someone had brought their fists down over several keys at once. He jumped as the hinged lid slammed shut over the keys, the force so great it vibrated the strings inside.

Delilah blinked into the ringing silence, her eyes darting between Gavin and the piano.

"I guess it was tired of playing," he said. He crossed the room and took her hand, lacing his fingers with hers. "Piano has always been a bit temperamental."

"I didn't mean—" she began, but he quickly cut her off with two fingers pressed to her lips.

"This is better anyway," he said with a shrug, pulling her forward and stopping only when his body was pressed all along hers. "I've been dying to kiss you."

Sunday was long and boring and seemed to stretch on forever. Gavin had to work, and Delilah did her best to stay busy, but her house felt too small, her parents too . . . *everywhere*. She watched TV and cleaned her room; she arranged all her books by size, then again by color, finally deciding to arrange them by the number and manner of deaths that occurred in each one.

But by late afternoon she was going crazy. She wanted to see him again, wanted to watch him smile in that way that made her stomach do strange things, wanted to run her hands through his wild hair and kiss him again until he looked at her in that savage way that felt positively obscene.

Delilah didn't normally text Gavin; her thoughts with him were usually too complicated to be contained in a few lines of text. There was also the matter of wanting to hear him speak, in that slow, unhurried way that he had. Gavin didn't say much, but he rarely seemed to filter the content in person, and Delilah was greedy for his words, preferring the sound of his voice to his stilted, monosyllabic typical-boy-text response. But desperate times called for desperate measures.

Are you home yet?

Thankfully, his response came only a few moments later. *Have to stay late.*

How late is late?

An hour or two?

Delilah considered this. She craved his company, but she had to admit she also craved the way she felt like she left this world and walked straight into another one when she went to his house. *Would it be ok if I went over? I could wait for you.*

She held her breath while she waited for Gavin's reply, the longest minute of her life so far. Uncertainty crawled under her skin as she wondered if her request was strange, or inappropriate. She liked the idea of being alone inside the house for a little while. She liked the idea of experiencing what Gavin had all these years.

You sure?

She smiled as she typed. *Definitely.*

• • •

Delilah waited until her parents went out for the night. She watched as her mother quietly got ready, applying her practically nonexistent makeup and just a spritz of Jean Naté. *Not too much,* she'd always said.

Her father puttered around the house, straightening things that didn't need to be straightened while the evening news droned on in the background. *So boring*, she thought, *and so completely different from where I want to be.*

Delilah followed them to the front door and waved as they backed out of the driveway, noting the way neither one looked up at her as they drove away. As soon as their blue sedan turned the corner, Delilah was off like a flash, grabbing the spare keys from the hook in the laundry room and sprinting out into the fading daylight.

With her father's car parked safely on the street, Delilah approached the gate.

Nothing looked different in the muted dusk light; the house was still a strange collage of colors and sizes, half the yard just as green as the other half was dead. The walkway leading to the front porch was as unusual as the building it belonged to—a winding path of earth-toned pavers, a sprinkling of colored glass and assorted bottle caps thrown in for good measure. Above the house, pink and purple clouds hung like cotton candy.

This time as she approached, Delilah noticed shutters on

the outside of the windows. No one had those anymore. They had fancy plantation shutters on the inside, with thick slats painted white or made of polished wood. These were weathered and thin, cracked in places and polished in others, as if the job of tending to them fell to a hundred different people each assigned a single strip of wood.

The only time Delilah prayed on instinct was just before she got back exam results. But this day she found herself murmuring a prayer as she moved down the path to the house. From this vantage, at the foot of the stairs, she felt like she was about to walk into another world. For a brief pulse she wondered if she would ever come out again.

Or whether she would ever want to.

Delilah gripped the rail and climbed the steps, pushing down the tickle of unease that flared behind her ribs. It was one thing to want to be here with Gavin, to remember the way the euphoric magic of the house seemed to seep into her skin. But it was another thing entirely to be here with the night approaching, without him, knowing the house could feel exactly how close she was.

Outside everything was quiet—unreasonably quiet, she noticed—and with her toes only inches from the front mat, she turned. Though winter seemed suspended in the yard and the trees were lush with leaves and more flowers than she could ever remember seeing in one place before, there were no birds. No bees darted from one blossom to the next.

No spiderwebs shook in the evening breeze. In fact, beyond the wind that rustled through the branches overhead, nothing moved inside the vine-covered walls at all.

She reasoned that the yard was creatureless because it was winter and not because organic life had opted to stay away from the house. Delilah reached for the brass knob, surprised when it turned and the door swung open easily.

To look around now, one could almost call the house cozy. Washed in the golden glow of the final throes of sunset, everything looked rosy and warm. But no fire crackled in the fireplace, and a glance at the floor revealed shadows stretching along the carpet and playfully nipping at her heels.

Delilah's gaze skirted over to the silent piano, and she wondered if Gavin was right and it had simply been tired of playing, or if it had stopped because of what she'd said. She certainly hoped not.

But just in case, she whispered, "Sorry about what I said. If I were him, I'd never want to leave."

A hollow silence rang through the room.

Not willing to stand around in the dark, Delilah crossed the carpet to where a tall lamp stood near the entryway. She reached out, flipping the switch that would turn it on, but nothing happened. She pulled again; peering up under the wide shade, even tightening the bulb to make sure it was secure. Still nothing.

Delilah bent at the knee, feeling around for the cord.

When she found none, she crossed to the television, kneeling to find where it plugged into the wall.

No cord, no outlet to plug it into. Her eyes moved around the room. No light switches, either.

Delilah pulled her phone from her pocket, swiping along the screen to wake it up. She turned it outward, where it cast a small puddle of light in front of her, but not enough for her to see more than a few feet radius around where she stood. She felt the dull thump of her heartbeat as her pulse picked up, and with it came the comforting rush of adrenaline, that feeling she loved from slasher flicks, from gory art. *This* was her element: the creepy, the unknown. It's why she wanted to come over in the first place.

"Calm down, Delilah," she told herself, trying out a laugh that came out breathless and a little tight.

Her footsteps sounded unreasonably loud in the silent house; the soft soles of her shoes against wood were like a siren announcing her presence. All around her the house remained eerily still. Delilah noted that if this were one of the movies she watched late at night while her parents slept, now would be the precise moment when the killer would jump out at the unsuspecting victim, slashing them to pieces. She couldn't help but glance over her shoulder, half expecting to find someone there.

Delilah had always believed she was more clever than the average girl, but in that moment, with so much space between herself and the front door, she wasn't so sure. Why was the house so still? Was it nervous? Was it confused? Or was it somehow lying in wait?

Delilah texted Gavin again: *I'm here. The house is so quiet. Are you sure this is ok? It doesn't mind?*

Her phone buzzed only seconds later with his reply: *Of course I'm sure.*

It's really dark, she told him, wincing in apology as she hit send. She didn't want to come off as nervous or needy . . . but the lack of lights coming on in the house and the lack of a fire blooming to life in the fireplace was starting to feel a little odd.

Really? he replied, and then immediately after, added, *I've never needed a flashlight before, but I know there are candles in my nightstand.*

At the top of the stairs, a hallway stretched long and shadowed in front of her. Framed photographs of a smiling Gavin—spanning from toothless to the tall, lanky boy she knew today—covered the walls.

She paused at a particularly large grouping of frames. In the first, Gavin stood alone with a much simpler version of the house looming behind him. In the second, both Gavin and the house had changed considerably: both had grown taller, and certain features had become more clearly defined while others had softened. And it continued: Each photo depicted a progressively older boy standing in front of a much larger and more complicated house.

Delilah realized she was standing in front of what could only be considered a series of family portraits.

Against the same wall stood a long, narrow table, a simple bowl of red apples she recognized from the tree out back resting on top. Delilah took a step back, her eyes following the ornate legs to where they ended, carved into what looked like the paws of some wild jungle animal, long claws digging into the wood floor. She wasn't sure why this particular detail stood out to her as strange, surrounded as she was by a house that lived and breathed and had raised a seventeen-year-old boy, but it sent a chill through her anyway.

She continued on and passed several rooms, doors ajar and filled with the same fading light as the rest of the house. Delilah hadn't paid much attention to them before—with Gavin nearby, it was hard to concentrate on much else—but now each one seemed to call to her, as if every corner held some new and deliciously dark secret.

Delilah cast the light of her phone into first doorway. It seemed ordinary enough: a large bed draped in fluffy white down, a nightstand, a rocker flanked by gleaming windows. The next held a set of twin beds, identical quilts covering each one. The wallpaper changed abruptly just before the third room, where a sea of hunter green abutted a yellow wall of dandelions.

She stopped in the doorway of a nursery, the space practically bulging with sloppily packed boxes, various toys spilling from beneath the cardboard flaps. Delilah remembered Gavin saying that the house provided whatever was needed, and she couldn't help wonder who all this was for. Gavin? Someone before him? Someone after?

The sun had all but gone, and the room swam with strange shadows. A doll peered at her from the top of the bookcase, its head lolling to the side, glass eyes dull and—thankfully—lifeless.

She moved down the hall, stopping short at a creak just behind her. She stood still, breath locked in her throat, the hair on the back of her neck standing up straight.

Delilah had always been the kind of girl who let her imagination run wild, and though she was certain that was the case now, it did nothing to stop the pounding of her heart inside her chest.

"Get a grip," she told herself, certain she would turn and find nothing but an empty hall, nothing more than stairs and darkness behind her.

Her brain buzzed with a memory of Gavin telling her that she was safe here, that the house would never hurt anything he cared about. She did her best to remember those words now, as the floorboards creaked again and an almost imperceptible growl sounded behind her.

With a deep breath she gathered her courage, spinning so quickly her skirt twisted around her legs. She blinked, searching up and down the empty hallway, shining her pathetic excuse for a light into each of the empty rooms.

Nothing.

Delilah narrowed her eyes, taking a shaky step forward. Then another.

She was almost certain the table had been much farther away.

This was the same house in which she'd danced and laughed with Gavin only yesterday, she reasoned, walking into his bedroom and closing the door behind her. This was the house she wanted to know, to trust, whose world she wanted to join. Still, on instinct she moved to set the lock, but of course there wasn't one.

Gavin's room overlooked the backyard—far from the only lamppost on the opposite end of the street—so it seemed darker than any of the other rooms. Delilah directed her light in front of her, following the white-blue glow to Gavin's nightstand. She found the candles right where he said they'd be—tucked near the back of the drawer—a yellow disposable lighter beneath.

Needing both hands, Delilah reluctantly set down her phone, saying yet another prayer as the lighter sparked in the darkness. It took two tries, but the wick eventually caught flame, the room gradually lightening as it grew.

As she placed the candle on the table, a sketchbook caught her eye. She picked it up and settled herself back against Gavin's pillows, opening it carefully across her lap.

The book was heavy and well used, the pages swollen

with ink and charcoal. The leather creaked in the silence, long spine brittle with age and years of use.

The first page held a bird drawn so realistically that Delilah couldn't help but run a finger along the wing, half expecting to feel the downy softness of feathers. There were a few drawings of her: under the tree at school, at the movie theater with Dhaval, listening to Mr. Harrington in English. She felt a wild, possessive rush at the thought of Gavin sitting on this bed at night, drawing her.

The book was nearly full, and Delilah continued to flip through the pages, her eyes growing heavier with each passing minute. Despite her earlier unease, there was something comforting about being in Gavin's room, on his bed and surrounded by his things. His smell was everywhere. The room was warm and a little humid, and it was easy enough to close her eyes and pretend that he was there now.

She fell asleep almost peacefully, slipping into the softness of flannel and down, feeling as if the blankets were arms wrapping themselves around her. *And maybe they are*, she thought, just as everything went dark.

Something was wrong.

Delilah opened her eyes with a start, wondering what woke her up in the first place. She blinked into the darkness, her eyes slowly focusing on the bleary shapes surrounding her, on the flickering candle next to the bed.

She shifted slightly, meaning to disentangle herself from the blankets now twisted around her legs and across her torso, when a sound came from somewhere in the dark recesses of the house. It started out small, nothing more than a single, muted thump, and was easy enough to ignore. Delilah closed her eyes and settled back in, waiting for sleep to reclaim her.

But it happened again. And again. Growing louder and more insistent . . . like a heartbeat.

"Gavin?"

Delilah waited, head still fuzzy with sleep, straining to hear any movement, wondering if perhaps Gavin had returned home while she slept.

A shiver moved up Delilah's spine as she continued to listen, her eyes wide and trained, unblinking, on the shadows around the large bed. She thought about the claw-footed table in the hall, the curtains that had closed so forcefully the first time she'd come to the house. She wondered what other kinds of things existed here, and what exactly happened inside these walls while Gavin was away.

The rational side of Delilah's brain chastised her, reminding her that she had a tendency toward the dramatic and insisting that if she intended to be a part of Gavin's life she would need to learn to deal with things and not let her imagination run wild at every creaking floorboard or bump in the walls. The house was alive after all; it was only natural that there would be the occasional sound or two.

Delilah peered through the dark and up to the fluffy clouds painted onto the blue ceiling. They floated peacefully across the plaster sky, and she tried to relax, to block out the steady thumping that continued from somewhere below.

The moon rose above the large tree just outside Gavin's window, its light breaking through the narrow gap in the curtains to stretch across the floor. The clouds were easier to make out now, the shapes mimicking small objects tucked into the fairy-tale sky: a teddy bear, a sailboat bobbing along the choppy waves. But with the added light came the realization that something had changed. The blue sky had turned stormy and dark, and menacing clouds began to roll across an increasingly turbulent sea.

Delilah shrank down into the blankets as she watched the scene above her, how the storm seemed to swallow up the imaginary sailboat, along with whatever calm she had managed to regain. Sweat made her clothes cling to her skin as her gaze traveled down the walls, over paintings and drawings that seemed to stop moving as soon as she looked at them.

Though Delilah could only imagine having slept for a few short minutes, the candle had practically burned itself out. It had been yellow—she was sure of it—but now bloodred wax slid down over the candleholder in smooth rivulets. The flame had dimmed, flickering slowly in the still air, and out of the corner of her eye she could see something moving along the wall.

Delilah strained to make out the shape.

The faint pattern inside the wallpaper seemed to stir, the edges becoming blurry before sharpening again. She blinked several times, certain she had to be seeing something that wasn't there. The pattern looked like spiders. Only a few at first, but then more and more, so many that the wall seemed to undulate with them. Their legs were thick, covered in coarse hairs, and their bodies were so plump and round that it turned her stomach with an instinctive panic.

"It's not real," she whispered, closing her eyes tight and hoping she could wake from whatever nightmare she was having. A flash tore through the room, and Delilah gasped, blinking up to where lightning streaked across the ceiling.

"It's not real."

Delilah's heart raced, the sound of her own pulse roaring in her ears. She tried to push up from the bed, but her limbs seemed locked in place, her mind unable to fire the impulse needed to move.

Spindly legs carried hundreds of black bodies skittering across the wall, so many that she could *hear* them. They moved in waves, scattering this way and that, finally arranging themselves into what appeared to be words.

The words formed as if they had been pushed from the wall before seeming to dissolve back into it again. Delilah was frozen, a scream caught in her throat. The blankets constricted around her, pinning her down, trapping her arms at her sides.

The bed vibrated, and she tried to peer over the edge, to see anything. The footboard began to tremble; the sound of groaning metal screeched all around her. For an instant the candle seemed to burn brighter, the flame and her own terrified expression reflected in the brass rails near her feet. Delilah watched in horror as they grew right in front of her, elongating, the ends sharpening like spikes as they reached toward the ceiling.

She began to thrash about, trying to break free, the binds beginning to cut into her skin. And all the while, above the sound of scurrying spiders and the deafening scream of metal, was the thump from downstairs, the recurring beat of a racing heart.

Delilah began to cry, hot tears streaking down her face. A scream tore from her, piercing the darkness just as everything grew silent. Her arms and legs suddenly freed, Delilah scrambled backward, pulling her knees to her chest.

The lights seemed to all come on at once, and the sound of a door opening and slamming shut again rang throughout the house.

Gavin.

Delilah blinked into the sudden brightness, quickly

scrubbing the tears from her cheeks just as her name was called from downstairs. Her eyes flew to the ceiling, where fluffy clouds now floated across the most serene blue sky Delilah could ever remember seeing. There were no spiders, nothing more than gray-blue paper covering the walls. The bed looked perfectly ordinary, too. Brass rails with a soft quilt tossed haphazardly across, not a single fingerprint to mar the pristine finish.

Her head hurt.

"Delilah?" Gavin called again, followed by the sound of his feet as he ran up the stairs.

"I'm in here," she said, surprised by the steadiness of her own voice.

"There you are," he began, his face falling as he took in her expression. Judging by the panic that quickly overtook his features and the way he raced across the room to sit at her side, she must have looked much less calm than she'd sounded. "What happened?"

Delilah gripped his hand, cool and steady in hers. "Nothing," she insisted, feeling herself calm as she realized she must have dreamed it all. "I fell asleep."

"Nightmare?" he asked, smoothing her hair.

"Just a dream. I'm okay, promise."

Gavin seemed to relax, bending to slide his lips carefully over hers. "Must have been pretty bad," he said, meeting her eyes.

Delilah shook her head and wrapped her arms around his waist. Gavin's heart beat strong and steady beneath her ear, chillingly similar to the sound that had woken her in the first place.

"Just a dream," she repeated, closing her eyes, trying to convince herself, too.

CHAPTER FOURTEEN

HER

D ELILAH DIDN'T SLEEP MUCH THAT NIGHT, afraid to close her eyes and find herself in the same nightmare. She'd had nightmares before, but this one was different. It felt real. *So* real.

She was crabby at breakfast, earning a reproachful look from both of her parents. She spilled milk as she poured it into her hot cereal, stubbed her toe on the table leg, and got caught rolling her eyes when her mother began discussing the long hair on the new male bagger down at the grocery store.

"Mom, his long hair doesn't make him a criminal."

Belinda Blue snorted, pulling her tea bag from her cup after a single, weak dunk. "I want this town to be what it used to be. Quiet, clean, and safe."

It was Delilah's turn to snort. "It *is* those things, Mom. A hippie bagger doesn't change that. Maybe it's good that we have someone here now who's from Portland, Oregon. Maybe it will open our eyes a little."

Her mother paused, planting a fist on her hip. "What do you want, Delilah? You want life to always be one adventure after another? Why can't you be happy here? Why do you always need adrenaline and wildness and things you can't predict?"

Delilah felt her smile straighten. So this was how her mother saw her: reckless, unpredictable, and rebellious simply because she'd stood up for a boy six years ago and didn't mind long hair on a bagger. The impression couldn't possibly come from anything else; her mother hardly knew her. "No, Mom. I just want life to be interesting."

"Well," her father mumbled from behind his paper, "whether your life is interesting or ordinary, you still have to live it."

Delilah felt strange and bent out of shape, annoyed at her inability to shake off a silly nightmare.

Because that's what it had to be, she decided, not wanting to recount the horrific images and sounds that played over and over in her head, but wanting to find some thread that didn't fit, any detail that would reassure her that nothing had *really* happened.

Gavin's house is good, she repeated to herself while walking to school. *His house is good and loves him; it would never do anything to hurt me. It's just protective, like a mama bear protecting its cub. Like any new person in his life, I have to prove myself.*

He was waiting for her at their tree when she turned the corner, a sketchbook open in his lap, head down, fingers smudging some part of his drawing. It was the same book

Delilah had been looking at before she'd fallen asleep. She had to push down a visible shudder.

She crossed the grass toward him, the thin layer of icy snow crunching beneath the soles of her boots.

He looked up, nose and cheeks pink from the cold, and smiled at her. "Hey," he said simply, pushing himself to his feet.

Delilah smiled back at him, reaching out to take his hand, warm and wrapped in thick brown gloves.

"Sleep okay?" he asked, a trace of worry in his voice.

Delilah shrugged, noncommittal, and they moved hand in hand toward the school. "What were you drawing?" she asked, nodding to the notebook he'd tucked under his other arm.

"Oh," he said, taking it out and opening it to a page near the back. "It's a weird one."

Delilah looked down at the familiar ivory paper, at the smudgy fingerprints along the edges. She felt her face grow pale, counted out the time in her heartbeat.

Gavin had been sketching a spider. The same spiders from her . . . *dream.*

"What is that?" she asked, feeling her heart make its way to her throat.

Running a hand through his hair, Gavin peered down at it. "I don't know, really. Just popped in my head, I guess. Like I said: weird."

Delilah closed the book and took his hand again. "Come on. We'll be late."

• • •

Delilah's headache still lingered from that morning.

She could feel Gavin watching her all through class, his gaze heated and pressing against her skin. For once she was grateful for the long lecture that day, boring as it was, because it gave her the perfect excuse to stay quiet, to try to sort out the tornado of questions in her head.

She tried to work out how Gavin could have known about the spiders, right down to the thick, hairy legs, the stripe of red along their round, brown backs. She ran her fingers over the insides of her wrists, looking for marks like the ones she'd felt cut into her by the blankets, but found nothing but the faint blue streak of veins beneath her skin. Intellectually, she knew it was just a coincidence, but why did it feel so strange? For a brief, terrifying moment she wondered if the house could have seen her dream, but pushed it away just as quickly, realizing how insane that sounded.

Delilah looked down to where a crumpled piece of paper had been tossed to her desk. She pulled it into her lap, glancing up to the teacher before opening it.

Are you ok?

A quick glance over her shoulder, and her eyes were met by Gavin's. He nodded toward the note, motioning for her to answer it.

Just tired. Didn't sleep much.

Mr. Harrington turned his back to the class as he began writing that night's homework on the board, and she slid the note back to Gavin. She didn't have long to wait. The note, paper creased and folded haphazardly, landed in front of her again.

Come over after school. I want to draw you.

She nearly choked on her gum. *Draw her?* A quick glance over her shoulder and she was met with Gavin's eyes, dark and serious. He motioned to the paper again.

Delilah bent down over her desk, face hot, the dream conveniently pushed to the back of her mind and obscured by a rush of heat. Gavin wanted to sketch her, like a real artist. The idea unleashed a cloud of butterflies in her stomach.

She swallowed, picking up her pencil with shaky hands, and wrote a single word:

Okay.

It was just a dream, after all.

The walk back to Gavin's house seemed longer than usual. Gavin held her hand the whole way, his little finger drawing the simplest, yet most distracting, circles against her palm.

"I'm home," Gavin called out as he stepped into the house, and when she followed him inside the door, Delilah pulled up short.

She felt as if the day before must have changed something in her. She was almost positive she'd never stepped foot in *this* house before.

The late-winter sun streamed in through the curtains just the same as it had before, and the trees gleamed emerald and green from the backyard. The fire stoked itself and burned brighter for Gavin, the room warming all around them. But the human eye is amazing at finding straight lines, and Delilah could tell at once that every angle was slightly skewed. Some were soft and sloped, others rigid but oblique. Nothing came together at right angles or with any standard metric. Doors tilted slightly or had one square corner, one rounded, much as Delilah knew her left foot had always been slightly longer than her right.

It was as if before the house had stood straight, paying attention, on its best behavior. Here she saw it as it was: an aberration, come together all wrong, with walls pushed together in wavy lines here, in sharp edges there.

The *thunk* of Gavin's backpack hitting the floor pulled Delilah out of her thoughts, and she blinked hard, looking away from the crooked walls and up at Gavin's relaxed smile. Behind him, the stems of a plant hanging near the front door began to sway gently, its leaves turning upward, leaning toward him.

"It's happy to see you," Delilah noted flatly, handing her jacket to Gavin with slightly shaking hands. She'd made the observation before, but somehow, this time, the house's reactions to Gavin felt syrupy, and—Delilah hated to admit it—*pointed*. As if it were reminding her what it had said the day before: *But he's ours.*

He looked around for a moment and shrugged. "Yeah."

They walked through the living room and into the bright kitchen. Gavin reached into the refrigerator to grab a pitcher of milk, setting it down next to a plate of cookies on the table.

The chair next to Delilah slid back, its feet barely making a sound against the wood floor. She sat down gingerly, almost as if she expected it to be pulled from beneath her at any moment. "So this is just waiting for you every day?" she asked.

Gavin poured milk into the two waiting glasses. "Pretty much. Or a sandwich."

Delilah took a cookie, finding it still warm. "Crazy," she said.

Gavin laughed and took the seat next to her, tossing an entire cookie into his mouth, saying, "I guess so," around it.

"And it's just always been that way?"

"For as long as I can remember, yeah." Gavin stood and they made their way into the dining room, where he pulled a pad of paper from a stack near the door. "I think I'll draw you in here, by Piano," he said, more to himself than to anyone else. "This room has the best light."

Delilah had to focus on not becoming distracted by the sight of him with his sketchbook, the way his fingers looked with the dark piece of charcoal clenched between them. He sat down next to her again and flipped to a blank page. "Look at me," he said, voice quiet and a little scratchy, sounding like his short fingernails might feel if he dragged them slowly down her bare back.

Blinking up to his face, Delilah felt her heart squeeze, wringing tightly.

"You're so pretty," he said to her mouth, and then he looked down, starting his drawing with the simple bow of her bottom lip.

Her "Thanks" came out tight and nearly silent.

"Wonder how I got such a pretty girlfriend," he murmured, looking up to study her again before starting to draw the heart-shaped outline of her face.

The room cooled in a silent rush, but Gavin didn't seem to notice, and Delilah had to wonder whether it was her imagination. *Stop it*, she told herself. *Don't be a baby.*

"I know you had a friend over that one time, when we were eleven. Just before I was sent away. But how many people have you had over here your whole life?" she asked, looking out the kitchen window. She felt like the trees were all leaning in close to get a look inside. Purple figs and red cherries blocked the late-afternoon sun.

Gavin shrugged, scratching his cheek with a charcoal-covered fingertip. It left a soft bruise of black on his skin, and Delilah reached forward, wiping it away just as he said, "Maybe two other people."

"And it was weird?" She could see how it would be weird now. She could barely see how it would feel normal. For a tight pulse, Delilah wanted the delirious, giddy thrill to return. She wanted to be enamored with the house again.

But Gavin didn't answer aloud. He just nodded, lost in drawing the determined point of her chin.

"And you're *never* lonely?"

This time she knew it wasn't her imagination when the room grew cold. Even Gavin looked up at the ceiling, at the walls, saying with quiet emphasis, "Sometimes for people but not for *company*."

The room warmed again. But it was as if her brain were on a roll and her mouth couldn't slow down the momentum: "So what *does* happen when you leave?"

Gavin stopped with a cookie perched at the edge of his mouth. "Leave?"

She nodded, wary of the way the walls seemed to be slowly pressing in. But it was as if she'd loosened a boulder and no longer had control over the course it would take crashing down the hill. She felt a little reckless, a little angry. Maybe her mother was right after all.

"What do you mean?" he asked, his eyes widening slightly as if to warn her.

"Well, this is our last year of high school," she said. Delilah blinked up to the window and swallowed, gathering courage to finish her thought. There was some tightness inside her, an itch to make the point. Maybe to provoke and see if she really was imagining things. Even though the itch was chased with an uneasy chill, she couldn't help herself: "What happens next year? Where will you live when you're at college or when you get married or whatever?"

This time the room cooled so quickly her breath puffed out like a cloud of smoke in front of her.

Gavin's brows drew together, and he looked up toward the ceiling again, his eyes narrowing at the chandelier that had started to sway above their heads. Abruptly, a great crack sounded through the entire house, and the walls of the kitchen began to pulse and throb, the house shaking so violently that Delilah braced a hand over each of her ears to muffle the sound.

"What's happening?" she shouted, looking around wildly.

"I . . . I'm not sure!" Gavin stood from his chair, and it toppled over behind him. "*Stop it*," he yelled. "She didn't mean anything!"

Delilah pushed herself from the table and began walking backward. "Gavin! What's going on?"

His eyes were wide and dark, his pupils so large they eclipsed the slightly lighter brown of his irises. "I think you better go," he shouted above the noise. "It's just upset. I need to talk to it."

The rug rolled beneath her feet, causing her to stumble, and she gripped the edge of the piano for balance. It shook her off, but Delilah managed to right herself again. The ceiling began to heave, and Delilah didn't need to be told twice. She ran instinctively for the door.

The handle wouldn't turn under her wildly shaking hand, and she stood there, madly rattling the knob until Gavin's hand wrapped around hers, gently prying it away.

He opened it easily enough, and with his house rocking all around him, Delilah raced out the door.

She didn't stop running until she was almost home, until the sun had fallen behind the houses and the light posts had flickered to life up and down the empty street. She pressed her back against the trunk of a large tree and looked back the way she'd come. The sidewalk behind her was empty, but it didn't feel abandoned. The street had an eerie feeling of fullness, as if the *awareness* of the house had somehow followed her all the way here.

Delilah closed her eyes and tried to still her shaking hands. Her lungs burned with each gulp of icy air. Her heart was pounding; her breath pushed from her chest in heavy gasps.

Gavin hadn't followed her. She began to pace up and down the sidewalk, occasionally glancing back in the direction of his house. Where was he? Why *hadn't* he followed her? Wasn't he scared? Wasn't he *worried*? Hadn't he seen the way the walls had bowed and shook, like someone taking a deep breath before bellowing out in rage?

She wondered briefly if she should go back for him, but her feet felt planted to the spot like they were encased in cement. She didn't want to go back, but she couldn't leave him there, either.

She'd left her coat at Gavin's house but had luckily kept her phone with her. She heard Gavin's familiar text tone from the front pocket of her skirt and fumbled to reach it. Her fingers were cold and numb, and she almost dropped it twice in her haste to read his message.

I'm ok, but it won't let me out. I promise I'll see you tomorrow. House is just upset, and I need to calm it down. I'm sorry.

Delilah wasn't sure what to do. Did she leave him there to fend for himself? Should she call someone? Who would she tell? Her parents? The police? As if he could read her mind, a second message appeared on the screen.

Don't worry about me, Delilah. House loves me. I'm safe.

CHAPTER FIFTEEN

HIM

G AVIN WONDERED HOW LONG IT WOULD TAKE for Delilah to find him.

He knew she was probably confused, or worried, or maybe even a little mad, having not found him waiting at their usual spot before school. In truth, he'd felt a bit like a criminal as he'd slipped out the front door, the sky still dark and the school halls still empty, early enough that he could escape into a windowless practice room unnoticed.

The music buildings were essentially a row of temporary trailers lifted from the ground by ugly blocks of cement and connected to an unreliable, rickety generator. The district had always intended to build a more permanent arts building—or so they said—but Gavin liked the hollow sound of his footsteps as he walked up the ramp to the doors, and the way the quiet seemed to seal him in when he closed the aluminum door.

For the past three and a half years the practice rooms had provided an odd sort of sanctuary: soundproofed and separated from the main buildings of the school by a long stretch of grass used for phys ed classes, it was where Gavin would go when he was mad at House for one reason or another, when he'd broken up with a girl or she'd broken up with him, or when he simply found people and their general assholery too much to bear and needed to really feel *alone*. Even now, when he was starting to suspect he wasn't ever really by himself, it was quiet enough inside the practice rooms to feel as if he were.

It wasn't that he was avoiding Delilah exactly, more that he wasn't sure what to say. He didn't know what had happened yesterday. He was still reeling himself and couldn't quite get past the look of terror on her face, the way she'd been so scared she couldn't even turn the doorknob to get out. Gavin wanted to apologize, and he wanted to explain.

The problem was, he had no idea what to say.

It was only a matter of time before Delilah realized he wasn't coming to class and would slip out, determined to find him. Which wasn't a bad thing, really—Gavin couldn't think of much he'd enjoy more than getting a few moments alone with her, but he was no closer to an answer now than he'd been last night.

Had House ever reacted that way before? Gavin tried to think back but couldn't recall anything. Neighbors had always steered clear of House; trick-or-treaters walked straight past its gate. Door-to-door salespeople might stand on the sidewalk outside, narrowing their eyes as they peered up through the wrought-iron bars and tangle of vines, but they never came any closer. The only people who came to the door were delivery-men bringing packages, the occasional doctor making a house call, Dave with his grocery delivery, and now Delilah. Gavin's friends were the kind he would talk to in class occasionally, or stand near during PE. He didn't have any who would think to come over after school or on the weekend; he didn't have relatives to speak of. It had been only him and House for most of his life. It had never seemed strange until now.

He'd never imagined when or where he would move someday. At nearly eighteen, he barely thought beyond the next week. But he also never believed House expected him to live there forever, alone.

After last night . . . he wasn't so sure.

Gavin didn't know much about religion—it seemed a thing people pulled out when they needed and disregarded when it suited their purpose—but he remembered finding an old Bible wedged under a loose board in his bathroom. A marble had fallen to the floor and rolled beneath the wooden armoire before he could reach it. It was his favorite—an oxblood swirl—and so he'd crawled over to get it, cheek pressed to the cool wood and arm stretched into the dusty shadows. His fingers had stumbled along the groove where two planks had lifted, and he'd felt the worn leather and embossed pages. He'd marveled over his secret find, somehow knowing he wasn't supposed to have it. The paper was so thin, like flower petals, and he wondered how something could seem so sturdy and also so delicate.

Over the years he'd read a few passages at a time, alone, sitting on the edge of the tub. "I am my beloved's, and my beloved is mine," *Song of Solomon* 6:31. Few passages had stuck with him, but that one had. He had likened it to how House felt about him and how he felt about it in return. They belonged to each other. And so Gavin had sensed the change—the slight shift in the air—long before Delilah had, and had known that something bad was about to happen. He'd felt it in the pit of his stomach, in the way the hairs on the back of his neck had prickled and risen along his skin. Fear inched up his spine, not for himself, but for Delilah. For a flash, he'd been afraid for her. And now he had to face her, *wanted* to see her, but how could he explain something he didn't quite understand himself?

Now, hunched over the piano in the music room, he pressed a few keys before erasing a series of notes on the sheet music in front of him. Penciling in a few more, he tried the combination again. It wasn't exactly what he heard in his mind's ear, but he was satisfied he was on the right track. Gavin had always had a knack for the arts, and his hobbies—music and sketching—filled most of his free time. Though he had a perfectly good instrument at home, he preferred the quiet solitude of the soundproof room when composing to sitting with Piano, who seemed to anticipate his moods and know what he was going to play before even he did.

Gavin's hands stilled at the sound of the door opening and closing behind him. Footsteps moved across the carpet and stopped a few feet away. He glanced over his shoulder, meeting Delilah's eyes.

He'd known that she would be worried about him, but he was unprepared for the wave of guilt as he took in her appearance. She looked tired. Her eyes were heavy, smudged with dark circles beneath. Left out of its usual braid, her light brown hair hung in thick waves that framed her face. His fingers itched to push it back, to feel it wrapped around his fist. He wondered if she had any idea how much older she looked right now—not a teenager but a woman, with passion and fire and a protective streak that rocked him—or how much it made him want to kiss her. And more.

Obviously uncomfortable under his gaze, Delilah gathered her hair over one shoulder and began to braid it. "I was in a hurry this morning," she explained.

"I like it down. You look pretty."

Delilah shook her head. "I don't feel pretty," she replied. "I feel sick to my stomach."

Gavin moved over on the bench and motioned for her to sit next to him. "I think that's my fault."

"Maybe a little. Were you avoiding me this morning?"

He considered his answer before saying it. He knew enough about girls to know they thought differently from boys and that Delilah might read into what he said. He wasn't avoiding her *exactly*, just trying to gather his thoughts.

"Yes," he said, before quickly adding, "and no. I wasn't sure what to say to you. How to explain what happened."

"It was scary."

"I know."

"Did it eventually calm down?"

"Yeah." What Gavin didn't say was that it had calmed down almost as soon as she'd vaulted out the front door, though it had taken hours before the strangeness had stopped entirely. The floors vibrated gently, and random doors opened and slammed themselves shut again for the rest of the night. It was like watching a parent rumble and grouse about a misbehaving teen. "It didn't mean to scare you," he explained, although the words felt a little sour on his tongue. "It's just how House . . . gets upset."

Delilah digested his answer, her eyes moving over his scribbled sheet music. He could feel the obvious question bubbling up inside her. "Has that ever happened before?" she asked.

"No . . . ," he hedged. "But I've also never brought a girl-friend home before, remember?"

It was such an odd feeling to be so protective of House and also of his relationship with Delilah. The warring feelings made him faintly nauseous.

"Then how do you know why it was like that?"

Gavin lifted one shoulder in a slow shrug. The casual

gesture felt wrong, dishonest somehow. "I just do. House is as much of a parent as I've ever had. It got upset when you brought up the idea of me moving away. It would never hurt anyone. It's not bad, Delilah. Just . . ."

"Just afraid of you leaving," she finished for him. She said it like it was a fact, as if she'd spent some time with this particular thought before.

"I suppose so. This is all new—this meeting new people. It's never had to share me before, not really. I've never brought up *wanting* to leave. I guess House isn't sure how to deal with it yet."

Delilah ran her finger along the glossy keys, applying just enough pressure to feel the smoothness against her fingertip, not hard enough to play a note. "Don't you ever wonder what happened to your parents? It's weird, after what happened yesterday, that we never talk about why it's just you and that house."

Gavin plucked at a few keys, absently, the F and G in six slow beats, then the E and G. The subject just sort of made him . . . tired. Delilah couldn't know how many hours, how many days or weeks or even months of his life he'd spent thinking about parents, about a mother to wrap her arms around him when he was sick or a father to help him build his airplanes, play music, just . . . talk to. "I used to think of them all the time. I went through an *obsessive find everything* stage when I was about seven, but I only have one picture. She had brown hair. That's literally the extent of my knowledge."

Delilah slid her hand over his knee and midway up this thigh. "Maybe you look like her."

It was only the solid weight of Delilah's hand on his leg that anchored Gavin to the room and kept him from slipping into that place he rarely let himself go, where he thought—*really* thought—about his mom. Gavin did have her hair. He had her pale skin and wide, dark eyes. He had the same nose he'd seen mirrored in a faded and crumpled photograph. She had a heart-shaped face—he remembered that much—and a guarded, wary smile. Gavin thought he shared that with her too.

"I found a picture in the bathroom a few years ago," he said. "The wood in there swells sometimes from the humidity, and I pulled out one of the drawers that had been getting stuck. The photo was taped to the bottom."

Delilah didn't comment on how odd it was to find a photograph purposely affixed that way, like someone had deliberately hidden it—a thought Gavin had had enough times for the both of them—instead asking, "But how did you know it was her?"

"There was a baby carriage in the background," he explained, "this rickety old thing that had to have come from an antique store or a flea market or something. I think she was—well, from the pictures I've seen—a little strange? Eccentric maybe? She had this long wavy hair and wore all these drapey things. She was beautiful but sort of a hippie, or something. Anyway, the stroller. It had these things hanging from the hood. An arrowhead, a feather, a wooden bear, some coins, and a few things I couldn't make out. I recognized some of them. I've had the arrowhead as long as I can remember. I'm pretty sure the carriage was mine."

Gavin wondered if Delilah would think this was too little to draw a conclusion from, but she was already bursting with more questions. Turning to face him, Delilah bent her leg and brought it up to rest on the bench between them, her knee pressed into his hip. And in what seemed like a completely natural move, she reached for his hand, holding it in both of her own.

"Have you ever asked anyone about your parents?"

"I don't honestly know where to start without making people realize that I'm alone there," he said, and then swallowed heavily. "I'm cared for. I'm loved. If Social Services or whoever knew that I didn't have parents, they'd take me away. They'd put me in foster care and take House apart. When I was old enough to realize that . . . I knew enough to know how bad it could be."

"So where did she go?" she said to herself, looking down at his fingers. "That's what we have to figure out."

This is where Gavin usually stopped thinking. It was just too much to imagine she had been in an accident, leaving House to care for him or—worse—that she'd *purposefully* left him there alone.

But in true Delilah fashion, she would not be deterred.

"There has to be an explanation we can find without letting people know you've been alone. . . ." She rubbed his middle finger with the tip of her thumb. "A way to keep you both safe."

This close it was impossible to miss the way her eyelashes looked resting against her cheeks when she blinked, or how her forehead furrowed in concentration. She twisted her fingers with his, examining them one by one. His hand looked positively massive next to hers, giant palms with long spindly fingers smudged with ink. His mind had started to bend away from the topic, and he was just starting to imagine how his large hands would look on parts of her body he hadn't seen before, when she spoke, snapping his attention back to her.

"You don't think," she began, then paused, chewing on her bottom lip. The parts of Gavin that were distinctly *boy* took notice; he even licked his own lips in response. "You don't think the house had anything to do with—"

Ice filled Gavin's veins, and he leaned forward, placing his fingers over Delilah's mouth to silence her. "Don't say that," he whispered, eyes darting around the room. Even the *idea* of House doing something malignant made his stomach do a hideous flip. To imagine House hearing them talk about it like that made him dizzy.

Had he just felt a shuffle from under the floor? A slither? The part of Gavin that had grown paranoid in the past twenty-four hours felt certain that something had moved—stretched or uncoiled—beneath his shoes. Carpet covered aluminum, aluminum rested on cement, cement covered dirt, and inside that dirt were rocks and bugs, the roots of trees. He froze, meeting Delilah's startled gaze.

"What is it?" she mumbled behind his fingertips, but he could only shake his head. Sweat pricked at the back of his neck, and Gavin closed his eyes, counted to ten before he stood and walked to the door, opening it just enough to peek out at the rows of trees that lined the sidewalk clear to Mulberry Street.

To his neighborhood.

Closing the door, he said, "She left me, Delilah. She left, and House didn't. That's all I know."

The walls had ears. The sky had eyes. And Gavin wondered if there were answers somewhere to questions he'd never thought to ask and where he would need to look to find them.

Gavin wasn't sure if he was going crazy. How was it possible to feel so warm and secure one day and so paranoid the next? House hadn't changed; *he* had. He'd become suspicious and untrusting, and as he made his way around the corner across from home, he felt a wave of guilt. House had protected him through winter storms and lonely days. It had fed him and clothed him and been everything he'd always needed it to be. Until Delilah.

He wondered if this was what every parent and child went through. Growing pains, he reasoned. That was all this was. Despite what House wanted, Gavin wasn't a little boy anymore, content with model airplanes and boxes of Legos. Things were changing, and they would both have to adjust.

The gate creaked open and the air seemed to warm around him. Vines unfurled and gripped his T-shirt as he passed. Front Door opened as soon as he started his way up the walk. Smoke puffed from Chimney in black, sooty spirals, the clouds heavier and more persistent the closer to House he got. It reminded him of a dog who'd just heard their owner's keys jiggle in the lock, and he could almost imagine a tail sprouting out of the back door, wagging wildly.

His steps sounded on the porch, and he walked inside, the scent of warm cookies filling the air.

"I'm home," he said, just like he did every day.

The furniture seemed to angle itself toward him; everything seemed to be listening. But for what? Everything was the same, and yet he couldn't shake the feeling that something was off. That House was waiting.

"Thanks for the cookies," he said, crossing the gleaming floor and reaching for a plate already piled with fresh-from-the-oven chocolate-chip cookies. His favorite.

House wouldn't have made cookies if it had heard Gavin talking about his mother; instinctively, he knew it. But TV didn't turn on. Piano didn't play. He found a glass of ice-cold milk on the counter and carried them both to Kitchen Table, taking a seat and trying not to think. His unease didn't come from a sense of fear, but rather that something had happened the day before, and both he and House were walking on eggshells.

The entire feeling made Gavin think of a housewife who discovers a secret about her husband but doesn't tell him immediately, instead letting him give himself away slowly, one word at a time, waiting until he makes a mistake. He just wasn't sure which of them—he or House—was the one with a secret.

Chapter Sixteen

HER

FOR THE NEXT FEW WEEKS, THEIR RELATIONSHIP felt a little homeless. Gavin didn't want to take her back to his house, and she insisted her parents would never let the two of them set foot in the door together. So they wandered the streets of their small town, talking about favorite candies and horror novelists, about movies and giant trees. He would sometimes kiss her on these walks—small touches and the occasional sharp nibble—but Delilah was almost constantly thinking about how she could find a way to press the front of her body all along the front of his. It was a tight sort of desperation that came from liking him more with every new piece of himself he shared and also needing to know that she stood a fighting chance if he ever had to choose between her and the house.

She looked up and noticed they'd reached the place their walks always ended: *her* house. This was the point when, in their new routine of wandering, he would ask her a question and she would answer, stretch for his last kiss of the day, and then walk inside to stare at the wall until she could clear her mind of him enough to focus on her homework.

What his question would be each day had become a game. On the days she demanded kiss after kiss on every street corner, he would end their walk with something innocent—*Do you prefer red or green grapes?* But on days she was wrapped up in talking, or thinking, he would invariably reel her in with something like, *Do you ever sleep bare, without a stitch of clothing on?*

When he'd asked this two weeks ago, his eyes had become so black and his voice so low that Delilah's skin caught fire and her soul slid from her body into his.

She'd finally answered, "No. But now I will."

But one drizzly Thursday, when her house rose out of the street so abruptly, and Delilah was neither overly hungry for him nor quietly thoughtful, Gavin leaned down, licked her bottom lip before kissing it sweetly, and asked her where her parents were.

She looked up, realizing the blue Chevy wasn't at the curb and the gold Cadillac wasn't in the driveway, and said, "I have no idea."

It wasn't like the three of them had mastered the art of comfortable dinnertime discussion where future outings were shared. Her parents expected her to be home by sunset, do her homework, and wash the dishes after dinner. She expected her parents to cook and then watch the nightly news or read worn copies of romance novels. So she didn't have a clue why both parents appeared to be gone, but nor did she waste another second. She grabbed Gavin's hand and pulled him inside. For some unknown reason, she wanted him inside *her* house this time.

His fingers shook a little around hers as they walked through the living room, dining room, and kitchen. He seemed more afraid of accidentally touching anything than she had been when *intentionally* touching things in his house, which, to be honest, Delilah found a little funny. Nothing here would reach out and grab him, tickle him, or shudder beneath him. Nothing, that is, except Delilah herself.

He looked down at his feet as they squeaked across the floor. "Why is there plastic on your carpet?"

"My mother doesn't like dirty feet in the house, so she put plastic down over the places people walk."

Gavin didn't say anything else, but his grip tightened until they reached the stairs, and he climbed up behind her as she grew hyperaware of the cloying scent: floral air freshener, cleaning chemicals, the plastic on the carpet.

Her bedroom was essentially the same as every ten-year-old girl's room anywhere, Delilah thought. Why had her parents never updated it between her visits home? It seemed funny that they should ignore Delilah's growth as much as Gavin's house seemed to ignore his.

She closed the door behind them, and his long, dark form

shadowed the entire room. It seemed like there was hardly space for them to move independently around each other.

"You make my room look tiny," she said, stepping up behind him. His attention moved away from her tiny bed and seemed to linger on a collection of ceramic unicorns on a shelf on the wall. The room was cluttered with her little-girl stuff, and she wondered if, for Gavin, it felt somehow both too dull in personality and too bright in color.

Delilah thought of all the nights she'd stared at the ceiling lately, waiting for the thoughts of him to slip away so she could sleep. She'd spent so many nights in the dorms or at Nonna's that even after being home for three months, she still felt like she was sleeping in someone else's house.

She didn't realize she'd been staring at her bed until Gavin said, "I don't think I'd be able to sleep here."

"Well, no. My father would kill you, for one, and we both wouldn't—"

"Not what I meant," he cut in, sounding embarrassed. "I mean, it's just so different. At school or work it's easy to handle being in flat, inanimate spaces. But this room feels like it should be alive . . . and it isn't."

"Most bedrooms aren't alive. Someday when we're older and we have—"

"It's okay," he interrupted her, shaking his head quickly. "It'll just take some getting used to when I'm over here."

Her brow furrowed, but she forced a small smile. The

truth was, she knew it wouldn't be easy for Gavin to ever live anywhere else, but someday he *would*. Whether he or the house knew it. "You know I'll just drag you with me anyway," she said, grinning, "so you may as well get used to houses being both this purple and this boring."

"Delilah," he whispered harshly, stepping close enough for her to feel the vibration of his voice in his chest. "You can't say things like that. I know it sounds crazy, but what if it can somehow hear you even here? I don't want it to have any reason to freak out on you again."

She studied him, hating how dark and anxious his eyes had become. "I think you're being paranoid." But deep down, she didn't. Not really. What she'd wanted was for him to agree with her, to tell her not to worry, that away from the house, they would be safe.

Gavin shrugged, but he also seemed unconvinced. "Maybe."

Suddenly the room felt too small and colorful, as if they were standing in the heart of a wilting wildflower. She took his hand and led him back out of the house, needing air and not wanting to be home yet.

"I want to walk some more with you." She wanted another question from him at the end of the walk, something about kissing her, or leaving this town together, or what kind of house they'd agree on. Definitely not a question about her parents' whereabouts.

They walked, without discussion, toward the enormous

park in the middle of town, with huge oak trees. She loved the idea of curling with him beneath one and reminding him that, in places like these, they *were* completely alone. And when she stopped in front of a tree and looked up at him, his lip snared between sharp teeth, her entire world reduced to the very simple desire to kiss him, for hours.

The groove formed by the enormous roots felt, to Delilah, a bit like sitting in the hull of a boat. She felt mildly subterranean when she lay down and tugged Gavin over her. He resisted, all long arms and forever-long torso trying to figure out how to position his body above hers.

"I'm worried I'll crush you," he said.

Delilah spread her arms and shifted until she was comfortable on her back. "I'm not." In fact, she half hoped he would.

"I don't feel like we're alone here." This time he whispered the words so she could barely hear him and looked back over his shoulder as if expecting to see a table, chair, or strip of spying wallpaper slithering through the grass.

"Gavin, no one is here except us. We never get to be alone; will you just come here and kiss me?"

Finally he gave in, shifting so he was over her, propped up on sharp elbows, the broad length of him making the space even darker and warmer. Gavin's kisses were never particularly gentle—all edge and growl—but Delilah could tell he liked this angle, face to face, where he didn't have to bend so far down or lift her from the ground. It was so new like this, and it felt wildly dangerous to be lying prone together in the middle of a public park on a school day.

The rustle of the branches overhead grew louder even though the sound of the wind seemed to disappear, and Gavin jerked above her, looking up and around them at ground level. When his lips returned to hers, it was with a new kind of determination that she didn't quite understand, but he turned slightly desperate and she found herself grateful for whatever seemed to have flipped a switch in him.

The kisses grew deeper, touches firmer and braver, and soon he was rocking above her and she was moving up from below—chasing the same thing he was—wanting more and more and needing to stretch this moment into days. The sky seemed to have disappeared now, too, and from behind her closed lids it felt like midnight in this tiny cocoon. When she opened her eyes just to look at him, his were squeezed tightly shut and the branches just behind him somehow seemed closer than before, making their spot perfectly secluded.

Delilah closed her eyes again and smiled against Gavin's mouth, sliding her legs up along his sides. She felt his fingers tease down her arms to wrap around her wrists and trap them beside her hips. When he did this, her need for him became heavy and tangible; the bind by his fingers caused her to dissolve into something dizzy, and incoherent, and shapeless. How did he know she would want him to be like this—demanding and capable and hungry?

But somehow the hands that pinned her were also moving up her shirt and over the soft fabric of her bra. His mouth grew hungrier, wetter on hers, with teeth and sounds. He had grown wild, but a tickling awareness pricked across Delilah's skin, as if she had touched a bare wire.

"Gavin," she murmured against his lips, trying to pull back and understand how he could pin her wrists while simultaneously touching her chest.

"Touch me back?" He pushed his words and breath against her lips, and when their meaning took shape in Delilah's head—he didn't realize she was bound at her wrists and *couldn't* touch him—daylight disappeared completely, and at once she had the sense of being surrounded. Delilah opened her eyes.

The darkness wasn't from the sun disappearing behind clouds or the simple cover of her eyelids over her eyes. It was the tree itself, bending to make a web around them of black, spindly branches that cut out the last beams of sunlight.

Dark twigs curled possessively around Gavin's back, their edges slipping beneath the hem of his shirt, into the sleeves and around his shoulders, spiraling down his biceps. Even still, he kissed along her neck, nibbled gently on her ear. "Delilah, please don't stop."

Delilah dug her feet into the soft earth and tried to push out from beneath him. Swallowing a scream, she felt the thick twist of branches around her skin, pinching her. When she started to struggle in earnest, they unwound from her wrists with a slow slither. Gavin sat up more slowly, impatiently pushing the branches out from under his shirt. They slipped away, slinking as if chastened.

He knew, she thought with horror. *All this time he knew the tree was moving, was crowding into his space and claiming him, and he didn't even care.*

"Why didn't you move?" she gasped, hearing the building hysteria in her voice. "How could you stand it?"

"It's not like I have a choice," he said, in a bleak and unfamiliar voice. "This park, House, the school—it doesn't matter where we try to be alone together. House will always be there. It will *always* see me."

"That's what you meant about it possessing inanimate objects. Anytime you leave the house, it can come with you, or—" Her breath caught, words tumbling out too fast. "Or in roots or power lines. You really think the house is always watching."

He didn't say anything, and Delilah looked away then, unable to stomach the anger and defeat on his face. She knew it wasn't directed at her, but even so the power of it felt despairing.

He scrubbed his face with his hands, then straightened his shirt. "We'll just have to accept that we can't really be alone."

The thought depressed her. She loved her time with Gavin just talking, but when she felt the way she did that day, she wanted more than just conversation. She wanted the weight of his hands on her sometimes too. "Why does the house hate me?"

"It doesn't hate you." He sounded tired. "It thinks you're a threat."

"You're not allowed to have a girlfriend?"

He looked up at her and swallowed a laugh, his face releasing the laconic grin once more. "I'm sure House isn't too familiar with a need for romance."

"How can you go home? Isn't it creepy? The way it doesn't want you to leave lately?"

Gavin shrugged, looking down the trail for a beat before bending to help her up from where she sat. "How can you go home to your parents?" he deflected. "Isn't it depressing?"

Delilah scowled. "Not the same."

"You're right, it's not. House holds me too close. Your parents barely hold you at all. They'd send you away again if they had the money, and you know it."

She fell silent—wounded by this truth—and Gavin shifted on his feet in front of her, his regret settling like a fog between them. "I didn't mean that, Lilah," he said.

Delilah looked up and his eyes seemed to darken. She loved what he'd just called her; no one had ever called her something so oddly intimate before. "I know."

"I know this is hard, but . . . I think everyone just needs time to get used to it. It's so new for all of us—including you," he reminded her. "There are some things you can't say. You can't expect me to walk away someday from the only family I've ever known."

That seemed to be the end of it. They walked silently, hand in hand, and when they reached the corner that would take them to Delilah's house if they turned left and Gavin's if they turned right, Delilah pulled him right.

"I'm walking you back," she said in answer to the skeptical rise of his brow. "That's got to earn me some bonus points, right? Returning you home?"

He smiled down at her and kissed the top of her head, and they walked until they reached the sidewalk in front of the gate. Delilah moved in carefully when it creaked open, pretending like she couldn't feel the house vibrating just up the walkway. With a quick glance to her right, she made sure the vines were wrapped around the iron, staying right where they should be.

And maybe she really *couldn't* feel the house vibrating, couldn't feel a chill slide up under her sweater and along her spine. Maybe it was all in her imagination because Gavin stopped and pulled her close. Close in a way *she* wouldn't have done if her parents were standing right beside them.

"Are you okay?" he asked, the tips of his fingers resting on the bare skin just below the hem of her sweater.

"Yes."

"I like you a lot," he said. She pushed up onto her toes, wanting to kiss him so thoroughly he'd have no question how much she liked him back, when the sound of scattering gravel and tires screeching pulled their attention to the driveway.

"Delilah Blue!" her father shouted.

Franklin Blue's car came to a dusty stop halfway into Gavin's long, pebbled drive.

Why did he have to drive down this particular street, today of all days? Delilah's stomach twisted, watching how several tendrils of vines slid down from the fence and snaked toward the tires.

"Dad," she said, taking a step forward.

"What on earth are you doing here? Get in the car."

"I have to go," she told Gavin, reluctantly pulling her hand from his.

His eyes were focused on the vines, too, brows drawn in confusion. "I'll see you tomorrow?"

"Tomorrow," she agreed, walking backward toward the car, eyes pleading. It had officially been the weirdest day of her life. "Good night."

Gavin looked up at her, expression unreadable. "Night, Lilah."

CHAPTER SEVENTEEN

HIM

GAVIN WAS ANGRY. IT HUMMED IN HIS VEINS, surging white-hot to power his lengthy strides as he walked away, back down the sidewalk and away from House. He was unable to go inside yet, feeling the anger bloom in his cheeks, leaving him flushed and too warm.

He could still feel the gentle scrape of the branches where they'd gripped him at the park, hear the rustle of leaves and see Delilah's terrified expression when she realized they weren't alone, when she realized *they might never be alone*. Rage rushed anew through his system, and his fists clenched and unclenched at his sides. This single thought ricocheted in his head, back and forth, louder and more unacceptable with every moment.

How long could this go on? Until he finished high school? College? *Forever?* He figured he was being dramatic when he'd told Delilah they'd need to get used to it, but was he really? And why was he only thinking about this now? He was young and the future had been so abstract, filled with unnumbered days and the vague idea of years that would stretch on and on and on, but would he live them all inside House?

Would it ever let him leave?

Gavin stumbled on an uneven piece of sidewalk and felt the bleakness of this idea wash over him. The walls would change, the rooms might shift or shrink or grow, but it would still be the same. *He* would be the same. He might get older, but he would never grow in that house. He would never learn anything different or know love or lust or hate. . . .

No. He would know hate. Years from now he would know hate and resentment because he could taste the bitterness of them swelling up inside him already. It felt like a cancer, this need to yell and shout and be angry. House had to stop; it had to stop trying to control his time and his life because as much as he loved it—would always love it—it would have to let him go. Not now, but one day. Soon.

He turned around, walking the long block back home. As if sensing his mood, Gate threw itself open, the hinges protesting loudly in the still afternoon. Vines didn't reach out to greet him this time; no tendrils wrapped themselves around his arms. Nothing breezed gently over the ends of his hair. Instead everything in the yard curled back in on themselves, the leaves trembling as if the wind had rushed in after him.

His footsteps thundered up the walkway, his eyes trained on the open front door. Gavin wondered if the entire house was waiting, on edge, for him to storm inside. It *had* to know what his reaction would be, that he'd be furious. If anyone else had stumbled on them, he and Delilah would have looked like any other pair of teenagers making out in a park.

But what House had done was *crazy*. Trees didn't wrap themselves around people; branches didn't twist into a person's clothes like the hands of some jealous girlfriend. Someone could have walked by and seen the branches up his shirt, forming a gloomy cave over them, and then what? How would that look? Someone would have found out.

Things had been fine with House when he'd left this morning—quiet. Just like they had been the last few days. And now that he thought about it, maybe things had been *too* quiet.

Like it had been waiting. Plotting until he'd left to meet Delilah.

In a rush, he took the steps two at a time, harder than he'd usually walk anywhere in House. Even when angry, he never stomped; it felt disrespectful. He never slammed drawers or dragged chairs across the floor, always careful of his feet or his voice. But right then, he didn't care. He wanted to be mad. It felt *good* to be mad. He was going to scream and yell and put a stop to this insanity before something bad really happened. He was suddenly worried that House *could* hear him in the music room or *anywhere* and may have been punishing him for more than just having a girlfriend. He knew it was impossible, but his paranoid brain seemed intent on replaying every conversation and thought he'd had over the last few weeks.

He stepped into the foyer and listened; it was his turn to wait now. Gavin kept his gaze on the floor, on the same rug that had covered the entryway for as long as he could remember. He'd raced Matchbox cars here, read countless books, and built Lego skyscrapers so tall he'd needed a chair to stand on. The soft beige and blue pile was normally a comfort—the pattern so familiar he could sketch it by memory—but it felt like a stranger in this moment. Everything did.

Gavin could still remember every one of those times he played by himself while House looked on. He never asked about the voices he could hear outside, the sound of laughter coming from kids who were probably his age. Sometimes he would see them through a window as they rode their bikes past Front Gate, or find a ball that had rolled from a neighboring house and stopped at the curb.

Once he'd seen a group of kids in a yard on his walk home. Over dinner he talked about what they were doing, how they were playing, and the next day after school, a trampoline had appeared in the backyard, already assembled and standing in the dewy grass. He'd stepped outside, blinking into the slanting light, positive he must be imagining it. Was it his birthday? A holiday he'd forgotten? He didn't think so.

Screen Door had given him a little push, nudging him down the steps and out into the yard, and Gavin realized the trampoline was for him. A gift. House had given him a present for no other reason than it wanted to see him happy.

Gavin had jumped all day. He'd taught himself to do backflips and front flips, turning only at the sound of laughter and applause from the other side of the fence. A group of kids from school were watching him, visible only on the highest point of each bounce. Gavin had smiled at them and waved, making it into a game each time their heads appeared and reappeared as he jumped.

They'd played along from the street, even calling his name at one point and asking if they could come play. Gavin didn't know what to tell them. Would House mind if friends came over? Nobody had ever asked before, and so Gavin wasn't even sure if that was allowed. He'd jumped down to the grass, stumbling as he regained his footing, and raced up the stairs and inside. But House had dinner waiting for him and had closed and locked Back Door, pulling down the shades until his new trampoline was hidden from view.

It was gone the next morning.

Gavin had never asked about it, in the same way he'd never really questioned anything House did.

When a book he'd been reading disappeared, Gavin would look for it, only to have another push itself from the shelves of Bookcase. When TV wouldn't turn on, he figured there had to be a good reason. He'd always assumed House did what was best for him.

But this was different. He was almost *eighteen*. He was allowed to have a girlfriend and date and even bring a girl home if he wanted. Gavin and Delilah had been making out in a park, not committing a felony. He'd always done what he was supposed to. He'd gotten good grades and stayed out of trouble. So why was House acting like this now? Now that he'd managed to find someone who didn't look at him like the weirdo he was—*someone who accepted House.* Didn't it see that?

And didn't it see how much he needed someone who was like him, too?

This thought finally pushed his anger from the pit of his stomach out into the room. "Why are you doing this!" he shouted, his voice echoing all the way up the stairs. "You scared her!"

Silence rang around him; only the sounds coming in from the street behind him pierced the eerie quiet. Gavin took another step forward, hesitating over whether or not he wanted to close Front Door. He didn't.

"Delilah's nice. She's good," he insisted, trying to smooth a layer of calm into his voice that he didn't feel. "I *like* her. She's my girlfriend, and you're going to have to figure out a way to be okay with it. With *her*."

Nothing.

Anger melted away and a trickle of fear slipped along Gavin's spine, a cold sweat that made him feel both too warm and too cool at once. A breeze wandered up the porch and inside, and he shivered.

Gavin had always lived here by himself—and other than Television or Radio, Delilah's had been the only other voice he could clearly remember hearing inside these walls—but he'd never actually been *alone*. House didn't speak with words, but he knew what it was saying as if it did. Right now it wasn't saying anything. It was the go-to punishment from House— being closed-off and silent—and Gavin felt a twinge of long-buried panic: What if he truly *was* alone? After all these years, what if he'd been abandoned? Again?

Fireplace was filled with nothing more than glowing embers. Piano remained quiet and still. Lamp stayed dark even as the sun began to burn itself out, slipping lower and lower in the sky. The image of a skull flittered through Gavin's thoughts, hollowed out and lifeless.

Don't go, he felt himself think, the words filling him with a sadness he didn't quite know how to handle. House *knew* this was his panic button. When he'd done something he shouldn't as a child—tiny things like not wanting to go to bed or leaving his toys scattered on the floor—the air would cool, the rooms growing as quiet as a grave. And now, at seventeen years old, it had the same effect as it had had when he was seven.

House knew how to play him; it knew how to get its way.

"It doesn't mean I don't love you," he hedged, and sensed an almost imperceptible flicker to his right, in the burning coals. Relief flickered inside his ribs, too. Until recently, he'd never really argued with House, and Gavin wondered if this was what it meant to fight with your brother or sister, to argue with your parents. "Can't I love you both?"

He didn't have time to examine this realization—the possibility that he *could* love Delilah—because Piano lurched with a huge clang, as if an anvil had been dropped from above, and the boom of every string snapped at once so loud he felt it reverberate through his chest.

"Don't be like tha—" he started to say, when his sketch-book flipped open on the coffee table. Gavin took a deep breath before walking over.

The book lay open to a drawing of Gavin smiling on a summer day, with House just behind him. He'd copied it from the photo that hung in the hallway and was still proud that he'd managed to duplicate it almost exactly, right down to the ice-cream cone and drips of melting vanilla running down the back of his hand. Silently, the sketchbook flipped to another page, one of Apple Tree in the backyard, his favorite swing suspended from the sturdy branches. Then another and another, all drawings of House and the many parts of it he loved.

Me, it was saying. *Pick me.*

Fireplace roared to life in the corner, warming the room as the flames grew and receded. Gavin could imagine the black smoke that was billowing from Chimney, the puffs like heaving, impatient breaths.

"I know it's hard, but I want Delilah in my life too. I don't want you to run her off. I'd be sad without her."

A chair pushed up behind him, buckling him at the knees. He dropped into the seat too quickly, and it teetered on two legs.

"Sorry," he started to say, before he was flung backward, Chair taking off across the room and stopping in Living Room. An old aluminum TV stand stood between Couch and Television, its worn brass finish rubbed down over time to a dull, coppery glow. But that wasn't what had his attention, because on top of the stand was a plate of food.

His stomach growled almost on instinct.

A tiny voice inside his head told him to slow down and think. Why was there a steaming plate of his favorite dinner—roast chicken, mashed potatoes and gravy, and hot rolls? He hadn't known he was hungry until just now, but his mouth watered as the scent of chicken floated up to him.

Pick us! See? Look at what we do for you.

Gavin didn't want to eat on principle, but the scent of roasted chicken was everywhere. His attention was pulled away anyway to the television screen when it suddenly flickered to life.

The neighborhood on TV looked surprisingly familiar: tall oak trees lined the empty street as a pair of bluebirds few past. Off in the distance, the top of an old church he recognized was visible, a statue perched on the tower looking down on the houses below. It was Gavin's street, and as the camera panned over, it was House, standing tall and crooked, and made of glass and stone and warm, worn wood, gleaming in the afternoon sun.

The screen zoomed in through the gate and up the walk, to a boy sitting cross-legged in the grass, an entire army of toy trucks surrounding him.

It was a drawing from Gavin's sketchbook brought to life, of Gavin playing while House looked on. Tree branches pulled in close, protecting him from the heat of the day.

House had gathered a hose, vines and branches, and the long, thin leaves of a tulip to push his trucks through the grass and up the little dirt paths he had made for them. Not once had it occurred to him that his world was different or *less* somehow because it was House playing with him instead of one of the boys that lived in a house a few blocks down. Gavin had just felt adored.

It had always been only *them*, so it wasn't surprising House was having a hard time dealing with the changes happening now.

As if it sensed his softening mood, the lights dimmed to a warm, cozy glow. The edges of a blanket brushed the curve of his cheek and wrapped itself around him in the closest thing to a hug it could offer.

Gavin took the first bite of his dinner and hummed in appreciation. It was perfect.

"Thank you," he said, tearing off a chunk of roll and running it through a warm pool of gravy. "It's delicious. I didn't realize I was so hungry. Thanks for thinking of me."

Lamp flickered in acknowledgment before brightening again.

Gavin let the feeling of contentment and hope wash over him. No one gets to pick the family they're given, and as far as families go—and despite what Delilah thought—he actually considered himself pretty lucky. House might be nosy and overprotective, but it was *his* and he loved it. You don't divorce your parents because they love you too much. You don't get a new brother or sister because you don't like the ones you have.

Somehow, he would make it work. House just needed to see how wonderful Delilah was; that was all. His love was big enough to share. He'd just have to figure out a way to show them both.

CHAPTER EIGHTEEN

HER

DELILAH FOUGHT SLEEP THAT NIGHT. EXHAUSTION weighed down the edges of her mind, making her thoughts syrupy and dense, but until her phone buzzed beneath her pillow to let her know Gavin was safe at home, she didn't want to close her eyes.

Instead, she climbed back out of bed at one in the morning and went to sit at her desk. Perched on the never-used surface was a shiny silver frame displaying a picture of Delilah with her parents, taken the summer before. It had been her shortest visit back from Massachusetts yet, but even though she'd been home for only a week, her father hadn't even taken a day off work to spend time with her. The picture was taken on a weekend, at a nearby park, where Delilah's mother had tried to put together a cheerful picnic of sandwiches and apples. Much of the picnic was decimated by ants, and her father left after only an hour, claiming he was needed at the office.

She pulled the photograph from the frame, staring at her

father's doughy face. In the way that words start to feel misspelled when one stares at them too long, his face started to look unfamiliar the longer she looked at him. Pulling a black marker from her bag, she began drawing thick brows over his pale ones, a black, angry frown over his indifferent mouth. In only a few minutes, her father had become a glowering gargoyle.

Delilah left her mother's plain, constantly surprised expression alone but drew blue lips over her own mouth, twisted black horns on her head, and crooked orange butterfly lashes over her eyes and reaching almost to her hairline as she thought back on the strange visit home.

"Don't they want to see more of me?" she'd asked Nonna when she'd returned to the silent stillness of a boarding-school town in the middle of summer.

"Do *you* want to see more of *them*?" Nonna had asked in reply. It was one of her more fluent moments, when her eyes cleared and she knew everything she'd always known, wasn't lost to a vague panic or searching for something she'd misplaced.

Delilah had grown quiet and unsure. She didn't know that she wanted more time with her parents, only that she'd hoped to feel more wanted whenever she went home.

"Baby, if I've learned one thing in the past sixteen years, it's this: When it comes to your parents, we both need to lower our expectations. Don't poke at anything you don't want to face." Nonna had left the room then, returning a few minutes later with a kiss to the top of Delilah's head and a giant platter of cookies in her arms.

Two weeks later, Nonna didn't even remember that conversation. If the Nonna of last summer knew that Delilah would be brought home just after Christmas that year—that she would be back living with her parents and finishing out high school in her hometown—she would have raised hell.

Unfortunately, Nonna didn't remember Delilah now, either.

Looking back, she was pretty sure she shouldn't have returned to Nonna's house at all that summer. Her forgetfulness and moments of blankness had been worsening at an alarming rate, and though her parents might not have put too much thought or effort into what she did on a daily basis, she was fairly certain they wouldn't have allowed her to return that summer had they known the extent of Nonna's illness.

But Delilah had loved Nonna and would have jumped at anyone like a wildcat had they tried to separate them even a day before it was absolutely necessary. The moments when Nonna hadn't remembered herself were terrifying, yes, but she had always been Delilah's favorite person in the world, the one person who made her feel truly loved.

Maybe that was exactly how Gavin felt.

Back in her own room, no longer near Nonna or the quiet boarding-school town or anything familiar, Delilah dropped the pen and closed her eyes. Was she doing it again? Poking something that was now, unfortunately, facing her? Could she behave herself better and make nice with the house? Away from it she just wanted it to *like* her, wanted it to let her have as much of Gavin as she wanted to have. But when she was there, it was almost like she couldn't help pushing. She couldn't help finding out what the reality of Gavin's life was, what it would someday be, and why the house couldn't set him free, even a little.

Unfortunately, the *idea* of scary things turned out to be so much better than the reality. The prospect of a living house, the potential it had for darkness and eerie moments had seemed perfectly adventuresome. But now her skin rose in gooseflesh and she felt like she was being watched by her own eyes in the photograph, by the windows and walls and carpeting. Did she just imagine a slight rumbling of the chair beneath her? Was she imagining the way the walls seemed to hum slightly now, trapping her inside? If she tried to escape and run downstairs, would her *own* house let her go?

Delilah shot up from the chair, consumed by a sudden, fluttering panic, and tore down the hall, down the stairs, and burst, panting, into the oddly bright kitchen. She pulled up short at the sight of her father seated at the kitchen table, his left hand wrapped around the neck of a bottle of amber liquid.

"Delilah." His voice came out thick, as if a balloon were lodged in his windpipe.

Her chest rose and fell as she struggled to catch her breath and take in the image in front of her. Franklin Blue, sitting drunk at his kitchen table in the middle of the night. The house faded into gray in her periphery, the idea that it was alive completely forgotten. She'd never seen her father anything but buttoned up and stern, but here he sat looking like he was almost melting into his chair.

"What are you doing up at this hour?" he asked, his voice bending the word "hour" into something that sounded more like "are." It took Delilah several beats before she translated in her head. He looked strange, not quite himself. A little dazed.

"I couldn't sleep," Delilah said, leaning against the counter behind her. "Then I got scared."

He laughed, staring at the table. "I know what you mean," he said, nodding before taking a long pull directly from the bottle. She could hear him swallow, stared at him as he winced a little. Even at a distance, the fumes from the alcohol burned at the surface of her eyes.

"Are you okay, Dad?"

"Sure."

"I didn't know you drank."

"I don't, usually." He pushed the bottle away from himself and rubbed his eyes. "I guess that explains why I'm sitting at the table drunk after two swigs. Have the worst headache."

Delilah thought about this as she eyed the bottle, tempted to point out that more than half the liquid was gone; it didn't seem like it was only two swigs that he'd taken. In fact, he'd been . . . off? . . . since he'd picked her up in Gavin's driveway. He'd barely said a word to her, and instead had kept prodding at his head, finally asking her to check the glove box for a bottle of aspirin.

"You seeing that boy?" He was staring at her now, and even with her eyes averted she could feel it. She'd never spoken to her father about boys or even girls. He'd definitely never seen her kiss one. He had always stayed safely in the father zone, discussing what was for dinner or whether she wanted to rethink wearing such a short skirt.

Delilah ran her fingernail along the gap between the aluminum and Formica of the kitchen table. "Gavin?"

"You think I know his name? The tall, skinny kid who looks like he climbed out of bed in the middle of the day. The old hippy lady's son."

Delilah froze. She could have sworn something rustled outside. "You know his mom?"

Franklin Blue snorted, shaking his head with contempt. "Hell no, I don't know her. Nobody really does."

She closed her eyes, took a deep breath. Her father was drunk, she reasoned. He didn't even know Gavin's name. How could he know anything meaningful about him? "His name is Gavin, and yes. I'm seeing him."

"You keeping yourself pure?"

She looked up at him then, surprised at the sharpness

of his tone. Her parents were strict and pious, but they'd rarely been as sanctimonious as he'd been with just those few, drawled words. Her father's eyes were glassy and unfocused as he stared, unblinking, at the chair across from him. She followed his gaze and then looked around the room. All around her the walls seemed to pulse, first quietly and then as if the sound were penetrating her head. "That depends on whether I'm still pure if I kiss him," she said finally.

"'Set me as a seal upon your heart, as a seal upon your arm, for love is strong as death, jealousy is fierce as the grave,'" he quoted, words slurring together slightly.

He didn't sound quite right, and Delilah wasn't sure if it was the alcohol, the fact that he was quoting Scripture as if reading from a script, or something else entirely. The wind outside dragged a branch across the kitchen window.

"Okay, then, Dad. I think I'll head back upstairs." Delilah watched him warily before she pushed away from the counter and walked back toward the door to the living room, and just beyond it, the stairs to the relative sanctuary of her room. To her right, a desk drawer rattled in its track, making her jump, and a gust of wind blew through the living room as if hitting her right in the face. A window had burst open across the room, letting in the frigid night air.

"'Do not suppose that I have come to bring peace to the earth. I did not come to bring peace, but a sword.'" Her father's voice rang hollow from the kitchen, but when she turned to look at him, he was asleep with his head lying in his crossed arms on the table.

Upstairs she pulled her phone out from under her pillow and finally gave in to texting Gavin again. *I need to talk to you.*

After ten minutes with no reply from him, she felt like her room was contracting in small pulses, breathing in and out. Strangely, unless it was directing its anger at her, she had never minded the idea that Gavin's house was alive, but the thought that such a thing could *spread*, that the house that hated her could also somehow take over her own home, was terrifying.

This is not okay, she thought. *Even if it was a nice house, a house that is alive is not okay. This isn't the same as Nonna's dementia.* She closed her eyes hard, squeezing them so tight she saw prisms of light. How was she seeing this only now? She'd wanted so much for the world to be wild and scary and unknown, but this kind of wild, scary, and unknown was *not okay.*

She texted Dhaval. *Are you awake?*

Her phone vibrated in her hand a moment later. *I am now because my phone buzzed right near my head.*

Sorry.

It's fine. What's up?

Delilah stared at her phone and then just dialed him, needing to hear a human voice that was familiar and didn't sound drunk or slightly . . . *possessed.* Dhaval picked up after barely a full ring. "Princess Delilah, it's sleepy time."

"I'm sorry. I'm having a really weird night."

She heard him rustle on the other end, as if sitting up in bed, and his groggy voice answered. "Okay. Tell me everything."

"Dhaval, have you ever noticed anything weird in this town?"

There was a moment of silence in which she could practically feel Dhaval's blank stare. "Are you serious right now? Everything's weird about Morton. It's like walking into the town in *Edward Scissorhands*."

"Okay, I mean things that feel like a haunting but aren't?"

"Someone needs to take your Netflix away."

"This isn't from a movie. This is from real life. I worry that things in this town are . . . possessed."

"I should record this conversation and play it for you tomorrow. You'll be mortified," he said. "Morton is weird, yes. But it's like too many people who are too much alike and who never speak to anyone from outside this town and never go anywhere, ever. "

"I'm serious," she said, feeling her throat tightening in the unfamiliar rising of tears. It was too much to take in. The tree in the park, and—worse—the way Gavin seemed completely unsurprised. And now her father's strange behavior downstairs, like something was speaking *for* him. She felt like the house was infecting everything and everyone around her. "I'm really freaking out."

The line rang with silence for several beats before he said, "Come over."

· · ·

Delilah hopped over cracks in the sidewalk and skirted every line in the pavement. The shadows of streetlights bent and arched over the path ahead, and she could feel their posts twisting behind her, their lamps turning to watch her like heads on long, curved necks. She was imagining it—she had to be; she was just spooked—but it was all she could do to not cry out and scream Dhaval's name the four blocks to his house from hers. The dim shade from trees and houses, cars and mailboxes seemed to cling to her own slight shadow until it was enormous in her peripheral vision, looming down the sidewalk beside her. She felt like she was dragging a black hole down the street.

Daytime sounds were absent, and in their place was only the odd buzzing of electrical wires, the occasional barking of a dog that seemed to grow farther and farther away, as if civilization were slowly ebbing away from her. Finally, Delilah gave in to her instinct to run and sprinted the remaining two blocks to Dhaval's house, feet slapping the pavement, arms pumping, and her heart pounding, a tight wail trapped high in her throat.

She hurled herself up the three steps to his porch, throwing politeness into the wind and banging as hard as she could on the door, looking behind her over her shoulder. She swore the branches of every tree leaned toward her; the sidewalk seemed to ripple in her wake.

But it wasn't Dhaval who answered the door. It was his

mother, Vani, in a deep green robe and holding the door open wide.

"Slow down," she whispered, pulling Delilah inside and shutting the door behind her with a quiet *click*. She reached to press her warm palms against Delilah's cheeks. "Slow down, *jaanu*. You look frazzled."

"I am," Delilah said, gulping in a huge breath of air and glancing shakily over at Dhaval as he appeared at the bottom of the stairs.

But Vani shook her head. "Mmm. That isn't the right word. I mean sizzled," she whispered, looking at every inch of Delilah's face. "Like you've been burned with electricity. You're scorched from the inside out."

"W-what do you mean?"

Vani closed her eyes, inhaled meditatively. Instead of answering, she said, "Let me make you some tea."

They never did get much information out of Dhaval's mother, who seemed more intent on calming Delilah down than talking about what had brought her there in the first place. While the teakettle whistled behind her, she told Delilah to breathe, told her everything was okay, and then sent them upstairs to Dhaval's room with a pot of tea and instructions to stay quiet—hinting to Delilah maybe she did know her son was gay after all, or maybe she just knew from the look on Delilah's face that the last thing on her mind right now was mischief of the sexual variety. She never once seemed surprised to find Delilah standing on her front porch at two in the morning, panicked.

Dhaval closed the door behind them and walked to his bed, sitting down cross-legged. "Do your parents know you're here?"

She shook her head.

"Your dad will kill you."

Shrugging, Delilah said, "I'm pretty sure Dad will still be asleep when I get home. He was *hammered* tonight."

Her best friend cocked his head. "You don't mean drunk?"

"I do."

"Is that what has you freaked out?"

She blinked away and studied the framed drawing of Brahma, Vishnu, and Shiva on his wall. "No. Not exactly. Well, sort of."

He waited for ten seconds. For twenty. Finally, Dhaval—never a patient person—exhaled loudly. "You realize I'm not going to be able to go back to sleep tonight and I have a calculus test in the morning?"

"I'm sorry."

"That isn't my point. Either tell me why you're here or just go to sleep and let me study."

Delilah closed her eyes and took a breath so deep she felt like if her lungs were balloons, she might lift from the bed. She blew out the breath and looked at Dhaval. "The Patchwork

House is . . . just about as weird and different as we always thought. It's—"

His dark eyes went wide. "Is that what you meant by haunted, earlier on the phone?"

"I don't know, okay? I. Need. You. To. Listen." She enunciated each word with exaggerated patience. "Maybe help me figure out what the hell is going on."

"You think because I'm brown I know about magic or voodoo?" he asked, shaking his head. "The only magic I know is the joy of watching Channing Tatum in *Magic Mike*."

"Dhaval."

"*Delilah*. That place is weird. Why are you even going there?" He leaned back and looked at her from head to foot. "Ohhhh. I see. Delilah Blue is getting some action over at the haunted mansion."

Shaking her head quickly and glancing out his window, Delilah whispered, "Can you focus, please? I just . . ." She leaned forward, gestured for Dhaval to do the same, and then very quietly whispered everything into his ear. That everything in the house—from the wallpaper to the silverware—was alive. That she'd asked what happens when Gavin leaves someday and how the house reacted. And that she feels the house following her . . . *everywhere*.

Dhaval pulled back and looked directly into her eyes. She could tell before he said a word that not only did he *not* believe her, but he thought she might be crazy. It made her think of

Gavin and all the years that it was easier to live alone than to try to introduce someone into his world.

"Don't," she said, her voice raspy, a thousand prickly pinpoints.

"It just sounds insane, okay? I mean, Gavin is weird. And let's be honest here. You're also a little weird."

She nodded. "I know."

"You haven't told anyone else this, have you? About the house? I mean, the way you talk about it makes it sound like he lives there *alone* or something. His parents wouldn't just let him live in a haunted house."

Delilah paused. Didn't everyone assume he lived there alone? Had anyone ever *seen* parents? She opened her mouth to confirm, but something stopped her. Some tickling instinct, some agreement, internally, that this could go bad for Gavin if people found out that he was a minor, living without another human for more than a decade. "I haven't told anyone else, and of course he isn't alone."

It wasn't a complete lie.

"So, I'm just saying, you have this amazing imagination and draw all of these really creepy things and watch way too many movies and maybe, I don't know." He looked past her, out the window. "Maybe it's two thirty in the morning and you should just sleep in my bed while I study."

With a tight nod, Delilah curled onto her side at the foot of his bed, pulling the comforter over her legs. Dhaval sat quietly near her for a minute before standing and walking over to his desk.

Would she ever be able to sleep again? Wouldn't she feel the need to be vigilant all the time, like anything in her room could come to life? But with the sound of Dhaval's pencil scratching across paper and her own even breaths in the otherwise-quiet room, Delilah slowly let herself fall asleep.

The room was black, pitch-black. Without opening her eyes, Delilah knew Dhaval wasn't at the desk, but had fallen asleep on the floor. He held her hand while she slept, and she smiled, squeezing it a little in thanks.

Fingers cracked together in her grip.

Fear spiked in her chest; ice filled her lungs. The hand was cold and hard, as if made of bones wrapped in the thinnest layer of brittle, dry skin. Delilah jerked her hand away, scooting back on the bed just as she heard Dhaval shoot up in the chair across the room and turn on his desk lamp.

"What?" he asked, eyes red with sleep and wide with alarm. "What happened?"

Delilah wiped her hand on the blanket, covering her mouth with her other one. A tight sob broke out. She knew she'd been holding a hand when she woke up. She knew it.

"I . . . ," she started, choking. "There was something in my hand. A hand. Fingers. Something." She was shaking so violently she could feel her breath fanning wildly across her palm.

"It was this, Dee. It was just your shirt."

She blinked from a sleepy Dhaval to the steel-gray sweater he held in his grasp. It *was* hers, the very same one she'd worn at Gavin's earlier that day.

She could still feel the stiff fingers between hers, hear the soft audible crackling of the brittle bones.

The house had climbed into her sweater and followed her home.

CHAPTER NINETEEN

HIM

DELILAH WAS QUIET AT LUNCH THE NEXT DAY. Though *quiet* might not have been the right description. She said she'd forgotten her lunch, so she dragged him to the cafeteria and then barely spoke, instead spending the majority of their thirty-minute break picking at her Salisbury steak and tearing the individual stems off each floret in her pile of steamed broccoli.

She looked tired, eyes heavy and body slumped forward. Like her eyelids were too heavy to keep open. Each of her blinks seemed to last longer than the last, and Gavin made sure he was close enough in case the elbow propped on the cafeteria table gave out and she went face-first into her tray.

He'd asked her this morning if everything was okay, and she'd waved him off. He'd asked again after third period, when he heard she'd fallen asleep and snored through most of Mr. Burton's US Government lecture.

On both occasions she'd given him a shake of the head and a small smile, even stifling a yawn. "I'm fine."

Fine. Gavin was starting to hate that word.

These were the moments he realized how little he knew about girls, about what they thought or felt versus what they said, or how to respond to any of it.

Of course he didn't know how to respond. He'd "gone out" with girls where it was implied they were together, for however brief a period that might be, but he'd never been in an actual I-am-your-boyfriend-and-you-are-my-girlfriend type of relationship before. There'd been Cornelia, but he'd only kissed her, dry and unfeeling. There was nothing wild about her—about *them*—and it had ended almost as quickly as it had begun. He hadn't grown up with parents to watch and model his behavior after. He didn't have brothers or sisters or even actual not-on-the-Internet friends to learn from, or ask questions. In fact, the only things he knew about male/female relationships he'd learned from TV or books.

But none of those stories was about a boy who had a house that was *alive* and had tried to scare his girlfriend to death, so he was pretty sure none of them would be any help to him anyway.

And besides, when had Delilah ever done or said what he'd been expecting? Gavin might not talk to a lot of people, but he was always watching, learning from others' interactions, and Delilah was about as different from other people as he was.

He supposed he should find some sort of comfort in that, but he didn't.

"Did you not sleep at all last night?" he asked, a pang of guilt gnawing slowly in his gut. He could still remember her face when he'd moved off of her and hear the confusion in her voice when she'd asked why he hadn't stopped when he knew what was happening. The idea that Delilah was so afraid because of what House had done that she couldn't sleep . . . well, that made him feel worse than he'd thought possible.

He didn't want anyone—especially Delilah—to suffer or worry or be hurt because of him. Because they chose to spend their time with someone who was so . . . not normal.

Delilah shook her head, and small wisps of hair that had fallen loose from her braid settled around her face, the ends fluttering in the warmed air pouring from the vents overhead.

"Not much," she said before pausing. Was she taking a breath? Was she concocting a story? Was she choosing how she would break up with him?

Gavin actually straightened in his chair at that last one, wanting to punch himself. He'd never felt this way about anyone before, and it was turning him into a twisty, emotional mess.

"I was worried," she continued. "When I didn't hear from you."

"I'm sorry," he said, eyes dropping to the table. "I didn't

know where my phone was and didn't find it until . . . until later. After House calmed down."

"I was afraid it would hurt you."

Gavin blinked up to the window, to the trees visible on the other side of the glass. Lately he felt like every conversation he and Delilah had should take place in the isolation of the music room; the cafeteria felt too exposed—too many students, too many windows. He swallowed before telling her, "House wouldn't hurt me." He wondered if she noticed that the words didn't seem to have as much conviction behind them as they used to.

"Have you ever noticed how often you say that?"

A smile twitched at the corner of his mouth, at that flash of fire he loved about her so much. "I said that it would have to behave itself. That I needed you to feel safe there for me to be happy. And that I needed both of you." The fluorescent-lit cafeteria felt bright and too full of other students for that kind of admission, but it needed to be said.

He swallowed, trying to ignore the heat seeping into his cheeks. His body felt too long and awkward for the table, and he stretched his legs in front of him, his shoulders relaxing almost instantly as his ankles tangled with Delilah's.

"And what did it do when you said that?" she asked.

He remembered how the walls had calmed almost instantly, the swinging chandelier slowly coming to a stop overhead. House had grown still and warm again, the chill in the air lessening with every breath. It felt like it was waiting. Or maybe thinking?

"It calmed down eventually."

"So you think House hid your phone?" she asked carefully.

Although Gavin didn't want to tell her that his phone had been with him one moment—in his back pocket; he was sure of it—and gone the next, he did. He hadn't thought much of it at the time—more concerned with calming everyone down than checking for texts—but he had later, when he'd climbed the stairs for bed and found it sitting there, waiting for him in the center of his pillow. Like it had been there all along.

"That's weird, Gavin. That's not normal."

He tried to ignore the way those two words together made him feel, distracting himself with the lid to his water bottle instead.

"Wouldn't your parents take your phone away if they were upset?" he asked.

Delilah opened her mouth to speak before she stopped, considering. "Well, it's not the same, is it?"

"Why? House is the closest thing to a family I've got, which is why I wonder if we've been doing this wrong."

"Wrong?"

He reached across the table, taking her hand in his. She had ink on her fingers, orange and blue and smudged black.

He wanted to ask what she'd been drawing and if she would show him.

"When you said you were walking me home, it got me thinking. What did couples do in the old days before they started dating?"

"The 'old days'?" she said, cracking a smile. "Exactly how far back should we go? Should I still be able to vote?"

Gavin rolled his eyes but smiled. "You know what I mean, smart-ass. Like your parents' age."

Her brows drew together, and he wanted to lean across the table and kiss her. He frowned. Another time.

"Ugh, I don't think my parents ever dated. They were just dropped here, fully coupled."

"Be serious, Lilah."

"I don't know," she said with a shrug. "Meet their parents?"

"Exactly."

"But I've already been there. It knows who I am."

"Sort of. Parts of House are new, but its foundation is old, *really* old. Maybe we should do it the old-fashioned way and introduce you properly." He squeezed her hand and gave her the most charming smile he could manage. "I can explain how wonderful you are, and my intention to court you."

"You're a dork," she said, but he noticed she was the one blushing now.

"There's no way it won't love you if given the chance."

Butterflies exploded in his stomach. "It's impossible not to," he added.

"So you want me to come over again?"

"Yeah. Let me make you dinner."

"Me? At your house? Maybe you missed the way I sprinted from there like I was on fire last time."

"Lilah—"

"I barely made it out and you want me to go back?"

He ran his fingers up each of hers, rubbed little circles into her palms. "I think it's possible you might be exaggerating a bit."

She chewed on her bottom lip, her eyes watching the way he touched her. "Maybe . . . ," she acknowledged.

"House is . . . It is what it is. I can't change that. But it's part of me. We're sort of a package deal."

"It's just so . . . How did it not creep you out before?" she asked, surprising him.

"It didn't creep you out at first," he reminded her.

"Yeah, I guess. It's just"—she took a deep breath—"odd, is all."

"Did you miss the last eighteen years where *I'm* odd?" he asked a little sheepishly. "House is strange and different, but it's mine. It fits me."

Delilah laced her fingers with his and squeezed. "Okay," she said finally. "But I expect dessert."

He nodded, already grinning. "Dessert, got it. That shouldn't be too hard."

Delilah tossed her silverware to her tray and wadded up her napkin. "I'm wearing my running shoes, and if stuff gets weird, I'm out of there. Dhaval's mom said I looked sizzled around the edges, burned, and I'd like to stay as unsizzled as possible, thank you very much."

Gavin stood as she did and followed her to the garbage cans. "Dhaval's mom?" he asked.

He watched as she scraped her tray and placed it on the conveyor belt that led to the kitchen. "Yeah. I was a little freaked out last night. I mean, for obvious reasons, of course, but . . . I don't know . . . My dad was all weird, sitting in the kitchen drinking and saying all this even weirder stuff. Like Scripture or something. I didn't want to be alone, so when you didn't answer, I texted Dhaval."

Gavin felt himself frown. "Your dad doesn't usually do those things?"

"Ha!" she said, looping her arm through his and leading them both out the double doors of the cafeteria. "My dad gets self-righteous when the neighbors bring over rum cake, for crying out loud. I've *never* seen him drink. He's more a piece of furniture in the house than a human."

"Maybe he had a rough day. Maybe it was that he saw you with me?"

Delilah was already shaking her head. "No. It was more than that, but . . . I can't explain it. Like he was there but . . . not. Anyway, it was creepy as hell, and so I snuck out and went to

Dhaval's. Though he's probably going to kill me for it today."

"So what did his mom mean by saying you were sizzled? Like physically, or metaphorically?" Gavin thought back to what had happened and couldn't remember any moment where House or the tree had *actually* burned her. *Had it?*

"Honestly, I don't know. It was the middle of the night, and she wasn't exactly a wealth of words. Maybe she meant I just had a weird vibe about me. After the park and my dad and the walk over there and my sweater—"

Gavin reached out, placing a hand on her arm to stop her. "What happened on the way over?" he asked, concerned. House had promised to be good, and he believed it. So why did it suddenly feel like he had a herd of horses galloping in his chest? "And your sweater?"

"Nothing. Well, it *felt* like something. But maybe that's because I was already freaked out and it was late and dark and—"

"Delilah."

"If felt like everything was watching me. The trees, the lampposts. Like at the park."

Gavin nodded, heaviness settling deep into his stomach. "So his mom didn't tell you anything else?"

"No. I went upstairs with Dhaval and talked his ear off. I'm sure he failed his math test this morning because of me."

"Did you tell him what happened?" *What happened.* What

a benign and completely inaccurate description of what was going on.

They stopped at her locker, and Delilah hesitated before she spun the lock and began putting in her combination. Gavin felt his brows rise, but he said nothing, waiting. "Not really. What I mean to say is, I told him what House is but . . . not *everything*."

"You could have, you know. If you trust Dhaval, then so do I. I don't want you to keep a secret from him because you think you're protecting me."

"It's not just that. He wouldn't understand. Besides, I think this is something we should probably keep to ourselves as much as possible. At least for now."

Gavin nodded again, slow and stiff, like his neck was a heavy weight set on a rusty hinge. He knew she was right. House had disappointed him, and he felt an odd unease, as if he wasn't entirely sure he could trust House where Delilah was concerned. But his chest ached, too, when he had these disloyal thoughts about his unlikely family. He wouldn't do anything that might put it in jeopardy.

"But dinner could be awesome," she said, clearly attempting to change the subject. "Impress me enough and I might let you kiss me again. I mean, I don't want a piano dropped on me or anything. . . ."

"Ha-ha."

"Okay, bad joke," she said with a small shrug. "But I'm sure House wouldn't object to a few kisses?"

And just like that, Gavin's brain went from doom and gloom to teenage boy and hormones. "How hard could it be?" he teased. "Google a recipe and boom. Dinner for two followed by kissing. My kind of night."

Chapter Twenty

Her

NEVER HAD A WALKWAY LOOKED SO HONEST and virtuous before: swept clean, steps gleaming. Even Dead Lawn seemed to have put in some effort: It was trimmed at least, and less muddy and brown than Delilah had ever seen it. If the front yard could make a noise, Delilah sensed it would be whistling innocently.

Come on in, Delilah.

Nothing strange to see here.

The effort it seemed to have put in for the dinner date did nothing to quell the nervous twist in her stomach as she stood in front of the door and knocked.

Delilah knew she should have shared her suspicions about the sweater with Gavin, that somehow part of the house had attached itself to it and followed her home. But she couldn't bring herself to do it. She hadn't been sleeping enough lately and had just woken from a dream. . . . She was groggy, not thinking straight. Concluding the sweater was possessed was no doubt a result of her wild imagination, because the alternative was too terrifying to even consider.

Gavin answered with his trademark half smile, motioning her inside. "Hey, Lilah."

Her palms felt sweaty and she couldn't shake the unease that crawled up and down her spine, but she put on her best smile—fake as it may be—and beamed up at him. "It smells amazing in here," she said, slipping off her shoes and shrugging out of her jacket as Gavin slid his hands to her shoulders to help her.

"Thanks," he said, and turned to hand it to the coatrack. "I, uh . . . I cooked."

She turned to look up at his blushing cheeks, feeling relief wash through her. It wasn't that she didn't think the house could cook; she *knew* it could. But if it cooked dinner tonight, there would be a part of her thinking, with every bite, that the house somehow slipped rat poison into her portion.

"Good," she said stupidly, and then added in a rush, "I mean, it's good practice for you. But not that you need practice, because the house will always be here to cook for you, *always*. I just mean—"

Gavin put a warm hand on her arm, whispering, "I get what you're trying to say. It's okay. Calm down, crazy."

Delilah blew out a nervous breath and looked around the foyer while Gavin stood patiently just behind her left shoulder, clearly letting her calm down. Back inside these walls, the comfort they shared on their walks around town or alone in the music room at school melted away, and even Delilah's natural confidence couldn't press away the jitters.

"House," he said into the room. "Delilah came back to see us. And like I told you"—he paused and leaned in close to her, meaningfully—"and *you,*" he added, "she's very important to me. I'm happy she came."

There was a small rustle in a plant near the front door—a wave? she wondered—and a lampshade tilted in her direction.

Delilah waved back, lamely, into the room and up toward the stairs. "Hi. Thank you for having me. Um, back," she added, wincing.

It felt like they were performing for an audience of dissatisfied customers, an audience made up only of overprotective parents. The night was just so *loaded.*

She looked up at him, wanting to say this out loud, to somehow contrast this moment with every other they'd spent together in the past weeks, walking in easy silence or admitting everything crazy and scary and secretive to each other. But the words died on her lips when he smiled the smile that showed his sharp teeth, which she'd never seen him give anyone but her. Gavin bent and, starting at the corner of her mouth, drew his lips across hers in a slow, soft line. They were parted a little and just a tiny bit wet from his tongue.

"You look so pretty tonight," he whispered once he reached the other side.

Delilah's insides melted, and she felt warm and heavy in her relief. She nodded when he tilted his head, silently asking if she was ready to come fully inside.

But the sense of relief evaporated as soon as Gavin's hand let go of hers and he moved purposefully toward the kitchen. More than she ever had before, Delilah understood the term "walking on eggshells." Of course, there weren't literal eggshells beneath her feet, but every time she took a step, the placement of her foot seemed to be a critical decision. One floorboard groaned when she stepped on it—low and splintery and the exact sound wood would make if it was *displeased*—and she very quickly skipped to the board beside it, which, thankfully, remained silent and sturdy. Another board pushed the wood nail up as she stepped down, poking her on the bottom of her foot through her wool sock. Delilah bit back a sharp cry and limped quietly behind Gavin. She felt as though the hallway was shrinking in on her, inspecting, expecting to be disappointed in whatever action she took. She was surrounded by hundreds of parts of the house every moment she was inside, and some seemed to have forgiven her while others clearly held a grudge.

In the kitchen, Gavin dished spaghetti into two bowls, handed one to Delilah and then grabbed a basket of garlic bread. With food in hand, they walked to the dining room. Delilah found herself glancing at everything on the floor, everything on the wall, every fixture hanging from the ceiling.

Everything—even the paintings—remained suspiciously still, but the dining room was absolutely freezing when they sat at the table to eat.

Looking around the room, Gavin asked, "Is it cold in here?"

She shrugged. "Maybe a little. It's okay." But her shiver revealed the lie.

Gavin looked up at the ceiling. "Are you trying to kick us out of here?" Beneath their plates, the table shook, and a wintery gust blew through the room. Delilah interpreted it as a clear *yes*.

With an irritated little growl, Gavin grabbed his bowl and the basket of bread and stood, saying, "Fine. Let's go," to Delilah, and led her into the living room.

It was much warmer here, and as soon as they settled down on the floor and set their plates on the coffee table, the fire roared to life in the fireplace.

Gavin seemed to be starving and, with this clear welcome from the room, immediately dug into his dinner. Unfortunately, Delilah's appetite was nonexistent. The fire popped enthusiastically in the fireplace and a few pillows slid across the floor to rest behind her, but Delilah couldn't take it as a sign to let her guard down.

She scoured her mind for a safe topic. Clearly anything having to do with the future was off-limits, even though most kids in their class would begin to hear back from college admissions offices soon. No doubt any discussion of their relationship was off-limits, too. School was an easy topic but also the last thing Delilah wanted to think about at the moment. She wanted to escape into the space they created together and lean in to him while he ate his dinner and run her hand over his thigh. She wanted to hear him tell her stories about junior year and his first kiss and what was his most fervent wish for life.

Studying her as he chewed, Gavin swallowed before saying, "You're so quiet."

"Am I?"

He gave her a playfully exasperated look.

"I'm just . . ." She trailed off.

"Nervous?" he offered.

"Yeah, a little." Glancing up at the ceiling—always as if the heart of each room was hovering above her—she whispered, "I don't want to do anything wrong."

"Tell me how it would go if you invited me to dinner at *your* place."

She smiled, pushed some noodles around on her plate, and said, "My father would be mute and weird."

"Like Dining Room," Gavin said with a small little tilt of his head.

Delilah laughed. "And my mother would natter on and on about the neighbors and groceries and her book club and the quilt she's making for the new baby on the block."

Gavin blinked over to the boisterous, popping fire and the pile of pillows behind her. "It's not really that different," he said, eyes wide with earnest pleading. "I think the protective parent is universal, you know?"

She wanted him to be right.

Gavin stood, stretching a mile above where she remained on the floor. His arms reached over his head, shirt riding up and exposing a slice of his torso: skin and muscle and the tiniest glimpse of hair.

She'd never seen a man shirtless before whom she so fiercely wanted to touch. And despite the fact that now was most certainly not the time to run her hands up and under his shirt, Delilah could almost feel the warmth of his skin she wanted it so much.

"Hey, Delilah, my face is up here," he said with a laugh. Delilah didn't bother to look away until he'd lowered his arms and waved his hand in front of his stomach. "Want to go for a walk?"

Delilah nearly burst into song. The oppressive weight of the house's attention had started to feel like individual pinpricks all along her skin, a steady pressure pushing in at her temples. On a walk they could speak in hushed voices, could pause on the corner of each block and touch and laugh and kiss. Unfortunately, she had to use the restroom and didn't think she could wait until they got to the park.

"Can I use the bathroom?" she asked as Gavin was nearly out of the room, their plates in his hand.

He paused, blinking down the hall in the direction of the closest downstairs bathroom before looking at her over his shoulder. "Yeah, but maybe use mine, upstairs?"

It was exactly the confidence killer she didn't need.

The stairs beneath her feet felt odd, like they were made of only the thinnest layer of wood surrounding frigid water. They were ice-cold and creaked beneath her feet; she kept expecting her foot to crack through, to fall up to her knee through sharp wood and splinters digging into her leg. At the top of the stairs she stopped, searching for a light switch for a breath before remembering she wouldn't find one.

With a wince, she called down to Gavin, "Hey, Gav? How do I get the lights on?"

She heard his feet stomp from the kitchen and the irritation in his voice when he yelled, "*Hallway!*"

Lights flickered on halfheartedly around her, buzzing and dim.

"Thanks," she mumbled. Her anxiety was slowly transitioning into irritation. She was here, wasn't she? Trying? Why was the house insisting on being so difficult?

Once she closed the bathroom door, she exhaled, remembering what Gavin had said about this room. She could see what he meant: It just felt like a bathroom. No sense that if she were quiet enough she could hear a heartbeat. No sense of invisible eyes watching her every move. It was amazing how blissful it could feel to be inside an ordinary room.

Moving to wash her hands, she stilled, catching sight of something behind her in the mirror. Delilah turned. On the windowsill was a tiny porcelain fawn, with golden dots on its beige fur, and with the same chip in its left hoof that her mother's had. That sensation was back, of phantom fingers pressing against her forehead, her temples. She blinked and the statue was gone, blinked again and it was back.

Her mind grappled to find the obvious explanation—Gavin had liked it, had taken it when he was at her house, wanting something of her home here.

But Delilah knew without having to dive too deep into the rationalization that it wasn't true. Mom kept the collection in the dining room. . . . Gavin had never even been in there.

This wasn't just the action of an overprotective parent. This was something far, far more sinister. Delilah would have never noticed the fawn missing from her home, so why bother?

Her mind bent away from the possibility that House put it right here, for her to see.

I can reach you anywhere, it was saying. *Even in this safe room.*

In the middle of the night even, her own fear echoed back. *When you think you're alone,* it reminded her.

No, she thought in rebellion. Maybe the House *did* take

it, but surely Gavin saw it somewhere—maybe on the piano, maybe in the kitchen—and knew it belonged to Belinda Blue. He brought it in here, into his sanctuary, to keep it safe. House wasn't above being threatening like that—Delilah wasn't lying to herself about that anymore—but this was Gavin's safe space at home.

Taking a step closer, Delilah pulled up short just before reaching for the fawn, distracted by a small bubble in the paint. A trick of the light or a hiccup in her mind made her think for a beat that it had moved from lower on the wall to just below her line of sight. Blinking, she looked back up at the fawn, reaching for it on the windowsill. Just beneath her hand, the bubble moved again, a tiny ripple skirting sideways barely a centimeter.

The bubble definitely moved, Delilah thought, heart punching her breastbone, blood rushing so fast in her veins that she felt dizzy, nearly manic.

Reaching forward, she touched the small blister with barely a fingertip to quiet her suspicions. It felt odd beneath her skin, more like stone than plaster or paint, and with a relieved exhale, she pushed a little harder, just to be sure.

But with the added pressure, the bubble gave, indenting the tiniest bit before it cracked open with a sickeningly wet squelch, and before Delilah had a chance to process what she was seeing, her hand was covered in scores of tiny, glossy black roaches. They spilled over her hand, between her fingers, and into her palm, thousands of feet making a tiny scratching noise on her skin, exploding up her arms and over her shoulders in a wave that sounded like a roar, scurrying into her hair.

Delilah screamed, throwing her arms, shoving her fingers in her hair to tear at the bugs, but there were so many. They were so small; she could feel their feet, could *hear* them on her skin. She felt the cold stream of them down her forehead, over her closed eyes, and slammed her mouth shut just before they began pushing, pushing, pushing at her lips.

In her shirt. Down her legs. She was *covered*, her skin pulsing from the outside in with their frantic scurrying. Finally, unable to take it a second more—they were still coming out of the wall, an endless stream; were they going to *eat* her?— Delilah opened her mouth, crying out in terror, running to the door and throwing her shoulder against it, hurtling herself out into the hallway.

But . . . she wasn't in the hallway at all. She'd left the bathroom only to enter a room she'd never seen before, with walls lined floor to ceiling with dusty books, a desk. It smelled old and stale with damp paper and the cloying scent of decay. Delilah could barely see past the creatures covering her face, but in the corner she caught a flash of a figure, hunched and dark, and she screamed, sprinting to the far end of the room to open another door that led her only into the nursery. Door after door she tried, wailing for Gavin, trying in vain to push the roaches from her skin. Where was he? What was she seeing? She tore open a door that opened to a brick wall. A door beside it opened to a mirror, revealing the horror of her body, covered head to toe in inky, slithering black.

She whipped around, running back into the strange library and feeling along the wall until she found another doorknob. It turned easily, flying open in the wind to a forty-foot drop directly onto the concrete below. Wind roared around her, pulling her off balance as the cold night air hit her face. Delilah jumped back from the ledge, gasping in terror.

"Gavin!" she screamed. "Oh my God, *help me!*"

She burst through a new door, falling forward onto her knees in the bathroom again, and crawled frantically into the shower, turning on the water, tearing at her clothes and hurling them across the room. Her jeans landed with a heavy splat, still crawling with roaches. Her top hit the blue wallpaper and slid into the sink, the pale yellow cotton turned black with insects. The spray was freezing, but she didn't care. She stared in horror as the roaches fled the clothes and, like an army, began moving in a river along the floor to the tub. They scaled the porcelain wall and spilled in an oily black wave over the lip, onto her feet again, this time crawling up her body instead of down. She stood in only her underwear, frozen in horror as she screamed.

The stiff shower curtain slid up her legs, over the bugs, inching up the fingers of her left hand and curling around her wrist, trapping it at her side. Delilah clawed at the plastic sheet with her free hand, pulling and pulling as the pressure tightened in stiff, biting straps around her arm. She cried out at the pain as it dug into her skin.

Gavin burst into the room, eyes wild and wide at the scene in front of him. "What are you *doing*?" he yelled, reaching to turn off the water. He leaped into the shower, gripping her shoulders and staring at her with black, terrified eyes. "Delilah, what did you *do*?"

"Gavin! I . . . It . . ." Delilah pointed down to the shower curtain, but there was nothing there, only her own hand wrapped around her arm and covered in blood where it looked as if she'd torn away the skin.

"I came up when I heard you turn on the shower," he said. "Why are you in the *shower*? Delilah, what happened to your *arm*?"

"No," she said, shaking her head wildly. "No, Gavin, there were *roaches*. They came out of the wall. And my mom's porcelain—" She stopped, staring wide-eyed up at the windowsill. There was no porcelain statue there. No bubble in the paint that had burst. No person or doors. No roaches scurrying back into the wall. But they had been there; she knew it. She *knew* it.

Now there was nothing but Delilah, in the shower in her underwear, with a handprint-shaped burn on her arm.

CHAPTER TWENTY-ONE

HIM

DELILAH WAS IN SHOCK; THAT WAS IT. OR maybe she was having some sort of episode. Gavin could hear her screaming down the hall, but he wasn't prepared for the sight of her standing there, half naked and soaked, scratching at her skin like it was covered in acid.

She was saying something about roaches, but Gavin bent to look under the sink and behind the toilet and he didn't see anything. Water swirled down the shower drain, and his shoes squelched against the porcelain surface. His socks were soaked clear through, the bottoms of his jeans, his T-shirt wet from trying to reach around her to turn off the shower and . . . wait, Delilah was practically *naked*. And shivering. And standing in his bathtub.

Gavin had hoped to maybe get Delilah in some stage of nakedness tonight, but in his imagination, it hadn't looked anything like this.

And shit, she was . . . Delilah was *bleeding*?

Blood ran between her fingers where they gripped her arm. It plunked to the bottom of the tub, one drop after another, forming a pink rivulet that disappeared down the drain.

Gavin stuttered out the beginnings of a few sentences, finally giving up and reaching for a nearby towel.

"G-g-g—" she tried to say, shaking violently now.

"Can I see?" he asked, motioning to her arm.

She shook her head wildly and pointed toward the window. "It was there; it was."

"I know. I know," he said, in a soft, placating tone. He tried to see where she was hurt, but she jerked away, cringing and shaking like she might crawl out of her skin.

Gavin tried to remember back to when they'd studied first aid in health class, specifically, the best way to respond to someone who'd just experienced an accident.

Pale skin, ragged breathing, disorientation. Delilah was definitely in shock. Her lips weren't blue and she seemed to be standing okay, so he guessed that was a positive. But it was freezing in here—colder than it had been downstairs, which . . . made no sense. This was his bathroom. House didn't come into this room.

Did it?

Delilah swayed on her feet, and he reached out to steady her. "Let's get you out of here," he said gently, placing a towel over her arm and wrapping another around her. He placed a hand on her shoulder and tried to lead her toward the edge of the tub. Delilah wasn't moving.

With no other choice, Gavin scooped her up in his arms, navigating the slippery floor and carrying her to his room. "Lights!" he shouted, at the end of his patience with all of them.

Bedroom Door flew open, and he stepped easily inside, hesitating a moment before placing Delilah on Bed. All he needed was for it to decide to prove a point and toss her to the floor, or for Headboard to rise up, towering over her like something out of a nightmare.

No.

He gave it a warning look and mumbled, "Be good," under his breath before he moved to the dresser, careful to stay close to her.

There wasn't much to pick from, being that Gavin was so much taller than Delilah, but he managed to find a pair of sweatpants he'd worn two summers ago and a T-shirt he suspected was the closest to her size he would find.

With the clothes and a pair of boxers he wasn't even sure he should offer, he turned back, approaching her a lot like he would an injured animal: keeping his steps light and making sure she knew he was there. "Here's some . . . if you want."

She nodded numbly, and he set everything down.

"Can we clean this up first? Can I at least see?" he asked.

When she nodded again, he pulled her arm away from

her body. Gavin knew Delilah was hurt and that he'd seen blood, but that in no way prepared him for the bleeding, oozing wound that greeted him when she lifted the towel.

A chill moved up his spine, and he snapped his mouth closed, intent on not saying anything that might alarm her. It was angry and red, jagged and singed around the edges in the shape of what looked like a handprint. It was as if the first layer of skin was just *gone*. Like someone had torn her open as they would a Christmas present, a single ribbon of skin at a time.

Gavin pushed the image to the back of his mind. Right now Delilah needed a doctor. He would try to figure out *how* this had happened later.

There was an old car in the garage behind House, a 1967 Buick Riviera. Gavin didn't drive it often. He preferred to walk or ride his bike when he needed something. Taking the car out of the garage meant the possibility of being pulled over, or maybe an accident, and he had absolutely no idea if the car was even legal to drive. *He* certainly wasn't.

It had faded blue paint and a bit of rust marring the finish, but Gavin loved that car and spent hours reading the owner's manual and researching how to fix things himself. He'd learned that gas would go bad after sitting for too long, so on a few occasions he'd had to remove the fuel tank and drain it. He'd changed spark plugs and wires that had deteriorated.

He'd rebuilt the carburetor and replaced gaskets and vacuum hoses, and he liked to imagine that it was as mechanically sound now as it had been the last day it was driven.

But Gavin didn't even want to think of when that had been.

"You have a *car*?" Delilah asked, lifting her head from where it rested on his shoulder. "And you don't have to carry me. I can walk."

"Maybe I like carrying you."

She was dry and dressed in his clothes now, and Gavin struggled to focus on getting her into the car and to the doctor without anyone seeing them.

"This house is chock-full of mysterious things," she slurred hoarsely. "A car seems so . . . *normal*."

Gavin studied her for a beat. At least some color had returned to her face. The bandage he'd wrapped around her arm seemed to have stopped most of the bleeding, but she winced when he lowered her into her seat.

"I don't drive it much," he admitted, slipping in next to her and fishing the keys from his pocket. "It's not really a good idea with the whole no license or parents thing, but I figured this was kind of an emergency."

When Delilah only nodded but didn't argue or needle him for more details about when he'd found it, how often he drove it, and whom he thought it might belong to, Gavin knew she must really be hurting.

The keys jangled in his hands as he fit the longest of them into the ignition, and he did the mental calculation, trying to remember the last time he'd started the car. He was pretty sure it'd been a few months, and so he held his breath as he turned the key, finally breathing again when the engine roared to life all around them.

The old Buick crept slowly out of the garage, the tires crunching over gravel and fallen leaves as he started it down the narrow drive. His palms sweated where they gripped the steering wheel, and he blinked up to the rearview mirror, wondering if he would see House rise up from the ground, roots pulled from the soil as it chased after them.

The car had never been more than a hobby before, but now—since Delilah—it meant more. It meant a freedom he hadn't known he needed.

Delilah's voice at his side drew his eyes from the mirror, and he turned to look at her, small and fragile, legs folded and arm cradled to her chest. "My parents will find out."

It struck Gavin that she didn't seem particularly bothered by this, more resigned to a fact she was just saying out loud.

"Do you have your phone?" he asked as a thought suddenly occurred to him.

Delilah nodded and pulled it from the front pocket of her borrowed sweatpants.

"Can you . . . ," he said, hesitating. He pushed his hair from his forehead and narrowed his eyes, watching the leaves that scurried across the empty street. "Can you send Dhaval a text? Ask him to meet us at Urgent Care?"

Confusion flittered across her expression. "Why?"

"Because everyone will think I did this to you." He heard her tiny gasp and the start of her rebuttal, but he stopped her. "You know they will, Lilah. Just . . . Maybe he'll be on my side."

"Nobody will think that. Are you kidding?"

"Just text him? Please?"

She was silent in the seat next to him, clearly unhappy with the idea of bringing Dhaval into any of this. But Gavin could see the moment she realized he might be right, and did what he asked, typing out a text for Dhaval to meet them there anyway.

Everyone would want to know what happened, and what would he say? That his house had attacked her? Because oh, by the way, it's alive? Or would they do what he most feared and assume it was him?

But another thought in Gavin's head seemed to be gaining weight and overshadowing everything else. Delilah had been alone in that bathroom. He was sure of it. There were no roaches and there was definitely no statue in the window, because that part of the House was *his*. It was.

Could Delilah . . . have done it to herself?

Gavin was sure whoever designed the Urgent Care at their small town's only medical center had intended for it to be calming. From the portraits of smiling children, with their pink cheeks and bright smiles, to the pastel-patterned chairs and bubbling fish tank, it looked like some deranged living room from a department-store catalogue.

He searched his thoughts and tried to remember if he'd ever been in a place like this before. The only memories he had of seeing a doctor involved one showing up on his front porch in the middle of the night, and now that he thought about it, wearing the same, dazed expression as Dave when he delivered the groceries every week. Gavin couldn't even think about what that meant. Not with the way everyone was looking at him, like he might leap at them at any minute.

Nothing about this place made Gavin want to stop pacing and sit down. *Nothing* made him comfortable. The chairs looked sticky, the carpet worn down to the plastic underside in some places and stained with random dark splotches in others. He was pretty sure he didn't want to know what those stains might be.

And the concerned, dare he say, *accusing* looks being aimed at him from the nurses' station weren't helping.

The staff had rushed Delilah off almost as soon as they'd arrived. One look at her tangled, damp hair, the clothes that were too big and clearly not hers, and the way she held her injured arm to her body—protectively—and they hadn't wasted a minute. Delilah looked like a battered woman, and Gavin, of course, looked like the culprit.

But she hadn't wanted to go alone, arguing with them and refusing to let go of his hand.

"I'll be back with you in a few minutes," Gavin had told her, brushing the hair from her face. He nodded to the front desk. "I just have to answer a few questions up here and fill out your paperwork, and then they'll let me come back."

He'd kissed the corners of her mouth, knowing it was a lie. Gavin knew, and maybe Delilah did, too, that they had no intention of letting him anywhere near Delilah as long as she was here.

Worn-out and still in pain, she had finally relented, turning to hug him a final time before pressing her cell phone into his hand. "Dhaval said he'll be here," she whispered. "Give this to him for me? My parents will take it."

He'd nodded and kissed her temple, watching as she was led out of the room, and the doors to the back of the facility closed behind her. Away from him.

"Maybe you can tell us what happened?" A nurse in her thirties spoke next to him. She looked pleasant enough, he supposed, but there was something about her—a pinched expression and almost gleeful look in her eyes at the prospect of possibly catching him at something—that made him dislike her almost immediately.

"Sure."

He took a seat at the front counter, his eyes flickering back and forth from the woman typing in front of him to the doors that led to the treatment area.

"Your name?"

"Gavin Timothy," he said.

"And you're the boyfriend."

He blinked back to the nurse, at the pointed way she'd said "the boyfriend," like there was accusation in it. "Yes."

"Can you tell me a little about what happened tonight?"

"I don't know," he said, and dropped his head into his hands. This was pathetic. Who would possibly believe him? "She went upstairs and closed the door. I heard her scream and followed. That's all."

"That's all?"

"Yeah."

"And you're sure nobody else was in there, Gavin?"

She was talking slower than she needed to, speaking as if he needed her to dumb it down for him. Her smile was pained and condescending, and when he didn't elaborate or tell her anything she wanted to hear, she tucked a strand of faded red hair behind her ear and made a note.

"We're going to need you to sit over there," she said, pointing the chewed end of a pencil to the waiting area. "We may need to talk to you again, so please don't leave." She gave him a glance that said *I'll be watching you* and *Stay where you're told*, before she picked up her papers and disappeared into the back.

And that's when Dhaval rushed in the door, in his soccer uniform and drenched in sweat. Gavin couldn't remember the last time he'd been so happy to see *anyone* other than Delilah.

"Is she okay?" Dhaval asked, panicked.

"They're cleaning her up now," Gavin told him.

"Cleaning her up? She said she'd had a little accident!"

Holding out his hands to calm Dhaval down, Gavin whispered, "It was, and she's fine. I promise."

"She's completely fine—you're sure?"

"I'm sure." Gavin led them over to a hallway just off the main waiting room and, apparently satisfied that Delilah wasn't moments from death, Dhaval followed.

"Can you tell me what the hell is going on?"

Gavin wasn't sure how to start.

"You know my house isn't . . ." He struggled to find the right word. Sane? Safe? Inanimate? "Normal." There, that was clear enough.

Dhaval narrowed his eyes. "You're saying your *house* did this?"

"Delilah's saying that," Gavin hedged.

Dhaval looked at him harder now. "But you don't believe her."

"I do, but . . ."

"But what? What exactly is wrong with her?"

Gavin told him everything he knew: how Delilah was wary of the house, how he'd invited her over for dinner, thinking maybe they needed to allow House to give them its blessing in a way. And then he explained what Delilah had said about the roaches and her mother's statue being in the bathroom, about getting lost in all the rooms and attacked in the shower. He admitted he hadn't seen any of it. He described how it looked like someone had branded a handprint into her arm.

Dhaval stared at Gavin for several breaths before leading them over to a vending machine. "I didn't eat after soccer practice. I came straight here, and this has me really freaked and I feel like I might pass out. You mind if I . . . ?" With a shaking hand, he motioned to the rows of colorfully packaged snacks.

Gavin shook his head. "You're sure Delilah wouldn't . . . ?" he asked, and immediately regretted it.

Dhaval stilled from where he'd been digging for money in his pocket. "Are you *serious*?"

Gavin winced, rubbing a hand over his face. "No. No. I know Delilah wouldn't hurt herself. It's just that, that bathroom is the only room where I ever felt like I was totally alone. If that's not true, it's a little hard for me to take. . . ."

"Where was your mom in all this?"

Gavin paused, blinking. Dhaval was obviously starting to believe what they'd been saying about House, but Gavin realized he also thought Gavin's mom was still around.

Everyone thought his mom was still around.

Deflecting, he asked, "Have you ever met her? My mom?"

Gavin watched as Dhaval pulled two crumpled bills from his pocket and tried to straighten them against the corner of the machine. "Well, no," Dhaval started. "I mean no one sees her." He looked up at Gavin's puzzled expression and added in a slow, patient voice, "Because she never leaves?"

"Right. Yeah," he said, suddenly light-headed. Gavin was starting to realize how much easier it was for people to believe his mom was so freaked out by strangers that she'd essentially lock herself up in her own house than to believe she could have abandoned her small child or that something terrible could have happened to her right in the middle of their nice, safe neighborhood.

Gavin knew this was insane. He should be horrified that everyone had essentially let him fend for himself, but it almost . . . made him feel better. Like he hadn't been abandoned by the entire town, after all.

The question was, where *was* his mom? All he had was a picture of her, but no memories. His stomach turned, and he closed his eyes, trying to breathe deeply enough to stave off the wave of nausea.

"But my mom knew her," Dhaval said. "Mom was friends with Hilary when we first moved here and I was a baby."

Hilary. His mother's name was Hilary.

Gavin took a step back, grateful that the wall was there to catch him.

Dhaval began to feed the bills into the machine, distracted. "Actually, I know my mom answered some questions she had about blessing a house. She's even been to your place."

Gavin's attention snapped to him, eyes wide. "The what now?"

"The blessing," Dhaval said, looking over his shoulder at Gavin. "I only know about this stuff because Grandma is always talking about it, but Vastu Shastra says all places are home to souls or spirits or whatever, and you have to pray and cleanse a space before you can live or even move stuff in. I know you guys were already living there before the blessing. If you ask my mom, she'll say that's bad juju."

Dhaval typed in the number of his selection and bent to retrieve a granola bar. Holding it up, he used it to point to his chest. "I have no idea what's going on here. I feel like this . . ." He looked to the side, breath coming out choppy and uneven. "Honestly? I feel like none of this can be real. But . . . I trust Delilah. I saw her that night after she thought it was following you guys everywhere. I saw her wake up thinking her sweater was possessed."

"Her . . . *what?*"

As if he hadn't heard this, Dhaval continued. "I mean, I don't know you that well, but we've been in school together since kindergarten and you seem weird but not *insane*. So maybe that *is* what happened. Maybe your mom did some crazy half-assed blessing in this super-old house and it all went haywire. Maybe your mom brought your house to life."

Dhaval didn't look entirely convinced, but Gavin's blood ran like ice in his veins. He hoped he was imagining the way the floor seemed to shift beneath his feet. He wanted to look outside and see if the trees had turned their leaves toward the windows, if the air had grown still, quieter so House could hear what Dhaval was saying.

Everything started to click into place, and Gavin was pretty sure he'd never been more afraid in his life. The memory he hated to revisit came flooding back to him, of the day he'd first found the car in the garage.

He could still hear the birds, smell the scent of dust and old gasoline when he'd finally been tall enough and strong enough to lift open the garage door. He could still see the car, feel the satin of the paint under his fingers, the softness of the leather.

And if he closed his eyes, he could remember the feeling of excitement, the thundering beat of his heart when he'd opened the door and sat inside. He would drive this someday, he'd thought, stretching his arms to wrap his hands around the steering wheel. Gavin had adjusted the seat and, of course, the knobs on the radio. He'd wiped a layer of dust from the dash and then looked up, tilting the rearview mirror low enough that he could see through the grimy back window.

But that's when his heart had halted in his chest, his pulse tripping in his throat. For a few moments it was as if the birds had stopped chirping outside; the leaves had quit shaking. It was so quiet he could hear the frantic thump of his pulse in his ears; and he'd had to close his eyes tight, shake his head to

clear it before he could look again. Because there in the backseat was a car seat—*his* car seat; he was sure of it. It was dusty
and forgotten, and an old bunny sat lopsided as it waited for
someone to come back and retrieve it.

Because his mom had disappeared.

Gavin hadn't thought about that car seat and what it
meant for years, and as he looked up, past Dhaval's worried
expression and out into the waiting room, Gavin realized he
wouldn't get a chance to think about what it meant now, either.

Delilah's parents were here.

CHAPTER TWENTY-TWO

HER

D R. MCNEILL LOOKED DOWN AT HER CHART, flipping up the top page with her insurance information to reveal the sheet beneath. It was covered with ink: three identical accounts of what happened to Delilah. Each was written in a different handwriting, of course, as each had been collected by a different nurse. One of the nurses—the one with LISA on her name tag—hung back, leaning against the wall.

Without having to ask, Delilah knew Nurse Lisa remained in the room so that Delilah wouldn't be left alone with a man.

"It says here you got wrapped up in a shower curtain." When the doctor met her eyes, she felt his concern and knew he was thinking the same thing the nurses were: *Your boyfriend beats you.*

She took a deep breath and then told him the same thing she'd already said three times before, the stupid, horrible story she was committed to now: "I spilled my dinner on myself. I went upstairs to shower and tripped on the tub and got tangled in the shower curtain."

"But only your arm got tangled?" he asked as if clarifying, even peeking back down at the accounts of the incident as if to confirm. She could hear the skepticism in his voice; he had to hear it for himself.

"Well, all of me was tangled. But just my arm got hurt."

"I'm having a hard time picturing this."

"I fell and it was hanging in the tub. It was plastic and sort of wrapped around me."

"And it somehow shredded so it looked like fingers?"

"No. It wasn't shredded. . . ." She trailed off.

He waited for her to say more, but she had no more. Her story was as weak as she felt. She could feel the heavy pressure of tears building behind her eyes, stinging across the surface.

Flipping her chart closed, the doctor sighed and rolled closer to Delilah on the wheeled stool. "Delilah."

She swallowed, meeting his eyes.

"You aren't alone, okay? If you need help getting out of this—"

"I know what you're thinking, but Gavin would never do this to me."

Dr. McNeill closed his eyes, nodding slowly. When he opened them again, he quietly asked, "Is there anyone you would rather talk to than me right now?"

Without hesitation, Delilah said, "Yeah. Gavin."

"Your parents might ask him to stay away from you. I'll be honest, Delilah. It doesn't look good. If you were my daughter, I'd be questioning Gavin's role in all of this."

As if on cue, a voice drifted down the hall from the waiting room to where she sat on a high cot. She couldn't make out the words, but her father's anger came across in the volume, in the short bursts of words fired at Gavin like bullets.

"This is awful for him," Delilah said in a choked whisper, and the tears finally spilled over as she stared at the curtain that was pulled around their small space, hiding the hallway from her view. "This is torture for him, and there's nothing he can do. It's killing him not being back here with me right now."

"But surely you understand why he's not."

Laughing without humor, Delilah looked him square in the eye. "I'll go home with my parents, and my dad will go watch the news and my mom will go read a book. The only person who really cares if my arm is okay is out there in the waiting room being yelled at for something he didn't do."

Dr. McNeill glanced back over his shoulder at Nurse Lisa. She shrugged, and he turned back to Delilah. "I want to see you back in here next week so I can make sure it's healing right."

When Delilah emerged from the procedure room, her arm wrapped in gauze and her blood humming with painkillers, she needed to take only one look at her father's face to know she shouldn't waste her breath asking what he'd said to Gavin. She realized she didn't have her phone; Gavin did. She couldn't even text him to find out where he'd gone or if he'd seen Dhaval.

The waiting room was emptier than she'd expected given the voices and commotion drifting to the back treatment room. When Dr. McNeill beckoned them, her parents followed him into an office adjacent to the waiting room enclosed with glass, through which Delilah could see him explaining the injury. He pointed to his arm, then patted it and spoke emphatically, curling his fingers in a scratching motion. Delilah watched him with wide, scrutinizing eyes, trying to figure out if he was representing her version of events. She doubted it. One look at Gavin in his dark, skinny pants, scuffed shoes, and wild, dark hair, and grown-ups would think he was two steps past odd and just shy of suspicious. Delilah was the only person around who knew for sure that the only rough touch Gavin would ever give her was a biting kiss she begged for.

And then the doctor ticked a list off with his fingers in the same way he had with her before releasing her to walk back to the waiting room. She knew what he was saying:

Don't expose the wound to water for the next twenty-four hours.

Remove the gauze after two days to let the wound breathe, and apply the antibiotic ointment every six hours.

No swimming, no baths, and don't let it stay wet or be submerged in water.

If it looks like it's getting infected, come back immediately.

The drive home in the backseat was suffocating. There wasn't enough room in the car for their three bodies, Delilah's leaden panic, her father's fury, and her mother's anxious nattering.

"Gosh, it's just been forever since we used that clinic. That Dr. McNeill is something—isn't he, Frankie?" she asked her husband. She went on without waiting for a reply. "He's been here since, what? The eighties? And before that it was his uncle running that office. Now, what was his name? Edwin something or other . . ."

"Miller," Delilah's father added flatly.

"Right! Edwin Miller. Oh, and he was a rake, wasn't he?" her mother said, voice practically dripping with scandal.

"You're thinking of his brother, Douglas."

"Messed around with at least five girls from our class, though. For sure Rosemary. Also Jennifer and Deborah."

"Mm-hmm."

"Whatever happened to him? I heard he got some young girl in trouble—"

"Never heard that."

"—moved across the river to Missouri, but that was from Jennifer, and you know she never knows what's really going on. . . ."

And even with the claustrophobic feeling in the car, Delilah still wanted Gavin to be in there with her. She didn't even have his borrowed clothes anymore. The nurses had told her parents to bring in a fresh set of her own. His things were probably lying in the Dumpster behind the Urgent Care. And now, away from there, away from the singular priority that she protect Gavin at all costs, the reality of what happened started to descend. The tremor started in her right hand and spread up to her shoulder, the panic burrowing into her chest and settling into a cold block of ice.

It was madness, wasn't it? That she'd been attacked by his *house* and he'd been blamed for it, and now she was bandaged and drugged and he was gone. Was he okay? Had he been arrested? Or was he home, back *there*, trying to reconcile what his house had done to Delilah with everything his house had done for him? This worry bounced around in her head, and even though it was nearly freezing outside, Delilah rolled down her window, simply needing air.

"Delilah Blue," her mother cried, interrupting herself. "Roll up that window this instant or you'll catch pneumonia!"

She rolled up her window but squeezed her eyes closed tight, trying to breathe, trying to think, trying to make sense out of any of this.

There was no family processing when they got home, no together time in the living room, asking what happened or how she was. Both of her parents moved to resume their nightly routine, but she stopped them with a calm, forceful, "Gavin didn't do this."

Silence rang back to her.

"I know you think that," she pressed onward. "I know Dr. McNeill thinks that too. I know you said something to Gavin in the waiting room. I heard you yelling at him. But you've seen him now. His hands are huge. If he'd grabbed my arm, he would have done much worse than this burn."

"They said your arm was . . . torn," her father hissed, repulsed by her injury. "Pieces of your skin, just gone."

And with those words, beneath her bandage, beneath the painkiller, her arm ached. "That doesn't mean he did it."

"Well, if you would tell someone the truth about what happened—"

"You wouldn't believe me, Dad."

Her father gave her a lingering, scandalized look before retiring to his post in the family room to watch the news.

"Try not to sleep on your left side, dear," her mother chirped as she headed upstairs to read. "And make sure you wash your hands and face before bed. God knows what you've been touching all day."

The Blue house grew quiet just after eleven. It was quiet in that way Delilah now recognized as normal, as a house sitting truly still. There were the noises of pipes tapping and vents blowing warm air, but no phantom heartbeats, no shifting, settling, or spying. She comforted herself with the explanation that maybe the spirits of the house—the life, the poltergeist, whatever was inside it—could move from object to object, from place to place underground or in wires, but the life itself wasn't contagious. It couldn't *really* spread.

But how does *it work?* Delilah thought idly. And then, more hysterically, as the pain medication was slowly wearing off and her arm throbbed, on fire with every heartbeat:

How does it hear us?

How does it follow us?

What is it, inside, that brings this crazy, menacing space to life?

She hadn't yet given the "how" much thought, and in the moment here, so many weeks after she should have considered it, it seemed so stupidly naive to just be thrilled by the miracle of its existence. But with the first inkling—in the private darkness of her thoughts—that she might someday need to destroy the house, she realized she would need to figure out how.

She closed her eyes, considering what she knew:

The house, and everything inside it, was alive.

The house followed them to the park, through some network of grass and roots and trees.

The house could possess objects that Gavin would take with him—the tricycle, little things he could put in his pockets. The sweater she wore to the house *had* been possessed. It wasn't a dream.

Something had happened to her father when he'd veered onto the property. Maybe the house possessed Dave the grocer, too. Had it tried to get into her mind that first day? What were those shadow fingertips she'd felt pressing in at her temples? Had they been trying to possess *her*? Was it angrier that Gavin wanted to be with her, or that it couldn't control her?

Could the house control anything that came onto its property? How far out of town could it spread?

Her heartbeat thundered a roaring storm in her chest. She had to talk to Gavin.

Delilah was suddenly certain that he wasn't home, that he wouldn't have gone back without first making sure she was okay. So when the grandfather clock in the living room struck midnight, Delilah pulled on a skirt and a plain top, opened her bedroom window and climbed out, gripping the rain gutter with her uninjured hand. She slid one leg over the ledge and then took a deep breath before pushing herself from the window, holding her body close to the pipe. Almost immediately, she lost her grip, sliding violently to the ground and landing so hard the wind was propelled from her lungs in a heavy cough. That was truly the last thing she needed tonight: to return to Urgent Care for a broken arm she'd obtained while trying to sneak out to see the boy her parents assumed was beating her.

Her head reverberated with the impact of the fall; her limbs felt heavy and slow under the diminishing effects of the

Percocet. On the lawn she paused, looking around as the cold seeped into the sleeves of her shirt and covered her skin, like the air itself was trying to tell her this was a bad idea.

Once again, the trees leaned in close, and the sky seemed to vanish into black. But this time Delilah looked up at the branches high above and hissed, "Touch me again and you'll lose him forever. Maybe you've lost him already."

Delilah wasn't sure how Gavin had learned to break in, but he was exactly where she'd expected he would be, closed in the dark practice room in the trailers behind the school, hunched over a piano. He looked up when she opened the door, eyes wide and full of wild relief. "I'm sorry I left," he blurted. "I wanted to stay, but—"

"I know," she said, cutting him off. "My dad was terrible to you, wasn't he?"

Gavin ran a long, wide-knuckled hand down his face. "Are you okay?"

"I'm fine. Got some drugs and bandages and I'm all set."

He nodded, letting his eyes move over every one of her features as if convincing himself that the only injury she'd sustained was on her arm.

"Hey, listen," Delilah said, taking a step closer. "I need you to do something for me."

He looked up to her, eyes pleading. "Anything."

Delilah held up the small pile of clothes she'd taken from

his locker. "I need you to put these on," she said, placing them on top of the piano.

Gavin blinked at her. "You want me to put my gym clothes on?"

"You trust me, right?"

Without a word, Gavin stood and began pulling off his T-shirt. Delilah motioned for him to hold on and searched inside the teacher's cupboard, coming back with an open garbage sack.

"In here, okay?"

Gavin dropped his shirt inside the bag and reached for his belt, his eyes flickering up to hers, brows lifted as if to say *you going to watch?* When she met his stare with a determined one of her own, he smiled and continued undressing.

He was down to his underwear, thumbs tucked into the elastic when he looked at her again.

"All of it," she said.

Gavin had wanted to get naked with her, but again, this wasn't exactly how or when he'd thought it would happen.

But Delilah wasn't quite as brave as she looked, because when he slipped his boxers down his legs and stood, dropping them in the bag before reaching for his clean clothes, her eyes were averted and her cheeks were definitely pinker than when she'd come in. He had never been undressed like this in front of someone else—not even close—even though he'd thought about it quite a lot. Gavin *liked* being naked in front of Delilah.

He liked how pretty she was when she blushed and how even though she seemed to be doing everything she could to not look, he thought he saw her peek, maybe just once.

"Delilah Blue," he said, smug as he watched her walk away. "Are you blushing?"

"Hush," she called over her shoulder, opening the door just enough to throw the tied bag outside, and quickly shut it again.

The air in the music room was cool on his skin, and Gavin quickly pulled his shorts up his legs. "Are you going to tell me what that was about?" he said.

Delilah crossed the room to stand in front of him. "You'll think I'm crazy."

"Is that even possible anymore?" he asked, shrugging into his clean shirt.

"You told me before that whatever's making the house . . . what it *is*, can attach itself to something before it's taken off the property. Like the way it used to with the tricycle or things it would leave for you to take if you had a big exam or needed some comfort?"

"Right," he murmured.

"Maybe the house has always been doing that with you, or maybe it hasn't. But since things started with us . . . I get the sense that it's *always* nearby, hijacking onto you whenever you leave."

Gavin nodded as if he had that sense, too.

"The other night at Dhaval's?" she began. "I fell asleep

and had a dream that I was holding a hand. Like I was holding someone's dead, rotting hand. When I woke up, screaming, it was just my sweater, the one I'd been wearing when I walked you home. But I knew I hadn't been dreaming. The sweater really did . . . *do* something."

"Jesus," Gavin said, knees feeling weak enough that he had to sit back down. "I can't believe it would . . . ," he started, and then glanced down to the new clothes he'd put on. "But these are from my house. I washed them there." He plucked at the collar of his shirt.

"I think we have to hope it has a purpose when it does it. What would be the point in attaching itself to your gym clothes? It wouldn't worry about that at the time."

"But why? Why would it follow me?"

"Why does any parent follow their kid? To watch them. To keep them safe. It's just . . . It's gone too far."

"But you think we're okay here?" he asked.

Delilah looked around the room. "I think so. I think the house can possess people too—maybe. . . . My dad was acting so weird that night after he pulled into your driveway. And Dave the grocer? You said he comes every week but then didn't recognize you later?"

"Anyone who comes to the house," Gavin whispered. "They all get this glazed look."

"But it can't do that with me and you. Maybe because we *know*."

Gavin seemed to take several quiet minutes to absorb what she was saying.

"I'm so sorry about all this," he said, carefully pulling her down to sit beside him. "For bringing you into this mess. For this." He brushed a thumb over the edge of her bandage.

Delilah was tempted to wiggle her arms playfully to show him that she really was fine, but he didn't look very lighthearted at the moment. She dropped the half smile and lowered her voice. "Honestly, I'm okay. I'm pretty hard to scare off."

He groaned and rested his head dissonantly against the keys. "I know how it looks. I can't even fathom hurting you."

"Of course you can't. None of this is your fault."

"Your dad thinks I did that to you. God, Delilah, I could never. I *love* you."

Everything else was forgotten—the pulsing pain in her arm, the fear of what would happen to their relationship, the terrifying unknown of the house—as her face exploded in a grin. "I love you, too."

He lifted his head, realizing what they'd both just said. Allowing a small smile, he said, "I do, you know. I have for, like, forever. And I usually don't care what anyone thinks, but it's different with you. I don't want anyone to think I could be violent with you. Especially your parents."

"Well, let me assure you that their opinion does not carry the same weight with me. But I'm pretty sure I convinced

239

them you didn't do it. Look at your giant hands, Gavin. You'd have left a handprint twice this size on my skin."

He stared down at his fingers propped on the keys and visibly relaxed. "Good argument, if not a little disturbing."

"Hardly," she said, grinning. "I spend hours thinking about your big hands."

He turned so he was straddling the bench and spread his fingers across his bent knees.

"Yeah? Tell me."

Delilah was so distracted by the sight of his long limbs, his enormous hands, the ends of his dark hair brushing the tips of his impossibly thick black lashes, that she forgot what she'd even said. "Tell you what?"

Swallowing, Gavin reminded her, "What you think about my hands."

"Right now?"

"Yeah."

"You're looking for distraction."

He smiled a little sadly. "Maybe."

"Shouldn't we talk about this?" she asked, taking a step closer to him. "I mean, not my arm. I don't want to talk about that. But about what happened in that room . . ."

He watched her for several long, silent seconds, his expression sliding from uncomfortable, to guilty, to defeated. "If it's all right with you . . . can we talk about that later?"

She sucked her bottom lip into her mouth as she studied

his slumped posture and his fingers gripping and releasing his thighs. So upset, wound so tight. They never did get that walk after dinner, and Delilah's hope they could have some time—talking, holding hands, letting the space grow warm and magnetic between them until he couldn't take it anymore and would press her against a wall or a tree or . . . *well*.

They were alone now; the school had been dark and full of shadows and echoes when she'd come in, and probably had been for hours. With her heart pounding ferociously beneath her breastbone, Delilah stood and reached under her skirt, wiggling her underwear down her legs. She stepped out of them, careful not to fall over.

Gavin swallowed. "Um. So." He reached back and scratched his neck. "So, Delilah? What are you doing?"

"Taking off my underwear."

"I can see that." He studied the pink cotton on the floor and blinked rapidly. The bravery he'd felt at his own nakedness just minutes before seemed to have abandoned him. "Lilah, I have no idea what to do with you . . ." Without looking up, he waved vaguely at her skirt, still in place, still hiding her most secret parts, adding, "Down there."

Delilah felt as though her blood had turned into a million fluttering wings in her veins. "So, I'll tell you."

She walked over to him, wishing he would just look up at her for a second, to let her know that he was okay with it, with this. And then she knew he was when he reached forward, put his hands on her hips over her skirt to draw her closer. He leaned forward and kissed her ribs, lips pressed just beneath her breast.

Pulling back, Gavin looked up at her and whispered, "I don't want to have sex for the first time in a practice room at school."

She worried for a moment that her chest might break open with her heart pounding so hard. "Okay."

"In case that's what you were thinking we were going to do."

"I'm pretty sure I'm not thinking at all right now."

"I guess that's what I mean." He smiled, and this time it crinkled the corners of his eyes. "You were in Urgent Care four hours ago, and now you're not wearing underwear."

"There's a lot of room between this and sex. Just touch me, Gavin."

He hesitated, but didn't look away.

"I'm scared," she admitted then, wanting to be honest with him but hoping he wouldn't stop.

His expression darkened immediately. "Of this, right now? Or of . . . House?"

She shook her head. "I know the house is all you've known. It's your *family*. I know it tears you up inside to see how hard it is for House right now, and how hard it is for me, too. The thing is, I'm yours. *I* don't belong to anyone but you. I'm scared that you'll never be mine the same way."

"Lilah, don't say that." He closed his eyes, pressed his face to her stomach.

His hands moved to cup the backs of her knees, and he arched his neck to kiss her. Delilah felt the familiar tumble of butterflies, the warm melting of her limbs. Nothing happened fast, but when she would look back on it later, in her innocent purple room, she would be unable to remember how it went from such a careful kiss to his hands moving up her bare thighs, slipping around to her hips and putting so much pressure there with the tips of his thumbs that she hoped he would leave small indentations she could find later with her own hands.

When he finally grew brave, and impatient, and kissed her with more teeth and growl than lips, he moved one hand between her legs. He'd said he didn't know what he was doing, but it didn't matter. Soon she had one hand wrapped around his wrist, showing him, and the other dug deep into his hair, ensuring his mouth never moved far from hers. The room reverberated with the quiet afterward, and he stared up at her for a long minute, unspeaking.

Delilah didn't think it was possible that anyone, ever before, had felt what she felt when Gavin carefully kissed her top and then her bottom lip and told her, "I *am* yours already. Completely."

"Are you sure?" she asked.

He nodded, glancing down at her bandaged arm, and already his eyes clouded over again.

He walked her home, lifted her so he could take his time and made her drunk with kisses, before watching her walk toward the dark quiet of her house.

Delilah had a lot to think about—Gavin's hands and smile, his confession that he loved her, and the relief in his eyes when she was falling to pieces—and it would have to sustain her for some time, because after he disappeared down the sidewalk, he didn't reappear for two days.

CHAPTER TWENTY-THREE

HER

STRANGE, OR MAYBE NOT, THAT SHE COULD FOCUS on her work when he was in class and was a useless mess when he wasn't. He hadn't texted to say he wasn't feeling well, hadn't called or e-mailed to give her the heads-up that he wouldn't be at school the next day.

Delilah ate lunch with an anxiously chatty Dhaval beneath the tree. He rambled on and on about math class, about what Kirk Teller said to him at lunch. He talked about his new shoes and his father's new car. He had a million words, and they all tumbled frantically out in a nonstop torrent.

Delilah felt acutely, painfully hyperaware. When Gavin was at her side, she felt safe, because even if House hated her, it cherished him. Until last night she didn't think it would ever *actually* hurt her, and if it did, it certainly wouldn't do it when he was nearby.

But now Delilah knew there was no safety anywhere. He

wasn't here, and even if he had been, apparently it wouldn't matter. Was *he* safe?

Life wasn't supposed to be like this; it wasn't supposed to be chronically terrifying. She wasn't supposed to wonder if the tree was listening to their conversation or if the grass would poison her skin if it could. She wasn't supposed to wonder what danger awaited her on the walk home, whether the sidewalk would crack suddenly, and just so, snapping her ankle. Or whether she should start trying to stay awake at night.

"Dee, are you listening to anything I'm saying?" Dhaval leaned forward, breaking into her trance.

"Sorry, no."

He exhaled slowly, looking out at the kids playing basketball in the distance. After several long beats of silence, he asked, "Are you going to tell me what's going on?"

She remained mute.

"You have to know how it looks," he said, turning and gesturing to her arm. "It looks like he hurt you, or *you* look insane."

Finally, she turned to him, glancing up at the tree branches—they didn't seem to be moving closer—before whispering, "I already tried to tell you how messed up it is, and you didn't believe me."

"So tell me everything again." After she gave him a skeptical look, he added, "I want to hear more. I think . . . I think I believe you now."

"Not here."

Delilah stood, brushing the dried grass and leaves from her skirt before pulling Dhaval toward the trailers and into the empty practice room. She sat him down on the very same piano bench where Gavin had been sitting last night. The very same bench where he'd touched her with such an aching, open tenderness. She could still feel the pressure of his fingers.

"Why are we in here?" Dhaval asked, looking around.

Blinking back into the present, Delilah said, "It just feels safe in here."

"That is—" He stopped himself just short of saying "crazy" and instead ended awkwardly with, "Really freaky, Dee."

Taking a deep breath and ignoring the bell signaling the end of lunch, Delilah told him about the day she met the house, about what it looked like, how it felt. She described how it loves Gavin, how it seems impossible that these hard, inanimate objects could be so, well, so animated, but it's true.

"I'd never seen anything more amazing," she admitted.

But then she recounted the afternoon she'd spent kissing Gavin in the park, the branches creeping beneath his shirt, trapping her wrists. She told him about the house reacting to her questions about the future, about how it felt like being thrown into a blender when it trembled and lurched beneath her feet.

Dhaval looked less skeptical this time and far more ashen.

"After that happened, Gavin wanted to make me dinner," she said, sitting down next to him. "I think he wanted me and the house to make up, or something. I could feel how angry it was at me. Some things—like the fireplace or the things in the living room—seemed to want to make nice, and so I thought maybe I just had to hang in there a little."

"Like, win it over," Dhaval added.

"Exactly." She told him about the plan to go for a walk, about washing her hands, and seeing her mother's figurine. She told him about turning, about her focus snagging on the small, seemingly innocent bubble of paint.

She told him, with growing hysteria, about everything that happened afterward: the roaches, the way the house taunted and played with her as she tried to escape. "I got in the shower, trying to wash them off. I threw my clothes across the room, and the roaches were coming for me and the shower curtain slid up my legs and wrapped around me and—" She hiccupped, squeezing her eyes closed. "It tore at my arm. When I screamed, Gavin burst into the room finally, but when I looked down . . ." She opened her eyes to look at Dhaval, and she could see in his expression that he already knew what she was going to say. "When I looked down, there was nothing there. No bugs, no crazy possessed shower curtain, no statue. Just the skin torn off my arm so it looked like I did it. Or Gavin."

"Dee, this is . . ." He swiped a shaking hand down his face. "I don't even know what this is."

"I know."

"And his mom?" Dhaval asked.

Delilah stared at him for several thundering heartbeats, finally answering truthfully though vaguely, "I don't know." Was there really a mother? If so, where in the hell was she? Scooting a little closer, she asked, "Dhaval, do you *know* his mom?"

He shook his head. "I told Gavin my mom does, sort of peripherally."

"He asked you?"

"Yeah. Mom answered some questions about blessing their house, a way long time ago—like when Gavin was tiny—and I only know that because she mentioned it to me the other night after you came over."

Delilah felt her brows pull close and tight. *"What?"*

He seemed oblivious to what had tripped her up. "She hasn't seen Gavin's mom in years. I get the sense that Mrs. Timothy is . . . a little eccentric. Mom wants to give her privacy, so she didn't ask you about her."

"Dhaval? Your mom didn't even ask why I came over so late. She didn't let me say a word. Do you remember? She told me to breathe, told me everything was okay."

"Yeah?" he said, confused. "So?"

"So," she said slowly, hoping he would understand, "did your mom know that I'm dating Gavin, or did you tell her that later?"

He paused, seeming to consider this for a beat before shaking his head. "Neither, actually."

"Then why did she bring up Gavin with you at all?"

"She said Hilary's son always has that same sizzled look you had." He looked at her with amused, incredulous eyes.

"Dhaval?"

"Mmm?"

"I've never *met* Hilary," Delilah said. "I've been inside his house four times—I even spent an hour in there alone one day—but I've never even *heard* her."

Unease tripped through Delilah's veins and opened up a space inside her chest that felt like it would keep growing and growing until she cracked wide open. *I must look like a crazy person,* she thought, as she practically ran home—avoiding cracks in the sidewalks, working to stay out of reach of branches, hoses, lampposts. Her temples ached and the entire sensation made her uneasy, as if it wasn't from thinking too much but from the house, somewhere, trying to press into her mind. She hopped up her front steps, exhaling a tight breath when she opened the front door and her house felt as flat and lifeless as it always had.

"Mom?" she called out.

"In the kitchen!"

Delilah dropped her backpack near the stairs and walked toward the back of the house, looking at things more closely than she ever had before. Nothing seemed to be obviously awry. The shelves were cluttered with hundreds of tiny porcelain figurines—including the fawn.

She closed her eyes, knowing now that it was all in her head. She never wanted to go back there. She would stay the hell away from the house, and the house would stay the hell away from her until she finished school and could get the hell out of Morton.

With Gavin in tow.

She pulled a chair away from the kitchen table and sat down.

"Long day?" her mother asked without looking up from the sink.

"Yeah."

"Did you keep your arm dry?"

Not *How is your arm*, or, *Are you in much pain*, but, *Did you keep your arm dry?* Delilah paused, looking down at the gauze wrap. "Yes."

"Good." Turning, her mother deposited a handful of washed spinach on top of a cutting board on the island. She reached into a drawer and pulled out a knife.

Delilah had seen it before, but it felt out of place here. The handle was ivory, the blade long and so clean it gleamed like a mirror. Dread chilled her hands, and the cold spread up her arms and into her throat.

It was from the shed.

"Mom, is that one of your knives?"

"It must be," Belinda said, lifting it to turn and inspect it for a beat before bunching some spinach in her hand to begin chopping.

Without thinking, Delilah reached for the knife, yanking it from her mother's grasp. It flashed hot in her palm, the pearly handle coming to life in a repulsive slither. With a scream, she hurled it at the wall, where it hit and stuck with a horrible, squelching thud. It didn't sound like a knife going into paint, plaster, or wood. It sounded like a knife hitting a chest and sinking through bone into something wet and vital. She stared, her heart thundering, expecting to see blood—or roaches—spill from the wall.

But instead the knife trembled from the force of the impact and then grew still.

The room was swallowed in shocked silence.

"Delilah Blue," her mother whispered, voice shaking. "What on earth is wrong with you?"

"That knife isn't yours, Mom. It's not yours. It's—" Her voice withered away into a soft gasp. The knife protruded eerily, the dim kitchen light slashing shadows along the blue paint. But instead of gleaming ivory, there was only wood, the wooden handle of an ordinary chef's knife.

Belinda threw up her hands, voice hysterical now. "Well, who cares whose knife it is? It works just as well as any other! You don't throw it at the bleeping *wall*!"

"But how . . . ?" Delilah said, stepping back, unable to look away from the object embedded in the wall. "I don't know what's happening, but . . . just don't touch it." Finally, she looked at her mother's face, her voice flat and hollow: "Don't even *look* at it."

Upstairs, fumbling for her phone, Delilah could hear her mother's hysterical voice on the house phone with her father. It drifted from the kitchen and up the banister as clear as a bell, sliding beneath Delilah's closed door.

"That's right! She threw it! At the wall! Frankie, I'm not sure this is the place for her. I'm not sure we can handle— well, no. First the injury and now throwing knives?" A pause. "I know." Another pause. "Yes, I'm fine." And finally a longer, heavier pause and her mother's relieved, choking exhale. "Okay. Yes, that's good, darling."

She closed her eyes and pressed her fingers against her temples, not even a little curious about what her mother had just agreed to do. Her head hurt again, like something was trying to get inside.

Stop, stop, stop, she thought, trying to push whatever it was out. She crawled from her bed, took all of the clothing in her laundry basket—not even bothering to sort through and find what she might have worn to Gavin's—opened the window, and hurled it out onto the back lawn, slamming the window shut again.

Her mom was still talking, her voice carrying up the stairs and down the hall.

"Send me away again," Delilah whispered. "Just send me anywhere."

And for a beat she relished the thought.

Until she remembered Gavin. Her birthday was rapidly approaching, and though that meant she'd legally be able to do whatever the hell she wanted soon enough, she wasn't sure he would follow.

She could feel the madness teasing at the edges of her thoughts. It brought back the strange memory of being a little girl at a party her father's business had thrown at the country club seven miles outside of town. Delilah had fingered the fancy table linen and then slowly lifted it—consumed by an overwhelming curiosity to just get a peek at the table beneath. The white Formica top was covered in an ugly web of scratches and stains.

She closed her eyes, imagining a tablecloth drifting over her thoughts, trying to keep all of her hysteria covered. If I do one thing at a time, she thought, it will be okay.

I'll text him.

I'll do my homework.

I'll sleep, and go to school, and forget that the house ever existed. I'm not crazy.

I'll talk to Gavin only about nice things, about pleasant things, and until we figure out how to get away, it will be enough.

The house will forget about me.

With shaking fingers, she sent Gavin a message: *Missed you at school today. Hope all is well. I feel like I'm losing my mind.*

Twenty minutes into her homework and with barely anything completed, Delilah jumped when her phone buzzed on her desk.

That's not all you're going to lose, girl.

CHAPTER TWENTY-FOUR

HIM

G AVIN HAD NEVER SKIPPED SCHOOL A DAY IN his life. He'd been sick before, of course, the occasional cold or stomach bug, that time he had the flu and could think of nothing else but his mom—or any mom, for that matter—to brush the hair from his feverish forehead or just hold him.

He would open his eyes and find medicine on Table, no name on the bottle, just a label with clearly typed instructions. Juice and steaming bowls of chicken soup were there one minute, then gone once they'd been emptied or grown cold. Piano played soft and soothing lullabies as he'd fallen into a restless, sweaty slumber.

And so he would miss a day or two, always returning once the cold had run its course or he was feeling better.

But he wasn't sick now.

The urge to wake that morning had tickled at the back of his brain, stirred in his sleep-heavy limbs. He'd shuffled into the blankets, restless and uncomfortable. Without looking, he could tell the room was still dark, and so he rolled over, ignoring his bladder and his stirring thoughts, intent on going back to sleep.

Voices in the distance drew his attention—familiar voices—the laughter and shouts of kids he knew, racing down the street near the end of the block toward school. But it wasn't time yet; he didn't need to look at the clock to know he had another hour, at least.

There were more shouts, followed by the sound of the garbage truck he passed every week as he left.

Gavin sat up, blankets falling to his waist and his brows drawn in confusion, as he stared at the heavy blue curtains across from him, at the sliver of yellow sun slipping in near the carpet. This time of year the giant tree on the other side of the fence outside his window was bare, all spindly branches and arching limbs. It allowed the light from the slowly brightening sky to fill his room each morning, one pastel shade at a time. It was why he never closed the curtains, why he hadn't closed them last night.

Pushing the hair from his forehead, he reached for his phone, pulling back at the sight of only the empty plug on Table. He paused and retraced his steps from last night, positive that he'd plugged it in before bed.

Gavin swung his legs from the mattress and crossed to the window. The floor was cold beneath the soles of his feet, the air biting against so much bare skin. With each step the curtains looked brighter, the light on the other side confirming his suspicions: At some point during the night, House had closed his curtains and taken his phone.

He pushed the drapes aside and looked down onto the frostbitten street. Up here in the house, he was high enough to see over the vine-covered fence, high enough to note that the driveways were empty, most of his neighbors having long since gone to work, a few stragglers in the distance on their way to school still hung back on the sidewalks.

It had to be almost eight in the morning and Gavin was late. He'd never been late.

"Why didn't anyone wake me?" he called out.

He pushed off the wall and went to the closet, swearing into the darkness when a light didn't turn on. "Light!" he shouted. The bulb overhead popped to life, and he began searching through his clothes, pulling a pair of jeans from a drawer, a hoodie from another. He collected a T-shirt and boxers and shuffled into the bathroom.

The shower didn't start. Gavin turned the knobs one way and then another, tossing his clothes to the floor before trying again.

"What the—?" he started, taking a step back before fingering the knobs again, watching them turn easily while the faucet stayed as dry as a bone. He couldn't remember a time anything had stopped working in House before. A leg might wobble on a table, a window frame might squeak, but it was always fixed the next day, and Gavin never really put much thought into it.

He checked Sink, even more confused when water ran from the tap, clear and cold. Toilet worked perfectly, too.

What the hell was happening? He'd been so tired when he got home yesterday. After what he'd done with Delilah—*finally* touching her—he'd wanted to question House somehow, to know what had really happened with Delilah in the bathroom. But House had been strange from the moment he'd walked in the door. Fireplace had roared to life, blazing hot in the hearth. TV turned on and off, and Chandelier over Dining Room Table swung wildly, silently demanding to know where he'd been.

So Delilah had been right after all: House had hijacked a ride, and taking off his clothes had made him invisible.

"I was just making sure she was okay," he said aloud. "You *hurt* her. Do you realize that?"

Silence.

The fire dimmed; Chandelier stilled.

"Sometimes I want to be alone with her," he said quietly. "Not to betray you, but just to be with *her*."

He'd climbed the stairs slowly, feeling the walls of the hallway bow inward in silent apology. Lights flickered on overhead, anticipating his path down the hall and into his bedroom, back down the hall and into the bathroom. Piano had even played while he fell asleep, and he couldn't remember the last time that had happened.

In the end, he'd been so exhausted he'd had to ignore, for the time being, the disloyal feeling he got when Blanket curled gently around him and Bedroom seemed to search for the perfect temperature that kept him from growing too restless.

House was trying to make amends, but as hard as it was to admit, Gavin knew that wasn't possible. After what had happened to Delilah, he wasn't sure he could stay much longer. He'd fallen asleep with a hollow pit of dread in his stomach, the pattern of "Once I graduate/I need to leave" pulsing with every other heartbeat.

Finally dressed—and unshowered, thanks to House—he walked down the hall and descended the stairs, stopping short when he reached the foyer. Gavin knew—*he knew*—he'd taken his shoes off when he'd come home last night. He *always* did. There'd been three pairs: the ones he'd been wearing, the ones he wore for gym, and the dark ones he had for work. Now there was nothing.

This wasn't just another coincidence, and frustration began a steady climb up his spine, humming in his veins. He tamped it down, reminding himself to hold his temper, to breathe. He didn't know for a fact that his shoes were gone. Maybe they were on the porch, he thought. Sometimes he'd wake to find the floors gleaming in the morning sun, a fresh coat of wax having been put down sometime during the night. On those days his shoes or backpack, or whatever else he'd happened to leave lying around, would be outside, waiting for him.

Gavin wasn't sure why he was holding his breath as he crossed the short distance to the door, but he was. His socks slipped easily over the polished wood floor.

There was no knob.

There wasn't even a place where a knob had been, only smooth, freshly sanded wood, freshly *sealed* wood. He took a step back like he'd been burned, closed his eyes and counted to ten, before opening them again. This wasn't an accident. Last night House was apologetic. Today it was punishing.

The smell of breakfast wafted in from the kitchen and over his shoulder. His stomach churned. How was he supposed to eat? Did it expect him to go sit like a good boy and stuff his face? Ignoring the fact that he was locked in? That he was essentially grounded without reason?

Gavin steadied himself, straightened his shoulders and spun on his heel, crossing to the kitchen. He ignored the trays of bacon and pancakes, enough food to feed an entire family, and stopped at the back door, heart slamming in his throat. His fingers fumbled on smooth wood, no trace of a patched hole or shadow of where the knob had been. Next he tried the window; there was no latch. And the next and the next, until he was sprinting from one room to the other. He considered breaking the glass, but some instinct wouldn't let him do it, the same one that kept him from running too loudly up the stairs or roughhousing inside.

He might hurt it.

Gavin slumped against the wall and slid down to the floor.

He spent the rest of the day in his room, and the next. This might have been House's ridiculous, over-the-top way of grounding him, but he wasn't speaking to it or even interacting unless it was absolutely necessary. He didn't come down for dinner and instead finished off the bag of chips he found in the pocket of one of his jackets, then sketched until he fell asleep, stretched the wrong way across Bed.

The next morning was much of the same—still no way out, no phone or shoes—but he was starving. He cursed his stomach the entire way down the stairs and into the kitchen, more grateful than he wanted to admit at the sight of his favorite breakfast waiting for him on the counter. He ate in silence, brushing off House's attempts to engage him in conversation or draw him out of his foul mood. But by the end of the day, Gavin was so tired of being inside, was so hungry to see Delilah, he said the only thing he could think—the only thing he *knew* House wanted to hear: "I won't go talk to Dhaval. I won't ask about my mom."

A huge, metallic pop rang from the front of the house. Gavin shot up, running through the kitchen and down the hall, skidding to a stop in his socked feet at the sight in front of him. The doorknob was back.

He took a step forward, looking back over his shoulder before he took another. Eyes closed, he reached out, his fingertips brushing the smooth metal. It didn't feel any different; it was cool beneath his touch, glossy even. He wrapped his hand around the knob and turned. . . . It opened.

"I don't want you to ever go back there," Delilah said in front of her locker the next day. It was, in fact, the only thing Delilah had said to him so far that morning, after practically leaping into his arms and knocking him back into the wall with the force of her small body. His hands lingered on her hips a moment longer than was appropriate considering the crowded hall all around them, his fingers brushing the smooth sliver of skin where her shirt met her skirt, teasing. She straightened, taking a step back, and took a moment to smooth her clothes and her hair before she turned and spun through the combination to her locker.

But Gavin didn't miss the pink remaining in her cheeks as she shoved an armful of clean clothes at him, the way she chewed on her lip as she turned and walked away. He loved that he could affect her that way. Anyone else might have thought she'd been embarrassed by their moment of PDA, but Gavin knew better. Delilah didn't have a shy bone in her body.

"Is this about me missing school?" he asked, trailing after her.

"We'll talk about it later," she said, stopping in front of

the boys' bathroom and nodding to the clothes in his arms. "I bought those at Goodwill. Let's hope they fit."

He didn't want to wait until later. He glanced down at the dark jeans, the black T-shirt, socks, and scuffed sneakers.

Gavin changed quickly, shoving his old clothes in his locker before following a group of other students into the classroom and sliding into his seat behind Delilah. He felt a little like he was in a fishbowl, surrounded by eyes and ears that might hear his secret, that might do something or tell someone and he'd be kept away from her. He realized for a moment that perhaps this was how Delilah always felt now, like someone was watching their every move, looking for a way to keep them apart. Gavin had grown used to the feeling—growing up surrounded by so many *things*—but to Delilah, it had to be terrifying, especially after the other night.

"I'm sorry," he said, and that got her attention.

She turned slightly in her seat, whispering, "Why on earth are you sorry?"

Gavin leaned in, kept his voice low. "Because this is our first fight, and it's my fault. *All* the shitty stuff happening to you lately is my fault."

Delilah frowned before her eyes darted to the window and back down to her desk. She tore a piece of lined paper from her binder and bent over it, scribbling something he couldn't see. A minute later, she reached back and dropped a note into his waiting palm.

He blinked up to the teacher, confident he was distracted enough writing a block of text on the board, and opened it carefully.

Where's your phone?

I don't know. I swear I plugged it in, but when I woke up that next morning it was gone.

He passed it forward and watched her shoulders tighten.

Gavin watched as she wrapped her phone in the piece of paper and reached behind her again to hand it off. He read the note first.

House has it. I know it does. Look.

The screen hadn't locked yet, and his eyes widened at the text in front of him: *That's not all you're going to lose, girl.* It was a text sent from his phone, after he'd fallen asleep. House *did* have it.

I didn't write that, Lilah. I swear.

She shook her head.

I know that! But do you see what I see?? We can't be together here in Morton. House may not hurt you, but clearly it doesn't have the same rules for me. I want to be with you, but the only way to do that is to leave & go far away. I'm going back East for school, whichever one I get into. I want you to come with me.

Gavin stared at the note, his heart rising to his throat and pounding, pounding, pounding so hard and fast he felt like he was choking. It was April. They would graduate in two months, and Delilah would move with or without him.

He pressed his palms to his eye sockets, pushing until he saw stars. He had to decide whether he would stay here or find a way to go. But now the idea of staying here indefinitely seemed insane. Every second he let himself really think about it, he saw House so differently. It had once been his own magical place, his safe haven when the outside world was terrifying and ostracizing. Now he still believed it loved him, but it did it all wrong. It wasn't human; it didn't operate under the same rules. It was willing to hurt the girl he loved in order to keep him.

But he couldn't just *leave*. He had nothing.

Lilah, of course I would come with you. But we need some sort of plan. We need money, and I need time to figure out how to deal with House. I still feel like there's a chance I can help it learn to understand, so that I can go without feeling like I'm escaping.

Delilah twirled her pencil around her long fingers, lost in concentration. He could tell she was frustrated by the way she took several deep breaths and pressed her hands to her face. But then she started to write again. He tried to ignore the sound of her pen moving over the paper, tried to stay calm while he waited for her answer.

He looked around the room, his gaze flicking on instinct to the window again, to the tree on the other side. He wondered if it was his imagination that the branches seemed to be closer to the glass than he remembered or if he'd really become this paranoid.

The note landed on his desk, and he opened it with slightly trembling fingers.

Then you have 2 months until school ends. Take money from the jar. You said it's always there, so start taking little chunks at a time. You'll give it to me in the music room and I'll hide it, so House will never know. If House doesn't come around before then, at least we'll have enough to get out of here.

The decision to actually leave had been easy in the end, because the prospect of being in House forever had started to feel wildly claustrophobic. A new routine began: As soon as he got to school he would change into clothes that had never been at House, and Delilah would take them back after school, to wash at her home. He took money from the jar, five dollars here, twenty dollars there, and would leave it in his desk, where Dhaval would switch it with bills from his own wallet and deposit it into his own account where House could stalk it all it wanted. Each afternoon Gavin would meet Delilah in the music room, and without talking, she would take the money, hiding it somewhere when she got home. Gavin didn't want to know where, having gotten so distrustful of House he worried if it ever knew what they were up to, it might use him to find out.

The plan was overly complicated, and at times they both questioned their sanity, hiding any clue of their relationship until they were able to escape to the windowless music room. It became a sanctuary of sorts, where they could be alone together and talk about their plans, where he could kiss her and touch her, where she would touch him. He lived for those tiny slips of time.

And it was working. After just a week they had ninety-three dollars. He got paid the next week and added another one hundred and sixty to that. If they could be patient, by the end of the school year they'd have enough that they could leave. House seemed to have calmed down. Delilah seemed less scared. Gavin didn't know what exactly came after graduation—he hadn't yet applied to colleges, and it was probably too late to do it anyway—but it was enough to hope.

It was the first time Gavin had let himself hope in a long time.

It was his first Saturday off in weeks. Gavin was home, cleaning his bathroom upstairs and enjoying the warmer air that fluttered in occasionally through the window. He always left a window wedged open these days with a small block of wood he'd managed to sneak out of Shed. He was fairly certain it wouldn't stop House if it really wanted it closed, but it made him feel better somehow. It helped him sleep.

The shower was working again and had been since he'd promised House he wouldn't go to Dhaval's or ask about his mom. A promise he'd kept so far. But for some reason the sink had been draining slowly. Gavin didn't know much about plumbing, and so he turned to the same source he had when he'd wanted to fix the car: books.

He had a bucket under the trap to catch any mess. He'd managed to get the rusted slip nut off and was in the process of getting the trap disconnected.

"Gross," he said, wiping at his nose with the back of his gloved hand; the smell was terrible. Trying not to breathe too deeply, he started pulling things from the curved pipe: a Lego, the tire from a Hot Wheels car, some sort of black gunk, and so much hair he actually considered shaving his head. What he wasn't expecting was the *plunk* he heard as something dislodged and dropped into the bucket below. He was almost afraid to look.

A key. Gavin stood and closed the door, looking around the bathroom before tugging off his gloves and starting the shower. With the key tucked protectively in his palm, he started stripping down to nothing. Once inside, and with the dark vinyl curtain pulled closed, he looked at the key under the spray.

It was maybe two inches long and silver, with VICTOR SAFE AND LOCK CO. engraved into the side. It didn't look like any house or car key he'd ever seen—there were no locks to anything in House—but maybe to a safe? Or some sort of padlock?

He didn't have time to think about it, though. When Piano began playing downstairs, it was time for lunch.

Gavin rinsed himself off and climbed out, careful to keep the key hidden in his hand while he dried off and dressed. Butterflies raced in his stomach, and he tried to tamp down the jittery feeling he got when he felt the sharp teeth pressed to his palm, the metal as it warmed against his skin. This key was critical. The doors on House never locked, and other than the small set he had for the car, he'd never even needed a key before. More important, he'd never held *this* key before, so unlike with the Lego or the Hot Wheels tire, if it fell down the drain, it wasn't because *he'd* dropped it.

• • •

As much as he hated to admit it, Gavin didn't believe he was ever really alone anymore, even in his "private" bathroom. He was pretty sure House knew all about his plumbing adventures on Saturday, but whether it had seen the key—or even knew the significance of it—Gavin couldn't begin to guess. It occurred to him, though, that House might decide to keep him locked up again Monday until he handed over the small treasure.

After he dressed for school, Gavin slipped the key into his pocket. He'd spent Sunday reading, finishing a term paper, and working a half shift at the theater. To play it safe, Delilah hadn't come to visit him once. Everything seemed fine, so in the back of his mind Gavin began to hope that, in fact, House hadn't noticed the key after all.

But as soon as he walked down the stairs, he knew it had.

The framed prints of his drawings that hung in the hallway had been replaced with photos of him as a baby. He followed the sounds of laughter coming from the living room and found Television playing old videos of him from when he was a toddler. In the kitchen, Curtain reached out to brush his cheek and Potted Plant ruffled his hair. Breakfast was already waiting for him, and as usual when House was up to something, there was enough food to feed an army.

Gavin's throat grew tight; his eyes burned with sadness and loss.

Maybe someday, a few years down the road, he'd be able to come home at Christmas and be with this unlikely family again. Maybe with some distance, House would understand what it had done and how it had broken everything that had once been so easy.

It had stalked them at the park.

It had terrorized and *hurt* Delilah.

It had trapped him inside for two days.

And Gavin suspected, deep down, that House was still hiding the truth about what had happened to his mother.

Gavin knew without hesitation that he would follow Delilah anywhere; she was the love of his life. His heart broke as he stared at the familiar and *magical* spread in front of him—enormous lemon muffins and fluffy scrambled eggs, plump wild berries and House-made peach jam. He knew once he left, he most likely wouldn't—and couldn't—ever come back.

"Thanks for trying to cheer me up," Gavin said, picking at some fruit. "I know I've been sort of off lately, but I got an e-mail from Delilah last night. Before work." He took a bite and tried to ignore the way the room cooled ever so slightly, bowing at the edges like a breath being held. "She got accepted to a school in Massachusetts. She's not supposed to leave until August, but she thinks she might go early. I don't know. . . . I think it might be a good idea."

House grew still for a moment, the leaves on the tree

outside the window unfurling in his direction, like a hand cupped around an ear, waiting. "She even suggested I go with her, but does she not know me at all?" he said, hoping he sounded angry, brokenhearted. "I'm not leaving. This is my home. You're my family. . . . I couldn't ever go." Meaningful pause. "I wouldn't want to."

He was actually a little surprised at how easy the lie was and how willing House was to accept it. Even Dining Room grew warm. The lights brightened everywhere, and the hands on Grandfather Clock began to spin wildly.

When Gavin slipped out the door fifteen minutes later, the key was still tucked inside his pocket.

CHAPTER TWENTY-FIVE

HER

GAVIN ARRIVED LATE. HE QUICKLY CHANGED into the clothes Delilah had left in a bag in his locker, and his long, loping strides carried him through the door and down the aisle to his seat. Silence fell over the room as Mr. Harrington stopped speaking while he got settled.

"Thanks for joining us, Mr. Timothy."

Gavin brushed his hair out of his eyes. "Sorry I'm late."

"By all means, let us run on your schedule."

With a tiny apologetic smile, Gavin bent to pull his tattered copy of *Ivanhoe* out of his backpack. He glanced up at Delilah, who unlike the rest of the class, hadn't yet turned her attention back to the front of the room, and the look in his eyes grew heated. "Hey, you."

They hadn't seen each other all weekend, and Delilah wanted to draw up a petition to make that amount of time apart illegal. Had Gavin changed? Had he been hurt? She worried about him being in the house alone and tried to catalogue even the smallest changes, but she couldn't seem to make it beyond the way he was looking at her.

"Hi." She shivered, turning back in her seat and sitting ramrod straight.

She knew they were trying not to anger the house further by spending time together, and she didn't think she'd ever take for granted again having Gavin back in school. But sitting in front of him was a torture. Especially since once Mr. Harrington started lecturing again, Gavin was leaning so far forward in his seat Delilah could practically feel his breath on the back of her neck.

"I need to talk to you."

"Lunch?"

"No," he whispered. "Before then." The words came out as punctuated spots of warm air on her skin.

She waited until Mr. Harrington turned to the board before angling slightly toward him to reply. "Okay. You okay?"

"Music room."

They skipped third period entirely.

Safely in the portable, he said, "I found a key."

"Do you have it with you?"

"Yeah."

The significance of this hit her slowly, in layers. First she remembered there were no locks in the house. And second, Gavin had left the house holding it.

"Do you think it knew you had it?" she asked, worrying her lip. "Do you think the house hijacked this?"

He shook his head. "If it knew I had this, it wouldn't have let me out at all." He handed it over to Delilah. It was only an inch or two long and very thin, with large, flat loops across the head and a row of small, sharp teeth up one side of the stem. While she turned it over in her palm, Gavin used her phone's Web browser to try to figure out what it might be for.

"It's not to a locket," he said. "It's too big." He scrolled farther down the page, mumbling, "Not a car, not a house, not a mailbox . . ." But then he sucked in a sharp breath and his head jerked back fractionally. "Oh."

"Oh?"

"A safe-deposit-box key."

Delilah took her phone from him and looked at the images he'd found. A few looked nearly identical to the key in her hand.

"Do you think it's from a local bank?" she asked, glancing up at him.

He lifted a broad shoulder in a shrug.

"Do we know if it's okay to do this in here?" She held up her phone. "Searching and calling? It can't hear us in here, but we're using the Internet. What if House—?"

He winced, but when he looked at her, his jaw was tight with determination. "Then it's too late now. Whatever you're thinking of doing, just do it."

According to the woman who answered the call, safe-deposit-box keys from Kansas National were flat-headed and smooth-toothed. The second bank Delilah called didn't even have safe-deposit boxes available to customers. But not only did the third bank she called, a Wells Fargo two miles down the highway, have keys that sounded identical to the one in her hand, they also told her—when pressed—they indeed had a box under the last name Timothy.

"Do you happen to have the first name?"

"I . . ." The reed-thin voice on the other end trailed off in an exhale.

"Please," Delilah insisted, before impulsively pushing the speaker button. "Gavin, tell him why we need to know the name."

Gavin cleared his throat, eyes locked on Delilah's. "Please can you tell me the first name on the account? We think it might be my mother's. I haven't seen her since I was little. I found this key and need to know if it was hers."

"Why don't you tell me her name, and I'll tell you if you're right."

Gavin closed his eyes, swallowing thickly. "Hilary? I think."

"You think? You aren't sure of your mother's first name?"

"Can you just tell me if it belongs to a Hilary Timothy?" Gavin growled, and Delilah looked up into the storm of his eyes. "I have the key. I have school identification with the same last name."

"Can you verify the address?" the man asked.

Gavin rattled off his address, and after a long pause, the man said, "Yes. It's registered to a Hilary Timothy. She opened the account in November of 1999 but has not accessed it since February of 2000."

"Thank you," Delilah said, robotically hitting the end call button. She looked up at his face. Gray-blue bruises formed half circles beneath his eyes. His lips seemed even redder than they usually did, against the backdrop of his ashen skin. "That was after you were born."

"I know."

"Gavin, we have to see what is in there. Everything I've heard about your mom tells me she wasn't a safe-deposit-box kind of gal, more of a 'keep everything in my magical trunk' kind of gal."

"I know," he said again.

"There are answers in there."

He closed his eyes, walked over to the piano bench, and sat down. "I *know*, Lilah."

Following him, she sat close enough that he could reach her but far enough to not be touching him. If she touched him, she would want to kiss him, and if she kissed him, she would want more. It was daylight outside, though none of it penetrated into the dark, soundproof room, and anyone could walk in here at any time.

"I had a weird thought the other day," Gavin said, running a long hand down his face. "What if we get out of here? What if we just run?"

"That's a weird thought? I thought that was the *only* thought."

"No," he said. "I'm not finished. What if we run and move somewhere new? What if we work our asses off to make ends meet? What if we make it through school working three jobs on no sleep? What if we do all that together, and things don't work out between us?"

Delilah pulled back a little. "So the risk of a failed relationship makes you think it might be better to just stay in the house forever?"

Gavin chewed a fingernail. "No," he said around it. "That isn't at all what I'm saying. I know I'll want to be with *you* forever."

She narrowed her eyes and studied his face, trying to figure out what he *was* saying. Was he saying it was scary that diving into this relationship had to also mean leaving? The house was possessive to the point of violence—*possessed*, too, with something dark and awful—but at least it would never break up with him. It would never leave.

"You could just as well fall out of love with me," she reasoned.

A tiny smile tilted his mouth. "I can't imagine falling out of love with you."

"I can't, either," she said quietly. "But maybe I don't get it. What are you getting at?"

Reaching forward, he took both of her hands, engulfing them in both of his. "Lilah, I'm saying that this is the nuclear option. That once we look in that safe-deposit box, there's a good chance we'll have to leave *that day*. House followed us to the park. You felt like it followed you to Dhaval's. We think we're being smart—changing my clothes every day, making sure we swap out the cash with Dhaval, trying to do everything we can so we aren't overheard—but we don't really know how any of this works. I know we have a plan, but I guess I wanted you to know that you don't have to do it with me. House might do something really terrible if we try to leave, and we may not have any idea what that looks like until it happens."

"Gavin—"

"I can leave on my own," he said, urgently trying to finish his thought. "You don't have to be in danger because of me anymore."

Her heart tripped into understanding. "I don't want you to do this without me."

"It could get messy," he said, and in his eyes she could see he was giving her one last out. "Doing this isn't the same as just walking down the street and not looking back. We don't know how far it can follow us."

"Do you think the house would hurt us where others can see?"

"I don't know," Gavin hedged. "But what if it tries? What if it's willing to play along until I actually try to leave, and then it fights us? Don't you get the feeling that at some point we'll have to break inside and . . . kill it?"

She couldn't believe he was the one to say it. She couldn't believe the words had actually come out of that full, kissable mouth. But her relief that they had was so immense, it seemed to expand inside her chest. He was well and truly done with it.

"If it comes down to that, I'll protect you."

One half of Gavin's mouth tilted in a grin. "Then as soon as we have enough money, as soon as we have our diplomas, we're heading to the bank and opening that box, and then we're leaving town. For now we're sitting tight. We're saving every penny, and we're pretending like you're leaving for Massachusetts and acting like everything is fine."

"Are you going to walk me home?" She stretched on her very tiptoes and kissed his chin. Outside, a drop of rain caught in the branch overhead, fell and landed on her scalp, and the wind whipped her hair all around their faces. "I mean, I'm leaving for the East Coast soon. You have only so many days left with me."

"I . . . ," he started, then shook his head, unable to say the words out loud, out in the open like this. He reached up and smoothed her hair behind her ear. "I can't."

"Whisper it," she said. "So soft, so close only I can hear."

Bending low, he pressed his lips right up against her ear. His words sounded like static, like air and the vibration of his voice deep in his throat: "I'm meeting with Hinkle today to talk about college."

Delilah pulled away, looking up at the trees overhead—a new instinct. But the world stayed settled: The earth didn't split open; the tree branches didn't thrash out to separate them.

"Really?" she asked.

"Yeah."

Frowning, she asked, "It's not too late?"

"It is for some, but he thinks we can swing something. My grades are pretty good."

"Do you have my list? You'll find something close?"

He nodded.

Delilah was so focused on the various scenarios—walking into a brick-and-ivy college building hand in hand with Gavin, setting up a home with him in a tiny apartment building, lying on a wide bed, her head on his chest and his voice rumbling against her as he talked for hours—that she failed to hear the fire.

Or maybe that wasn't quite right. She *heard* it, but it sounded like crackling leaves and then a flock of birds and then, finally, a haze of gunshots overtaking the town. This was when Delilah looked up and saw the choking black smoke rising over the Hendersons' house, which meant either their house was on fire . . . or hers was.

She took off in a sprint, her backpack bouncing heavily on her shoulders, slowing her progress. When she turned the corner, she pulled up short, crying out. It *was* her house on fire, flames flogging the back wall, looking as if it had started on the second floor and spread lower. The blaze didn't yet reach the ground; it poured from her window like liquid and was only inches from snaring the broad oak in the backyard.

Sirens screamed behind her, and she was nearly knocked over by the force of the fire engines hurling past.

It was mayhem. Firemen everywhere, water and smoke clogging every inch of air. She could feel the soot on her face as the first blast from the hose lashed the house, could feel the water ricocheting back at her.

"Stand back!" A huge hand grasped her shoulder, guiding her behind the fire engine. She looked up into watery blue eyes, an enormous face with red stubble, a nose red from too much alcohol over the years, and breath smelling of nicotine and mint. "Is this your house?"

Delilah strained to look around him, to the house in the distance. "Yes."

"Where are your parents?"

"I don't . . ." She closed her eyes, swallowing to catch her thoughts and line them up into some sort of order. The smallest ones first: *It's Wednesday. Mom is volunteering at the library. Dad had a job interview in Emporia.* They weren't home. They were safe. And then the larger ones: How did the fire start, and why is it only my room? She had nothing in there to spark a fire—no curling iron or candles she could have left lit. Not even a night-light left plugged into the wall.

Delilah slapped a hand to her mouth, but a sob broke free, raw and sharp. "The money. Oh my God. All of the money we've saved."

"Okay, okay," the fireman said, in a low, soothing voice. "No one's home—is that what you're telling me?"

"But the money!" she cried, struggling to push past him. He held her steady, murmuring words he meant to be calming, but the panic had gripped her. It had curled its fingers around her heart and was making it beat and beat and beat until the blood churned in her veins in an agitated frenzy.

Delilah could see it, high in her closet: the shoebox filled with cash. Hundreds of dollars now, and all of it gone. There would be no easy escape. No brick-and-ivy buildings. No apartment just for them, light and white and empty but for their bed and their little dining table and the possibility of anything, anything in the world after this. Gone.

Delilah felt herself sliding down the side of the fire truck, felt the hot rubber of the tire on her back, the cold asphalt of the street beneath her, and buried her face against her bent knees. The fireman halfheartedly reached to pull her back to her feet and then gave up, standing close enough for her to feel the cuff of his heavy, scratchy pants against her calf. She assumed he meant it to be comforting, so she resisted the urge to scoot away. But it wasn't comforting. The last thing she needed to be reminded of right at that second was how close she was to everything, to everyone.

Heels clicked on the street near her head, and her mother's hysterical voice rang too sharply in the air, like a knife cutting through glass: screechy and shattering. "I'm Belinda Blue! This is my house! What is happening? What is going on?"

"There's been a fire, ma'am." The same fireman pulled Delilah's mother to the side and explained in a low voice everything he knew. "We got a call only about fifteen minutes ago. Said the back of the house was on fire. Looks like an accident, though we'll know when we get inside. We think it was started from the wires overhead. . . ."

Delilah stopped listening. She knew it was no accident.

In the end, the fire was put out in minutes, and the whole process felt wiltingly anticlimactic. A swarm of police and delighted, idle town officials took only a half hour to deem the fire an accident caused by overheated electrical wires stretching in unsightly ropes above the backyard. Delilah stared up at them, sagging as if exhausted and innocuously silent. Shut off for now, most likely. She had no idea how danger could have leaped from such a mild-mannered tangle of wires into her bedroom, but she seemed to be the only one left unconvinced. Her hands remained clenched into nervous fists at her sides. She startled at any small sound behind her.

Pulling out her phone, Delilah texted Gavin a simple, *Call me.*

She walked around to the front of the house and through the front door. The firemen had closed off her bedroom from the rest of the rooms with a thick plastic tarp. Even so, everything smelled like soot and ash and wet, dripping wood. For the time being, Delilah's new sleeping quarters would be the living room, but nothing could be salvaged from her bedroom to put down here with her, so it looked as it always did: dim, polished, cluttered with hundreds of ceramic statues.

Belinda looked like a stranger, or a crazy person. Who else but a person who has lost her mind comes home to her house on fire and then two hours later smiles as she emerges from the kitchen with some sliced apple and a pill for her daughter?

"This'll help you calm down." She handed Delilah the pill and some water and put the apples down on the coffee table.

Calm down? Delilah hadn't said a word since her father got home with his surprisingly expansive collection of curse words, since the firemen had stomped back out through the house—"See? Glad I have those plastic mats down!" her mother had chirped as they padded in boots and heavy gear across the virginal cream of the living room floor—since the police had been through and officially deemed it an *accident*, and since the plastic tarp separated the mess of Delilah's room from the rest of the house.

"I don't want it," she said, taking only the water from her mother's hand.

"You'll take the pill or you'll be grounded." Her mother smiled, but it did nothing to cover the bite in her voice. "You've been through a trauma. *I've* been through a trauma. I want to go lie down up in my room and not worry about what you're doing down here."

Delilah's brows went up in understanding. "I'm fine." But she took the long white pill anyway, curling it in her palm. "I'll call Dhaval. I'll do my homework." *And wait for Gavin to call*, she thought.

The sound of the television filtered in from the other room, and it occurred to Delilah that she had no idea whether her father actually got the job today. If his evening routine wasn't changed by a fire in his house, of course it wouldn't be altered by good news, either. Belinda blinked away, out the front window, and her brows pulled together in concern. Without having to look, Delilah knew what she saw out there: neighbors still standing in front of the house, pretending to worry but more than anything relishing the chance to gossip. Nothing out of the ordinary ever happened around here. At least not that they knew of. Imagine the slobbering frenzy that would break out if anyone really knew about Gavin's house. If they knew it wasn't just an odd feat of architecture but something wicked, possessed, malignant.

"It wasn't an accident, Mom."

Delilah wasn't sure where the words were coming from, but she needed some sign, some nudge that Belinda could *be* a mother. That maybe she would hear the desperate, hysterical edge that made Delilah's voice faintly metallic and it would trip some wire in her mother, turning her nurturing and communicative. Instead Belinda drew her eyes back to Delilah slowly, disappointment pulling her features into a sagging frown. On anyone else, the pink cardigan she wore might have looked feminine or soft, but on Belinda Blue it was too pink and too harsh against her pressed-powder skin. She looked like a disapproving piece of salmon. "Don't start."

"It wasn't, Mom. What they're saying doesn't even make sense. A spark flew into my closed window and started a fire? Seriously? It *rained* earlier today."

"You're going to tell the firemen how to do their jobs now?"

"Maybe, if it's obvious they're wrong."

Her mother pointed to the fist holding the pill. "Take it or you're grounded. No phone. No sketchbooks. No time with that weird boy."

She watched as Delilah placed it on her tongue and took what must have looked like a long gulp of water.

What her mother didn't see was that Delilah spit it out moments later.

CHAPTER TWENTY-SIX

HIM

G AVIN HAD NEVER BROKEN INTO AN *ACTUAL* house before, but really, how hard could it be?

From the shadows he watched as the last window of the Blues' house went dark, and he waited.

The air grew colder near the curb, and from where he sat he could see the final, lingering onlookers shuffle away from the sidewalk and back to their cars or houses. Neighbors took one more glance around their curtains before they gave up for the night, and the windows of their houses went dark too.

There wasn't much of a moon tonight, just a round slice of silver against the black sky. The air was damp, and Gavin wished he'd thought ahead to bring a heavier jacket, or something warm to sit on while he waited. He wondered how House felt about him not coming home for dinner and whether it had sent its *feelers* out to look for him.

He'd been in the Blues' shed since the last fire truck had pulled away from the curb, soot and smoke-stained firemen congratulating one another and already arguing over whose turn it was to make dinner.

There was no way Delilah's parents would let him anywhere near her, and so he'd snuck into the backyard, hoping the screams of the siren and all the busybody neighbors would distract House long enough for him to hide in the cement outbuilding.

When he'd left school and walked to Delilah's—intent on telling her Hinkle thought Gavin would be able to get in nearly anywhere Delilah had already applied, only maybe a year after her—he could smell the fire long before he could see the damage. But once he was closer, he saw where pristine white siding met charred wood and the precise distinction between what had been damaged and what hadn't.

His knees felt weak when he glanced at the intact power lines overhead and back to the tape that had been strung through the Blues' once-immaculate backyard, cordoning it off to anyone trying to get a better look. From the mumbled conversations he'd listened to since sunset, the firemen blamed fallen power lines, an electrical short, or some freak accident, but Gavin knew better. House had done this, and the key hidden in his pocket suddenly felt like it weighed a thousand pounds. House had set a *fire*. This wasn't like a parent getting angry and locking him in. This wasn't the same as taking his keys or hiding his cell phone or his shoes. This wasn't the same as it trying to scare Delilah off. House wanted Delilah to know it could get to her at any time.

It knew what time school ended, and if Gavin was right, then Delilah had been in the music room when the fire started, because she'd stayed later than normal to be with him. If she'd gone home when she usually did . . .

He couldn't even *think* about that.

He held his breath, quietly placing one foot in front of the other as he slipped out of his hiding spot and crept into the yard.

It was easier than Gavin imagined to move around without being seen. Delilah's house couldn't feel his footsteps in the wet grass, or hear the squelch of his sneakers as he moved to the back door. It couldn't feel his fingers as he searched for a spare key along the top of the doorframe, or his hands as he skimmed the side of the house, where he found a single window that had been left unlocked.

It took some work to get the window to move—the frame was clean but kept getting stuck on the track from lack of use—but it finally gave, sliding open just enough to let him slip inside.

Delilah's house was eerily quiet, and without a single window cracked or the fan blowing, it felt stuffy to the point of suffocation and smelled of cleaning solvents and artificial flowers.

It was all wrong. Delilah smelled like apples, and whenever they were together—and close—he had to resist the urge to rest his head in the crook of her neck and breathe her in. This place didn't smell like Delilah at all.

She was right where he thought she'd be: on the couch, blanket wrapped so high around her head there was barely a tuft of tangled honey hair visible at the top. Gavin took a seat on the coffee table next to her and leaned over, pulling the duvet down just enough to see her face.

He was struck again by the realization that Delilah could have died. And even in this house, there was no one here watching over her, no one worrying about the toxic fumes in the room or the heat pressing down from the ceiling.

"Lilah," he whispered into her ear, so quiet he was sure only she could hear.

He pulled back just in time to see the flutter of her lashes, and the moment she woke and realized he was there.

"Ga—" she started, but he pressed a gentle finger to her mouth and shook his head. Delilah blinked, sitting up carefully and searching the room with wide eyes, almost as if she expected to find someone standing nearby.

Gavin stood and reached out to help her up, taking a step back as she extricated herself from the mountain of blankets. Only now did it occur to him that he didn't actually know what would happen next or where they would go, only that they couldn't stay here. He didn't want her alone in this house. Really, when it came down to it, he didn't trust House enough to let Delilah be away from him at all anymore.

He shuffled through the small list of options—park, garage, car, school—before settling on the only place they could go where they could really talk.

When Delilah had her shoes on, he took a step toward

her, admittedly crowding into her space while he brushed her hands aside and zipped up her jacket for her. She glared at him, but it carried no heat. Her hands were shaking, and her eyes were wide.

"I was so scared," she admitted, barely a whisper.

He nodded, bending to kiss her forehead. He'd always been tall, and growing up he'd hated how it was just another thing that made him stand out, but standing this close to Delilah and towering at least a foot above, he liked it. He liked feeling like he could lean down and wrap his arms around her body, hiding her from anything that might come looking. Delilah wasn't small, and she certainly wasn't helpless, but in this way, he liked that he could protect her, whether she wanted him to or not.

The sound of Gavin's squeaky old bike cut through the silent neighborhood as they made their way to the school, Gavin pedaling as quietly as he could and Delilah perched carefully on the handlebars. They didn't speak or even say where they were going out loud, but focused every bit of energy on watching the road ahead of them . . . and listening for any sounds behind.

It was too silent, as if the world all around them held its breath. House had made its point today: *I know what you're doing. I could stop you anytime I want.* And now it waited to see what Gavin and Delilah would do. The thought that House might escalate this made Gavin feel queasy.

The school was a little terrifying at night; Gavin was man enough to admit that. It was old, with strange angles and squat, cramped buildings eerily surrounded by streetlights dotting the parking lot with yellowed spots of light. Gavin had broken into this room many times over the years to play music alone, to lie in the quiet and feel the strange stillness that comes with a building without life, and so it didn't take long for him to pop the screen from the window and jimmy open the latch.

He unlocked the door from the inside before following Delilah into Mr. McMannis's office. Together they found a couple of gym mats that would work nicely as a bed, some emergency candles, two bags of Doritos, a couple of Capri Suns, and even a chocolate bar. Once they were safely in the music room, they locked the dead bolt and moved bookcases in front of the air-conditioning vents before turning off the flashlight on Delilah's phone.

Delilah had lit a candle near the center of the room and got to work putting their bed together while Gavin checked everything again. They hadn't said more than five words to each other since the last time they were here—earlier that day—too concerned with whether they were being watched and getting to safety than anything else. But now the weight of it all seemed to be pressing in on them, and Delilah sank back on the mat, closing her eyes with shaking hands pressed to her face.

"Lilah?" He'd never really seen her melt down. Was it silent, or earsplitting? Wincing, he ran his hand up her forearm, pulling one of her hands away from her face. "Look at me."

"Just . . . breathing," she explained. He watched as she took five deep breaths and then dropped her other hand, looking up at him. Calmer now. "This is pretty cozy." She sat up and looked around before breaking off a chunk of chocolate and settling back into their makeshift camp, surrounded by all their pilfered supplies and the faint glow of the candle. "This is definitely where I'm coming when the zombie apocalypse happens."

"*When* it happens?" he asked, grinning.

"It's inevitable. Gene manipulation, biological weapons, voodoo. Don't you watch TV at all?"

Gavin shook his head but smiled. "Only about three stations ever seem to come in, and *Leave It to Beaver* usually seems to be playing on all of them."

"God, I have so much to teach you," she said. "Food, water, shelter, a bathroom just next door. We're all set here."

Gavin stretched out next to her, hands folded on his stomach as he looked at the drop ceiling overhead. She couldn't be that far off: There wasn't much else he'd want right now. He had Delilah, some snacks, and a locked door. What else could there possibly be?

"Hmm," he said, playing along. "What about guns? A giant baseball bat?"

"Well, yes, of course. But even with just this, we'd be good." Delilah grew quiet for a moment before she added softly, "We'll always know this place is here in case we need to come back."

And there it was: the elephant in the room. This wasn't just pretend anymore. House wasn't a secret they could hope to keep from the rest of the world. They were talking about running away, *running for their lives,* if he wanted to get technical.

Along with that realization came the slow, creeping feeling he'd had earlier, the dread that had clawed at Gavin's stomach when he'd seen the scorched side of Delilah's house.

Gavin closed his eyes but nodded anyway. He knew for as much as Delilah hated this town or how uninvolved her parents were, they were still her parents and Morton was still her home. Of course someday she might want to come back.

"We have to leave, Lilah. Tomorrow. It's not safe here anymore."

He heard Delilah swallow. "I know."

"We need to figure out how far away we need to get, and we need to just go. We can't wait until we have enough money."

Delilah took a deep breath, like she was readying herself for something big. "All the money's gone," she said. "All of it. It was my first thought when I saw the flames."

Gavin rolled to his side and looked down at her. "I don't

care about the money. I thought I'd lost you. That was *my* first thought when I saw what happened."

Delilah's fingers played at the fabric of his shirt. "Where should we go?"

"I don't care if we're living in a box under a bridge somewhere. As long as I'm with you, I don't care about the rest."

It was one of the few times they'd been alone like this, without the threat of a bell ringing or having to be home for curfew. Gavin knew there was so much *more* going on—the need for a plan, the reality that tomorrow they would be running for their *lives*, for God's sake—but right now, with her breath on his neck and her hands making fists around the hem of his shirt, the *alone* part was the only thing he could focus on.

He could kiss her where no one could see them; he could touch her in places *he'd* never seen before. He wanted to care about the bigger things—the terrifying things—but at that moment, the reality of Delilah beside him was all he could think about: her lips, her hands, her body stretched out on the mat.

As if Delilah was thinking the exact same thing, her grip on his shirt tightened. He bent to kiss her, slow at first. Always some teeth, always some growl, and then he would suck her lips and tongue and her tiny, gasping sounds.

She pulled his shirt up and off, and with a little smile, he returned the favor.

He could kiss her all day, he thought, his eyes closed as her teeth dragged along his jaw. He could get drunk on the taste of chocolate still on her tongue and the heat of her skin along his entire body.

Gavin exhaled against her neck, his brain slanting at the soft smell of her skin. "Where do we stop?" he asked, moving to kiss her slightly swollen bottom lip. His hand slid beneath her, and with only a few fumbling attempts, he managed to unclasp her bra.

It took nearly a minute before she answered—because she arched into him and made a quiet, pleading sound when he pulled the straps down and off her arms—and in that time he continued his gentle assault: lips to neck, to collarbone, fingers spread across her chest.

Finally she asked, voice tight, "You *want* to stop?"

"No. It's why I'm asking you to tell me when we do." He swiped his tongue over her ribs, slid a hand up under the hem of her skirt, over her soft thighs.

"We don't."

"I'm not exactly sure what to do," he whispered, hovering above her. "With you, I mean."

"With me specifically?" she said, smiling.

Gavin felt himself blush to the tips of his ears, but he refused to look away. "A little. I've never done this before."

"Me either. But . . . I've thought about it a lot."

Gavin groaned and let his head fall to her shoulder. "Delilah."

"What? Am I not supposed to say that?"

"You're not if you want me to last at all."

"I think . . . ," she said, running her hands down his bare back. "I think it's okay if you don't? Like, maybe . . . I like the idea of you losing yourself for a few minutes."

"Let's hope it's longer than a few minutes," he said, laughing into her skin. It felt so right to laugh with her about something like this, when everything else was so big and dark and looming over them. Delilah was his sun, and he'd smiled more because of her in the last few months than he had in his entire life.

He pushed himself up and looked down at her again as she worked his jeans down his hips. "You're sure?"

"I'm *positive*. You have . . . something?"

He gulped. He knew she meant a condom, and the question made this seem more real than anything else could have. "I do."

Sex was and wasn't what he expected. Of course he expected it would hurt her, and he expected it to feel unlike anything he'd ever known. But he didn't expect the calm confidence that took root in his thoughts when he felt her relax beneath him, heard her gasp, "I'm okay; I'm okay," and beg him to start, to move, to do something because, she said, she felt like she was losing her mind.

He didn't expect them to move together so easily, as if they shared a heartbeat.

He didn't expect to be able to slow and stop in the middle of everything just to kiss her and feel her laugh when she said, "I can't believe we're doing this." And then she stretched to kiss him, adding, "Do you like it?"

"Like" was such a strange word. Gavin liked peaches and the color black. This was a bliss he didn't think he could go a day without now.

Afterward, it felt like he had no bones, like every bit of strength in his nearly eighteen-year-old body had been drained from him.

The room was too hot for them to stay pressed together like this, but Gavin didn't care. With his head resting on her stomach, Delilah played with his hair and his eyes grew heavier and heavier. He wished they could stay here forever.

"So we'll go to the bank tomorrow." It was the first thing she'd said since she made those broken little sounds of relief, and goose bumps broke out along his arms at the memory, only a few minutes old.

Gavin pressed a kiss next to her navel, another just above it. "I'll go get everything from the safe-deposit box and meet you outside at eleven," he said. "Get what you need from your house and then walk there, using a route where people can see you." He pulled away to look up at her.

"I don't have much left to take with me," she reminded him.

"Just get whatever you can. And, Lilah, if I'm not at the bank, leave town without me. I'll find you."

Delilah balked. "Why wouldn't you be there? You're not going back to the house, are you?" she asked.

"I want to get the car, but I don't think . . ." He hated to say what came next: "I don't think House would let me out. I'll go to the safe-deposit box. You're just going to have to get whatever money you can from your house and meet me at the bank."

"That sounds way too easy," Delilah said.

Gavin pulled her on top of him, ignoring the sick dread he felt when she said this. Instead, he slid her legs to either side of his hips and closed his eyes at the warmth of her skin. "It doesn't matter. We just have to make it through tomorrow and that's it. The rest will figure itself out."

Gavin had kissed Delilah good-bye before the sun was even up. They'd cleaned the music room, stacked the mats back in the gym office, and tied the trash into a tiny bag to take with them. He'd watched her dress, surrendering his casual glances for outright staring as she'd pulled on her skirt and then her bra. He wasn't embarrassed when she caught him, and he hadn't looked away when she'd laughed and thrown his shirt in his direction. She'd told him he was hers and she was his; he was *allowed* to look, encouraged even.

And that's how they ended up here, Delilah pressed to the wall while he kissed her long and slow, while he tried to make it last. Gavin knew he'd never be the same after what happened in this room, that his life would forever be divided into two separate halves: everything before last night and everything after.

When he finally pulled away to breathe, Gavin pressed a kiss to her nose and the corner of her mouth before resting his forehead against hers. "You remember what I said?" he asked her.

Delilah nodded but kept her eyes closed. "Meet you at eleven."

"And?" he pressed, lifting her chin gently so she would look at him.

She blew out a shaky breath. "And . . . if you're not there . . . I'm to leave town by myself."

"Okay, good."

"But—"

Her phone chimed in her pocket. "Dhaval," she said. "That's his alert."

Where are you? No idea what's happening, but Gavin's mom called. HIS MOM.

Delilah blinked up to Gavin with eyes so wide he thought they might burst.

"What?" he asked. She started typing so fast she almost dropped the phone twice. "Lilah? Did that say . . . ?"

WHAT DO YOU MEAN HIS MOM? she typed back.

His reply came only a moment later. *JUST WHAT I SAID. She called and told my mom he didn't come home last night. That she was worried.*

"Your mom called," she mumbled. "Your . . . *momandI-don'tknowhow!*"

Gavin felt like his legs might give out from under him. He reached for her phone, not bothering with text, and just pushed Dhaval's contact picture, closing his eyes while it rang.

"Dee!"

"Dhaval, what happened?" Gavin asked, his voice hoarse and trembling. "She called? Where did she call from?"

Gavin listened as Dhaval explained, his arm slowly falling to his side until the phone fell to the floor. He could still hear Dhaval's voice shouting through the line, but he didn't care.

"Gav?" Delilah said. "What did he say?"

"He said she called from my home phone. She's inside House."

CHAPTER TWENTY-SEVEN

HER

I'M COMING WITH YOU," SHE SAID. SHE COULD FEEL the stubborn set of her jaw. If anyone asked her right at this second, Delilah would swear she was eight feet tall and four feet wide. Nothing was getting between her and Gavin.

Gavin shook his head emphatically, and Delilah felt a rough growl escape her throat. "Lilah, *no*. I need to go back there, and you need to go to the bank."

"Don't you see that's what House *wants*? It's pretending to be your mother!"

"Look," he said, his long fingers gripping her shoulders. "House has never mimicked a voice before, okay? If my mother . . ." He let the words trail off, closing his eyes. "I can't leave town without knowing who called Dhaval."

"It will hurt you. Remember what you said? This, today, is the nuclear option. House just declared war."

"I know House hurt you. I will never forgive it for that.

But House has never hurt me. Ever. All I need to do is get in there. . . ." The rest of the plan seemed to be still out of his mental reach, and Delilah felt a scream build deep in her belly and fill her entire chest as he thought it through. She clenched her jaw to keep it from erupting and frazzling Gavin even more. "I just need to *see*. Don't you understand? I never thought she was there, so I never *looked*."

"I don't like it."

"It's not even six in the morning. Go home. Get on the couch. Pretend you've been there all night. Pack up a few things when your parents leave for the day, and then head to the bank. I'll meet you there at eleven, just like we planned. I may even get there in time to go with you, but if not, you need to get into the safe-deposit box."

"It might have nothing," she reminded him. "Maybe it has some of her hippie books and crystals."

He took a deep breath, staring her down. "It might have my birth certificate, with the names of *both* of my parents. It might have money."

"I really, *really* don't like this."

"I can't do this if I'm worrying about you," he told her. "If House was tricking me, I'll know right away and I'll get out. I've never broken a window out of respect, but that doesn't mean I won't throw a table through one if it means the difference between being with you or not. I have to do this."

• • •

Delilah was beneath the covers on the couch when her father came downstairs to make coffee just after seven. She tried to feign sleep, but her heart was beating so fast it seemed to nearly choke her airway. She felt every minute ticking by, etching like a razor slice into her skin.

Gavin is almost home by now.

Maybe he's walked inside.

Maybe he's already trapped.

When her father came in and woke her, she stretched and looked around the room, trying to figure out what she could possibly take with her. There were the clothes that had been in the washer or dryer when the fire happened. There was some cash from her mother's antique vase on top of the fridge. She would pack a knife. Some food. She would leave her parents a note, telling them she was leaving for college early. In the time it would take them to find her—even if they jumped into action and found her in only two days—she would be eighteen.

They had exactly seventy-three dollars between the two of them. Most of it in fives and ones, rolled into a log and shoved in Delilah's jacket pocket. She added another two hundred from her mother's vase. If the house was going to take anything from her now, it would have to light *her* on fire too.

By eight fifty, Delilah was standing on Mercer and Main, duffel bag slung over her shoulder as she paced, waiting for the bank to open. She felt every shift in the breeze, heard every rustle in the trees overhead. The safe-deposit-box key was clenched so tightly in her fist it might leave an impression in her flesh forever. And if it did, every time she would look at the imprint, it would remind her of this biting, freezing terror: *How on earth am I meant to walk in there and open this box without the building crumbling down on me? How does Gavin expect to escape today and meet me out front?*

It was the perfect trap. His faith in the house had left him blind.

She couldn't believe she'd let him go. What if the contents of the box told them nothing? What if instead of money or important papers, it held a few dusty trinkets or old photographs. What then? She was here, wasting time when she could have been with him, *fighting*.

The stress was too big for her, physically. It seemed to spread past her skin, in a haze of panic she couldn't seem to shake. Delilah resisted the urge to glance at her phone again. She knew it hadn't been more than a couple of minutes since she last looked, when she'd calculated the bank would open in ten minutes.

How long do I stand here, she thought, *before I decide something has happened and I go to the house? How can he possibly expect me to move forward without him?*

She thought back to the night before, in the music room, with Gavin's hands and body all over her in a fever. She still felt tender from what they'd done, and she let herself remember every bit of it for just a moment, only a heartbeat: his breath warm and fast on her neck, teeth dragging to her collarbone, the sight of his smooth, muscled shoulders moving over her first slowly and then with abandon. How he'd started so carefully but listened to her when she told him she wanted none of that.

And then later: his warm, satisfied mouth pressed to her bare stomach and his promise that he would be here today. But that was before he knew his mother had called.

"Take everything worth anything," he'd said as he'd backed away toward the door leading out of the music room, "and if I'm not there by eleven, get out of town. I'll find you."

Delilah swallowed, looking down at her phone just as the doors to the bank clicked open.

She'd held on to the hope that Gavin would be here now, that he would have gone in and escaped easily, or changed his mind at the gate and managed to dodge all of the trees swiping at him as he ran back to her here, in the middle of town.

It was only nine.

He wasn't late.

She shouldn't worry yet.

But her panic was a cold, slithering thing, as if the house had crawled into her this time, finally possessing her. But she knew it hadn't. She was completely alone on the sidewalk outside the bank, because if Gavin was trapped there, House had everything it needed already.

• • •

The bank was empty but for a few tellers, a manager speaking on the phone in a glass-enclosed office, and a smiling, clean-cut, fair-haired man behind a desk. Taking a deep breath, Delilah walked over to him and sat down with shaking legs.

"I need to access a safe-deposit box."

The man, whose desk had a name plate with KENNETH engraved into brass, smiled again and turned to his computer. "Well, great. I can help you there. What's your name?"

"I'm Delilah Blue." He began to type her name into his computer, but she quickly added, "But it's not my box."

Kenneth's smile faltered as he looked back at her. "Whose box is it?"

"Hilary Timothy."

He typed in the name and then shook his head, eyes genuinely apologetic when he looked back to her. "You're not listed as a user on this account."

"I have a key, though," she said, hope causing her voice to crack halfway through.

"Unfortunately, it doesn't work that way. You need to be an approved user."

Was it something in Delilah's expression that made him so sincerely concerned for her? Something in the way her voice shook and she looked like she'd seen a ghost, maybe a thousand of them? She could see it in Kenneth's face that if this rule could be bent, he might just do it.

"What if . . . ?" She paused, taking a deep breath before saying, "What if Hilary died?"

Kenneth blinked, surprised. He collected himself quickly enough. "Well, she does have someone else on the access form. Maybe you can contact them?"

Delilah shook her head, not understanding. A key was a key, after all. She only needed to open the box, not take anything with her. "I just need to see what's in there. There are answers in that box, sir."

"There are standard security features set up with a safe-deposit box," Kenneth explained patiently. "You can't access the box with only the key. Whoever requires access to the box needs to be present with their identification when the box is created, because they have to sign the signature card. Only the individuals that have signed the signature card have access to the safe-deposit box. Everyone who signs is given a key to the box. Does this make sense?"

"Yes," Delilah said, closing her eyes to think, think, think.

"Although you have a key, you are not on the list of registered users, so I know that key is not yours."

"Is Gavin Timothy on the list?" she asked, ignoring the gentle admonishment in his words.

Kenneth glanced at the computer screen in front of him. "Sorry, no. It may help to remind you that a *signature* is required when the account was first established. If Gavin is Ms. Timothy's son, he likely would have been—"

"Right," she said, cutting him off. He would have been only a toddler when she opened the box. Delilah bent over, pressing her hands to her face. She could feel tears rising, making her throat feel thick and her face grow tight. Gavin had gone back to the house and she had no way of knowing if he was okay, but she couldn't imagine a scenario where House welcomed him home with cookies and warmth. She couldn't get into the box to find out what, if anything, his mother knew, and all of their money was burned to ashes. Her parents were as warm as glaciers; Nonna was lost to dementia. The risk of coming here had been a waste, and Delilah had never felt more defeated in her entire life. "Sorry. I'm leaving. I just need a minute."

"Delilah." Kenneth bent closer so she could hear when he whispered, "I'm sure you're looking for information for a very good reason, but unless you can come back with Hilary Timothy or Vani Reddy, I'm sorry to say I can't help you."

"Vani Reddy?" Delilah looked up into Kenneth's warm, hazel eyes, blood thundering in her ears. Hope. A faint glimmer of hope sparked in her chest.

"Yes," Kenneth said with a polite smile. "She's the other person listed on the account."

Delilah knocked on the door to the Reddy house with a clammy, shaking fist. Dhaval answered, wearing his soccer uniform and eating a sandwich.

"Oh shit," he said around a bite. "You look like hell."

Delilah made a minor attempt to finger comb her hair. "I need to speak to your mom, D."

Vani appeared from the kitchen, wiping her hands on a linen cloth. "Delilah?"

"Auntie, I'm so sorry to come by like this without calling."

The other woman hushed her, told her to come inside.

"Vani," Delilah started, putting her backpack down beside the coatrack. "You knew Gavin's mother?"

"I know her, yes."

"I think Gavin's in trouble. I don't know who else can help me."

Vani waved Delilah farther inside, leading her to the living room. "Hilary called looking for him. Is that what this is about?"

Delilah looked at Dhaval, asking, "What have you told her?"

He swallowed his bite, eyes wide, and then said, "Nothing yet."

"Told me about what?" Vani draped the dish towel over the back of a chair and sat down. "What are you two up to?"

"Have you ever been to the Timothy house?"

She nodded. "Years ago. Hilary and I were once . . . well, we were close acquaintances, if that makes sense. Not really friends, more than strangers. I haven't seen her in a while."

"You talk about her as if she's still alive."

Vani paused, tilting her head as she let this sink in. "And you speak about her as if she isn't. The dead don't usually make phone calls, Delilah."

"So you *did* talk to her this morning?"

"I did. What is this about?"

Delilah swallowed, leaning closer. "Vani, I've been to Gavin's house before, but I've never met her. I haven't even *seen* her."

"You must understand Hilary is a very private, eccentric—"

"*No*, Auntie," Delilah said, interrupting with apology in her eyes. "*Gavin* has never seen her, either. At least not since he was small. He lives there alone."

Vani's hand pressed to her chest, her eyes wide. "That can't be true, *jaanu*."

"I mean, alone with the house," Delilah explained slowly. "The house is . . . possessed, or haunted. It's raised Gavin. It's been good to him, all his life. But when he and I started seeing each other, it didn't react well."

"She's telling the truth, *Amma*," Dhaval whispered.

"I think it was the house that called you," Delilah told her. "It's a trap. I think the house did something to her."

To Delilah's horror—or possibly her relief; could it somehow be both?—Vani seemed to want to believe her. "You knew something was different about the house," Delilah said.

Vani didn't answer, instead asking: "Why didn't Gavin tell anyone?"

"It was all he knew. When he was little he didn't know anything else, and when he figured out he was different, he was afraid he would be in trouble, or something would happen to the house. That people might take him away."

"Why didn't *you* tell me, Delilah?"

"I've been gone for nearly six years!" Delilah cried. "We all thought the house was creepy, but none of us ever got close enough to see more. It wasn't until I came home and started following him—"

"Stalking, more like," Dhaval teased, and both females threw him a look.

"—and he took me inside," Delilah continued. "At first I thought it was amazing. I mean, it seemed like a miracle. I wish you could see what I saw. I didn't say anything then because I didn't want it to be dissected or studied. But when Gavin and I became closer, the house . . . It started to resent me."

Vani's eyes narrowed, concentrating. "*Resent* you?"

"It's horrible, Auntie. It stalked us. It was the house that hurt my arm, not Gavin, not me! It set my room on fire to destroy the money we'd saved so we could go somewhere else together. It can possess objects, like Gavin's clothes. It can possess people who go onto the property. That's how no one has ever taken Gavin away: Social workers come to the porch and the house makes them think everything is fine."

Horror crept into Vani's voice. "How does it do this?"

"I don't know," Delilah admitted in a shaky whisper. "I

don't know if it's one spirit or a million inside, but it feels like there are a lot. Everything has its own personality. Some things are nice—like things in the living room. Some rooms have never liked me, like the kitchen or the dining room. Or," she added, feeling her cheeks heat, "Gavin's bedroom. They just want Gavin. I swear. If he never left the house, it would never bother anyone."

"And he wants out now?" Vani asked.

"Yes, but even if he didn't, I would burn it down to get him out of there."

Vani stood, walking over to the mantel where she had a line of family photographs: a portrait of Dhaval kneeling with a soccer ball, a framed photo from her wedding. "Hilary played around too much with blessings and cleansings, souls and spirits. She came to me hoping I would know more—my mother was a very spiritual woman, you see—but I assured her I simply follow Hindu teachings. There isn't anything mystical about me."

Delilah glanced at Dhaval. He'd mentioned a blessing ceremony before, but this was the first time Delilah felt dread trickle like ice into her blood when it was mentioned. "Do you think she might have done this? With the blessing ceremony?"

"Hilary dabbled in a lot of different religions, chose what she liked about each. She talked to me about blessing her house. She had a . . . power about her, but it seemed innocent enough. She was a free spirit, maybe a little flaky, but she had good intentions. She'd left her husband, who I think wasn't a very good man, and moved here to buy the house. She wanted to grow her own food out there, wanted to live differently from the way most of society does. When she started talking about blessing the house, I told her it wasn't a good idea. I had family who knew about that stuff, but I didn't. Not enough."

"See?" Dhaval whispered to Delilah.

"The last time I saw her," Vani continued, "she needed someone to help her open a safe-deposit box in town for her documents. She was wary of those places—banks, government offices, anything official, you see. When we were downstairs, she mentioned she thought she'd done the blessing ceremony wrong. I asked what she meant, but she only said the house felt fuller. She was thrilled by it, though. And that was that."

"You didn't see her after?"

"No, Delilah. She was always a bit of a hermit; I just assumed it had grown worse. You want to let people have their oddities."

"We found Hilary's key to the box," Delilah explained. "After the fire, that was it. We were going to check the safe-deposit box to see what his mother had left there and try to get away from the house. From town. But then his mother called, and he went there looking for her and told me to go to the bank."

Dhaval leaned forward, shock all over his face. "You were going to leave?"

Delilah stared at him with wide eyes. "Hell yes, we're going to leave!"

"Dee, your grades are so go—"

"Dhaval! This thing set my house on fire! I don't care about my grades right now! I can finish high school somewhere else!"

Vani's eyes cleared in understanding. "You tried, but couldn't get into the safe-deposit box."

"No, I couldn't."

"And you knew before you came here that I have access," Vani said quietly.

"Please, I need your help."

Vani stood, nodding. "Let me get my things."

Delilah stopped her with a hand on her arm, eyes already apologetic. "Auntie, I can't leave town without Gavin."

"I know, *jaanu*."

Delilah's voice dropped to barely a whisper. "Can you help me get him out? I don't know what I'm dealing with here."

"I can try. The bank is on the way. It won't take more than a few minutes, and then we'll go to your Gavin. But, Delilah, it's more than getting him and leaving town. If this is all true, we'll also need to get rid of the haunting, and I can rely only on very rusty knowledge for that."

With Vani at her side, getting access to the safe-deposit box was simple. A flash of identification, a signature on a form, and they all followed Kenneth down into the belly of the building.

"When you're done," he said in his quiet, warm voice, "put the box away and come on upstairs. Or, if you prefer, I can help you store it."

The box itself was long and flat, and it felt too light to hold all of the answers Delilah needed.

And, in fact, the box held only seven pieces of paper: two photos, three handwritten pages that looked as if they'd been hastily torn from a notebook, Gavin's birth certificate, and the deed to the land beneath the house. They took it all and headed back to the car.

"Do we wait here for him?" Vani asked. "It's only ten, Delilah. He told you he would be here at eleven."

"I can't sit here and do nothing. There's no way everything is going fine over there."

With Dhaval driving and the calming hum of the engine all around them, Delilah went through the pages. Hilary was beautiful, in a wild sort of way. In one picture her brown hair was pulled from her face with leather ties and jeweled clips. She wore a flowing, layered blue dress. Her black eyes gleamed in happiness, and she held a baby Gavin in her arms as if she'd won the entire world when she had him.

In the second Gavin was older, clearly barely walking as he tilted—nearly toppling—and Hilary crouched on the sidewalk before him, arms open in welcome. Behind them, the house loomed, the window eyes staring down at them on the street.

Delilah could already feel the life there, and a violent shiver ran down her arms.

"Here," Vani said, handing Delilah the notes. They were short, written in a giant, looping scrawl. The edges of the first two were jagged as if hastily torn from a notebook. Delilah read them aloud:

> Finished the blessing today, and I can feel the love this house has for me, for Gavin. All around us things seem to have come to life and it's glorious! I sat down with Gavin in the living room and simply breathed in and out and meditated on images of our future here. We have a lifetime ahead of us inside these walls. I've never felt so surrounded.

The bottom of the page was missing, as if only this section mattered.

"If I remember . . . there is a part of the ceremony," Vani said quietly, "where you welcome life to the house. But it's a subtle difference, okay, where you welcome your life to the house, or you simply welcome life. I fear Hilary has done this wrong. Terribly wrong. I fear she brought life to everything in the house."

Delilah moved the second note to the front, scanning it.

> I've met a man, a loved, a beloved. Will we move? Won't we move? Ron hasn't been to the house, and I don't know

that I want him here. It's our safe place, our wonderland. And what would he think? There are so many things in this world that we can't understand. But tonight at his apartment he asked me to bring Gavin and move in with him. I don't want to leave our house! But I love him! I said I would think about it. And now I'm home and House is being awful. It's cold, and I keep getting lost trying to find my room. Gavin was in the nursery and then he was downstairs. I brought him upstairs with me to get some medicine for my headache, and when I turned around he was gone again. I found him in the kitchen walking toward the counter with the knives. I yelled at the house. I told it to keep away from my baby. I hate that I did it. House loves Gavin. I know it does, but it had never scared me like that.

I write these things because I'm afraid to say them out loud. I thought if I saw them on paper I'd realize how silly I'm being. Looking at them . . . they don't seem silly at all.

"See?" Delilah whispered. "Oh God." She knew what happened. She knew. She knew.

The last note was a mess, more so than the others. The writing looked hurried and panicked, the words pressed too hard into sterile bank stationery.

Something has changed. My thoughts aren't my own.
My head hurts all the time now. I'm afraid of what I've
done. I've tried to cleanse the air with sage. I've tried
a frankincense smudge and pickled garlic, put salt all
around the house. I've done any incantation I can find,
and nothing works. The house scares me now. Last
night I went to the basement to get a jar of peaches,
and I was stuck down there for hours because the door
locked. It LOCKED. It's never locked before, and this
time it did, with Gavin upstairs alone! I came out,
finally, when the door clicked open, and Gavin was in
his room, playing quietly. I feel . . . It sounds crazy, but
I feel like this house thinks Gavin belongs to it. Not me.

Delilah glanced up at Dhaval in the rearview mirror, feeling grim. "This is awful," he whispered.

"I think she's dead," Delilah said, with a feeling like a
heavy anchor settling in her stomach.

"It was her," Dhaval said. "I'm sure of it. We'll get to the
house and you'll see. Everything will be fine."

Delilah returned to the note:

I don't know what else to do. It punishes me in odd,
terrifying ways. Hiding my things, making me get
lost on my way to bed or the kitchen or the bathroom.
It's like it's playing with me. Like I'm a mouse and

it's batting me around with its paw. It grows quiet, or trembles so subtly while I'm working or cooking. I'm not sure if I'm imagining it. It trips me on the stairs, drops paintings near me when I walk past, and the nightmares. Oh, Gaia, the dreams. It gives me dreams straight from hell and then makes me realize I'm awake.

The photos in the hallway are all of Gavin and the house. There was one of us together, him in his stroller and me at his side. A part of the photograph had been burned, my face nothing more than a scorch mark. I took it down, hid some of the others, and have started to make a plan.

I'm going to take Gavin to Ron's until I can clear this up. In case something happens, I'm leaving our documents in this box and leaving tonight. If someone finds these . . . help him.

Delilah laid the note back down in the box and gave herself to the count of ten to panic.

1 . . . 2 . . .

Gavin is in there.

3 . . . 4 . . . 5 . . .

Gavin is alone.

6 . . . 7 . . .

Hilary was probably killed by the house and this is all a trap.
It will never let him out now.

8 . . . 9 . . . 10.

The house wouldn't hurt Gavin.

It wouldn't.

It wouldn't.

It wouldn't.

Delilah inhaled sharply, swallowing her fear, her sick, slithering panic. The sound of the tires on pavement filled her head. The house loved Gavin and wanted her gone. It wanted her to leave. It wanted her to run away and leave Gavin behind.

There was no way in hell.

"Dhaval! Take this turn first. Stop by my house!" she said.

Delilah looked out at the houses as they pulled onto her street. The neighborhood felt deserted in the late-morning sun: The sidewalk was flat, and the street was empty. There wasn't even much of a breeze. Instead, the brightly colored houses down the blocks looked like innocent toys, or candy, lined up obliviously and vulnerable.

Her mother was gone, but Franklin Blue was home in the family room, watching the news in the middle of the day. He didn't even call out to her as she dug through her duffel bag in the living room, changed into black jeans, a long-sleeved black T-shirt, and a thin down vest. She strapped on boots and glanced at herself in the dining room mirror.

Dhaval stepped into the room. "You look badass."

"I need to."

"The house doesn't care how you look, does it?" he asked, trying to bring in some of his trademark swagger, but it fell flat.

"No, but I need to feel like someone who can do this. Someone in a little skirt and polo shirt won't beat down the demons."

He followed her out through the family room—Franklin complaining only when they blocked his view of the television—and into the backyard.

"Where are you going?" Dhaval hissed, trailing behind her into the shed. His eyes went as wide as saucers when she reached for an ax on the wall. "Delilah, are you out of your damn mind?"

"You think I can get him out with my bare hands?" She sounded braver than she felt, and gripped the weapon in both of her hands. Was it any good to take this along, or was she better off leaving both hands free, simply to defend herself? She imagined shards of wood and plaster; she imagined fire and wind and the enormous tremors of the house shaking all around her. Any weapon she had, would the house simply take it over? Could she control anything?

"An *ax*?" he yell-hissed. "This isn't the zombie apocalypse, girl! Your dad doesn't have a gun?"

"You think a gun is going to work on a possessed house? I don't need to reload an ax!"

"What's going on out here?" The gruff, deep voice of Delilah's father tore through the crisp, bright air, and both teens whipped around to face him, eyes wide.

"We need an ax to take down this diseased tree over at Dhaval's." Delilah recovered smoothly.

Franklin leaned against the doorway, looking skeptical as he crossed his arms over his chest. He was so enormous that for a tiny beat Delilah wished he were just a little more crazy, a touch more adventurous; he would make an excellent addition to the team they were putting together. "Ravi doesn't have one?" he asked.

"No, sir," Dhaval said. "My dad believes in gardeners to take care of ax-related events."

Franklin all but ignored Dhaval. "Not sure I want you taking an ax out of the house, Delilah. Seems like a lot of trouble to be had."

If he only knew.

"You can drive it over there for us," she said, holding her breath. It was a gamble, but the odds were in her favor. Her father's physical laziness was nearly as limitless as his antisocial tendencies.

Delilah watched as her dad grumbled something and headed back toward the house. They had everything they needed and were about to leave when something on the workbench caught her eye. The shed was the part of the Blue family home that Delilah's mother didn't scour and disinfect within an inch of its life. And there, in the layer of dust covering the neglected workbench was a heart and the words "Gavin loves Delilah" written in Gavin's handwriting.

In the backseat, Dhaval sat beside her and reached over to take her hand. "You okay?" he asked.

She wasn't.

Vani started the car, taking a deep breath. "We're leaving if anyone gets hurt."

"Okay," lied Delilah. She wouldn't leave until Gavin was with her.

This is all happening too fast. But . . . why didn't we do this sooner? This is crazy.

"I know you think the house won't hurt Gavin," Vani continued, "but we're calling the police as soon as anything seems off."

"If the police come, the house will crumble." Delilah closed her eyes and took as much air into her lungs as she could manage.

"I'm assuming the spirits are more concerned with Gavin and won't care where we are," Dhaval said quietly. "I think the first thing we need to do is find him."

"I'll find him," Delilah said. "You two stay just outside the gate until I bring him out."

Nodding, Vani glanced at them in the rearview mirror, making a left on Sycamore. "Once you bring him out, we'll need to pull all of the spirits to where he is and then . . ." She shook her head, and for the first time Delilah could see that Vani was trying to seem far braver than she felt. "Maybe then I can banish them? I don't know! I've never done this before! God, if only my mother were here."

"You can do it," Delilah said. "We all can. So first we need to gather them all around *us*, too?"

"Yes, *jaanu*."

With a little, terrified laugh, Delilah whispered, "They *hate* me." She closed her eyes after she said it and could barely imagine what she would find when she got back to the house.

It would be like trying to cross the gates of hell.

It would be like walking into the ticking heart of a bomb.

When she looked up again, Delilah caught Vani glancing at her in the rearview mirror. "We don't have any choice, do we?" Vani said.

Delilah sat up straighter and took a moment to check in on Dhaval. Throughout all of this, he was so quiet, so uncharacteristically thoughtful, just taking it all in. But when he met her eyes, he looked determined . . . and fearless. When her eyes caught his, she felt it like a physical shove, like he'd grabbed Delilah's heart and reminded it how to keep beating.

"Gavin's in there," he whispered. "In that crazy-ass house, Dee. It'll hurt anyone who gets in its way. Nobody's safe while it stands. We have to do this. *I* can do this."

"I'll get inside and find him," Delilah said. "It can change things around and confuse us, but at least I've been there before. You two stay on the sidewalk out front until you hear me call for you. No matter what, stay outside. There's a shed in the back. That's where I'll take him. It's small, but it's probably the safest place for all of us. As soon as we get there, you'll need to be ready."

Vani met her eyes once more. "We'll be ready."

"And then, Dhaval?" she said, looking at her best friend.

He looked up, dark eyes luminous in the waning sun. "Yeah?"

"You still know how to hot-wire?"

When Dhaval had come home from visiting his cousins in California, he'd e-mailed Delilah, bragging about how one of them had taught him how to hot-wire cars. Judging by her gasp and the way Vani's eyes widened, her son hadn't filled her in on that part of his vacation.

"Sure do," Dhaval said, grinning proudly.

"House has the keys, so you'll need to get the old car started. Gavin and I are going to get the hell out of town."

They parked at the curb, and Delilah stepped out. The damp leaves on the ground looked like bruises, blue-gray against the drab concrete sidewalk. The once-lively yard was silent; there was no breeze, no bobbing, reaching vines; there were no birds in the trees anywhere near it, no sounds of life other than the terrified pounding of her own pulse in her ears.

She looked up at the looming building in front of her. All at once she had the impression of looking at two separate houses: the brilliant structure it might have once been and the crooked, gloomy monstrosity it had become. The house was dark and heavy, and the thick, putrid air outside gave the impression of waterlogged wood, cracked cement, and dried-up grass.

But the details of the house itself were hidden behind a haze of fog, and she had to step closer to get a better look. The house came into focus when she was right there, barely two feet from the iron gate, which opened easily beneath her hands with a piercing groan. Darkness sealed up behind her as she stepped onto the paved walkway, and Delilah's confidence curdled. As she walked in, the once-thriving yard looked exactly like it would if it had been left untended for two decades. There was no green lawn, no yellow. There were no flowering trees or beds full of blooming tulips. Everything was brown. The house was run-down, dilapidated, as if all of the life—like the birds—had simply vanished.

But Delilah knew better. She knew everything had simply gathered inside, waiting.

CHAPTER TWENTY-EIGHT

HIM

THE FIRST THING HE'D NOTICED WAS BLUE SKY. Not that a blue sky this time of year was out of the ordinary—it was spring, after all—but on *this* corner, looking down the tree-lined street to where House stood, the blue above him stood out.

The sky above House was always dotted with puffs of dark smoke, even in summer. A steady spiral continually emanated from Chimney and dissolved away as soon as it reached the clouds. Today, however, at barely seven in the morning, every inch of the world above House was as black as night, as if something hateful had stained the sky and the morning sun was unable to penetrate the shadow.

The ground was littered with leaves and fallen branches that crunched beneath the rubber of Gavin's bike tires as he braked to a stop. Even in the strange, early-morning blackness, he could tell there was no smoke billowing from Chimney because there was no fire. There was always a fire.

House never did anything without a reason, and Gavin knew beyond a shadow of a doubt that *he* was that reason. House was waiting for him.

The sun had just started to filter through the neighbor's trees, and though he could feel the warmth of it beginning to seep into the back of his dark hoodie and warm the tips of his ears, Gavin shivered in the eerie chill surrounding his home. He had no idea what he would find when he opened that door, but he knew it was time.

He'd been debating not coming back at all, knowing how easy it would be to stay in the music room with Delilah, to ignore all of this and remain lost in her. They could have caught a bus later this morning, left town with very little fanfare. Maybe they would have been able to drive that unknown distance that would put them truly out of reach of House. Delilah would be eighteen in a few days. He would be eighteen in just over two weeks. He wasn't sure which of the two of them would be less likely to find someone coming after them.

He knew leaving would have been the *smart* thing. He knew he should have tried. Dhaval's text had changed everything. But the farther away Gavin was from the music room and his conversation with Dhaval, the more certain he became that House was toying with him, finding a way to mimic a woman's voice on the phone. But if there was a chance—no matter how small—that his mom was there, inside somewhere, he had to look.

His heart seemed to be trying to claw out of his chest. His pulse was jagged, leaping and unsteady, and it was distracting enough for Gavin to wonder whether he could take the panic of facing this dark beast in front of him.

Closing his eyes, he struggled to steady his breaths as he made a small mental list of tasks:

Get inside. Listen for my mother. Gather what I need and get out. Find Delilah.

Find Delilah.

Delilah.

He didn't have much in the way of possessions and had never considered himself to be overly sentimental—he'd never really felt like the things in House belonged to him anyway—but now that he was standing outside, there were a handful of items he couldn't bear the thought of leaving behind. He wanted the Bible he'd found and he wanted the photograph of his mom. He couldn't dream of leaving his sketchbooks behind, and if it were possible, he wanted to find the keys to the car. If he could somehow manage to get those, he could have his things and a way for them to leave town, too. Running away would be a lot easier in the Buick than on a bike.

To be safe, he parked the bike outside Iron Gate in case the worst happened and he couldn't get the car, and he headed for House.

Gate didn't open on its own the way it usually did, and

so he pushed it open with a groan, coming to an abrupt stop when he stepped into the yard. Not only was Chimney silent, but the lawn looked . . . dead. Really dead, both sides. The grass was brown and brittle, and weeds grew in the cracks between the pavers that led to the front door. House looked well and truly abandoned—abandoned for *years*—as if his entire life had never happened.

The vines that wound themselves around the columns on the front porch were spindly, and the purple petals of the new blossoms as delicate and dry as old paper, dropping one by one into a small pile on the top step. Gavin wasn't sure what to make of all this, and he briefly wondered if maybe House had . . . left? Maybe his mom had come home and House was gone because he didn't need it anymore.

He didn't know how to process that. On the one hand, that was the point of all of this, wasn't it? To get away? To live his own life? So why did he feel that familiar panic? That tremor in his hands at the thought of being alone?

"I'm home," he called, standing in the foyer, and clenched his jaw when the urge to shout *Mom?* became almost too much to bear. He did his best to keep his hands steady while he unzipped his hoodie and hung it on a hook near the door. He kept his shoes on.

Gavin looked down the hall and listened for the sound of footsteps in one of the other rooms, or from someplace upstairs. Nothing.

"Where is everyone?" he asked, careful to keep the quiver from his voice.

Fireplace flickered to life, the low flames sputtering around the ever-present log.

So *something* was still here, but no mother stepped out of the shadows. He tried to ignore the feeling in his stomach, as if a trapdoor had opened in his diaphragm and his heart had dropped straight through.

"Everyone okay?" He looked up the staircase at the dark hall beyond. "Things are pretty dark outside."

He kept his steps even as he walked to a table—careful to look like he didn't understand why anything would be amiss—and went through a stack of mail that was sitting there. His hands shook as he flipped through the flyers and envelopes of coupons. They received junk mail and neighborhood flyers shoved into the box at the curb, but no bills. Nothing personal or that required a response had ever been delivered to House. He assumed since House didn't really run on metered electricity or gas, and there was no cable TV, there were no bills. He didn't even know if they paid taxes. House powered everything itself; there was nobody to pay.

But standing here now, clinging to the unreal possibility that his mother had been here in the house, he wondered: Weren't there some things that required a signature? Who had enrolled him in school? Who had signed off when the doctor arrived, dazed and robotic, at the door? And why had he never thought to question any of this before Delilah came into his life? Gavin always assumed his reality was *different* from those around him, but beneath that assumption had always been a dark, secret belief that House also made him special.

A single word stabbed at his thoughts: *How?*

How could a boy be orphaned without people all over town knowing what happened to his mother?

How could he be so lucky that his house happened to step in and raise him?

How could he not immediately wonder, when the house began terrorizing Delilah, if the house had also hurt his mother?

What if House had never been good? What if he'd been here all his life, trusting and blind, and the only family he'd ever known was simply . . . evil?

Struggling to stay calm and choking back the tight swell of tears, Gavin continued to listen for any sound of human life in the house. He dropped the stack of mail on the table and went to Kitchen, pulled down a glass, and filled it with water from the tap.

As he drank, holding the glass with a trembling hand, Gavin tried to ignore the odd darkness outside. The resurgence of a fire in Fireplace had warmed the front rooms. A fresh plate of cookies sat on the counter. Daisies on the windowsill unfurled their petals and faced him.

"Think I might go upstairs and get a bit more sleep," he said.

He reached for an apple in the crisper drawer and straightened, polishing the tender red skin on the fabric of his shirt. "I fell asleep practicing for the spring concert and have this horrible crick in my neck. A nap might do me a world of good. Maybe we can look at the sprinklers out front when I'm done? The twins aren't looking so good."

The daisies nodded their heads but made no movement to reach out for him as he placed his glass in the sink.

Gavin climbed the stairs one at a time, hoping he didn't look as anxious as he felt. It was so quiet. There had always been an energy about House that he'd grown accustomed to, a tiny vibration, the sense of movement all around him that used to ease him to sleep at night and remind him that he wasn't alone. He could feel it in the walls and the wood beneath his feet. He could feel it in the air. Today it was still there, but it was different.

It was tighter. Tenser. He felt like he was trapped in the belly of a clenched muscle, knowing House would do anything to keep from hurting him but sensing its pulsing fury.

The lights in the stairway illuminated, but they buzzed dissonantly. The stairs creaked with each step he took, somehow less solid, nearly brittle under his shoes.

"What's going on?" he asked, swallowing so thickly he could hear it in the eerie silence. "Are you mad at me?"

Dread began to build in Gavin's stomach, and he climbed the rest of the stairs quickly, his eyes on the bedroom doorway at the end of the hall, ears still straining to hear anything.

There was a duffel bag in his closet, and Gavin thought briefly of filling it with clothes and toiletries and other things before trying to flee, but dismissed the idea just as quickly. The only reason House hadn't snapped was because Gavin hadn't tried to run.

He sat on his bed, picked up his sketchbook and a short stick of charcoal, struggling to look calm and relaxed. How did he do this? How did he search House for his mother when it could see every single move he made? He'd never seen House look this way—dark and dead and *sinister*. Was there really any way to fool it?

Gavin remembered the mornings he'd been grounded, how the doorknobs had vanished from the front doors, the latches had been removed from the windows. Delilah swore House morphed and physically transformed the night she came over for dinner. Was it possible there were parts of House he didn't even know were there?

Spotting an old box on a shelf in his room, Gavin took down a model airplane he'd never finished and muttered something about finding glue. He was able to rifle through old drawers, peer into cabinets he hadn't opened in ages, even check under couch cushions and beds. House even seemed happy to help, moving furniture out of his way and opening cupboards for him. He opened every closet, dragged casual fingertips down walls as he passed, feeling for any edges or bumps that shouldn't be there.

He found a bunch of old bottles of migraine medication that must have belonged to his mother, but no glue and no hidden rooms.

With two hours to go before he was meant to meet Delilah, Gavin had pretty much given up hope of finding anything.

He climbed the stairs again and headed back into his room, stopping dead in his tracks when he crossed to the bed. There, in the center of his perfectly straightened comforter, was the photo of his mom that he kept taped inside the bathroom drawer.

House knew all along what he was looking for.

The air cooled, the room darkening as if the sun had tucked itself behind the clouds, hiding. Pinpricks of sweat broke out along his skin, and he felt gooseflesh rise along his arms, his legs, the back of his neck.

Outside in the distance he could see blue sky and the leaves of trees fluttering in the breeze, but close to House, everything felt dark. The yard was cast beneath a shadow. Wind whipped through the dead branches of his favorite cherry tree.

There was a sound in the hallway behind him. Not footsteps, a *growl*. It was a sound that could come only from the belly of a beast—low and angry—vibrating along the boards below his bedroom and climbing up the walls. The tremor went higher and higher, like a shiver passing through the entire house.

Gavin closed his eyes, visualized the stairs and how many steps it would take to get there.

If he ran, he knew Bed might move and he would have to jump. Dresser might try to block the doorway. The hallway was clear, but Table was fast and could block any door it wanted. It would try to slow him down, trip him, knock him down the stairs if it had to.

Oh God.

Gavin tried to push the thought of this type of physical battle from his head, but he couldn't. He closed his eyes again and could see the image of him there, at the bottom of the stairs, limbs bent at grotesque right angles, neck turned oddly, eyes open and glassy. Would House prefer that Gavin died, because then he would never leave? The air left his lungs in a rush, and he moved to cover his mouth, swallowing the rise of bile in his throat. This wasn't House being frustrated or wounded. For the first time in his life, Gavin knew that House was prepared to do whatever it took to keep him there.

It never had any intention of letting me leave.

He eyed his bedroom windows, covered with heavy curtains that could easily snare and trap him. He looked directly across the hall, into the open bathroom and the window he'd left wedged open with a block of wood.

It was still there.

If he was fast, he might be able to reach it and climb out. If House slammed the frame closed, he would shatter the glass. It was the only clear path. He narrowed his eyes and calculated the distance. Fifteen feet. That was as far as he needed to go. Fifteen feet from where he stood to the bathroom.

He stared out into the hallway, took a deep breath, and then ran.

Hallway Table scraped along the floor and planted itself between his body and the door, and he dove under it, sliding along the icy wood floor and out into the hall. His shoulder collided with the wall and it rippled, changing color and then shape right before his eyes, and suddenly, he had no idea where he was. There was supposed to be a hallway on his right, a door *right there* that led to the bathroom—to the window—and now there wasn't. It was wallpaper he'd never seen before, covering walls beside a set of doors he'd never opened.

"Mom!" he screamed. "Are you here? Mom!" The scratchy, hysterical cry was a sound he'd never made before. He pounded on the wall, sliding his hands along the smooth surface as he struggled to make his way down the rippling hallway.

With no other choice, Gavin sprinted in the opposite direction, toward the stairs and the front door. The floor bucked up in front of him, the wooden planks parting with an earsplitting crack, and rose as if standing, melding into a solid wooden wall, forming door after door after door. He reached for one and then another, throwing them open to find a crooked staircase that rose up to nothing, a brick wall, a freezing black abyss.

Behind him, the entire house shook, and it was so cold

that Gavin could see his own breath, feel the burn of frost beneath his fingertips. The floor started to tip, and he felt himself slide backward, calling out for his mother the entire time. His fingers scrambled to find purchase on the slick wood, nails digging into the icy surface.

A rope latch swung from the ceiling behind him, the pull for the door to the attic. Although he'd never been inside, he knew from the outside that there were windows up there, and Gavin struggled to roll over and reach for the catch. After three tries he managed to get his footing and caught it, watching as the door swung down, the ladder unfurling and crashing to the floor in front of him. Shrill screams tore through the air, but *whose*? Gavin had never heard another voice in this house besides Delilah's and yet . . . they sounded familiar. Were these the voices Delilah had heard? The ones from her nightmare? They were saying his name, sobbing it, screaming it from every direction. The walls bowed, and light shone behind the cracks in the plaster, like a train was barreling down from the sky, zeroed in on the house.

Gavin lunged for the ladder and began climbing, his hands slick with sweat and blood and God only knows what else. His feet slipped on the rungs, and beneath him, his legs felt limp and deadened with fear. Gavin had seen every horror movie played in the last four years at the Morton movie house but had never imagined anything like this. Terror gripped his heart in a solid fist, and his body didn't seem to be his own.

Pain pulsed in every muscle, and his hands wouldn't steady, his feet missed nearly every rung as he scrambled to climb.

"Stop!" he heard himself beg. "Please, *please*, stop."

Sooty dust covered the attic floor, nearly an inch thick, and as Gavin climbed inside, it billowed up, blurring the air like snowflakes in a storm, swirling. He'd tried to get into the attic when he was younger but could never manage to get the door open; the latch had been sealed shut. He wondered if something had dislodged it, if the shaking he felt under his feet had been enough to finally let it open. Or if whatever kept it closed had abandoned post, following the higher-priority order: Get him.

He frantically searched the space, gaze landing on two dormer windows on the far side of the attic. If he could get to them, somehow manage to pry them open, maybe he could get out onto the ledge, slide down the eaves, or at the very least cry for help.

He'd taken only one step when he felt something slither up his leg, cold and rough as if covered in thorns. He looked down to see a vine wrap itself around his calf and pull, knocking his feet out from under him. Pain radiated along the entire front of his body as he landed heavily on the floor. He coughed violently, and his lungs filled with dust, gagging him.

Gavin rolled to his back, trying to catch his breath. He blinked into the darkness, his vision black and fuzzy around the edges. There were shapes above him, vague shadows flitting through the trusses and exposed beams.

Sweet Gavin.

Our Gavin.

She couldn't have you either.

The vine's grip tightened, wrapping farther up his leg and around his waist, slowly dragging him back toward the attic door.

"No!" He tried to scream, still choking and gasping for air. His fingers clawed at the floor, nails dragging through the grime, splinters digging into his skin as he searched blindly for something to hold on to.

He felt himself being pulled back toward the ladder, felt the shaking all around him and wondered how the house was even still standing. Voices he'd never heard before—scratchy and thin, thick and wet—filled the hallways and rooms just below him.

Gavin.

Look what we did for you.

Gavin didn't want to die here, and he knew that if he didn't fight back, he would. The image he'd seen of his body broken at the bottom of the stairs wasn't just his imagination; it would happen. If not the stairs, it would be a tangled shower curtain holding him underwater in the bath, cookies made with rat poison, or maybe a fire while he slept. This wasn't the house he'd grown up in. It wasn't the same house that had taken care of him when he was sick and that had listened to him talk for hours about airplanes and given him books to answer his questions about the planets and stars.

Like one of Belinda Blue's little figurines in her hutch, House had kept him here as a toy under glass, and whatever was inside House would kill him before he could ever leave it.

And then it would kill Delilah.

He reached for one of the rungs on the ladder, using the leverage to kick at whatever had him. Gavin slipped part of the way down, slamming his chin against the wood and screaming out in pain. The sound must have distracted House enough that the vine's hold loosened. Gavin fell to the floor and was able to jerk away, scramble to his feet and stagger down the hall. The sound of a whip cracked through the air, and a sharp breeze snapped by his head only a pulse before the sound came again and something sliced sharply into his face. Crying out, Gavin raised his hand to his cheek and felt liquid running in a hot stream down to his neck. He could taste his blood, smell the dust in the air and the scent of rotting wood and fresh earth everywhere.

"Mom!" Tears stung at his eyes and made it hard to see in the darkness; he didn't know where he was anymore. He reached out to feel along the wall, but it seemed to undulate under his fingers, wiggling cold and wet.

He jerked away and ran blindly toward a light in front of him, the glow from a window. He could see his yard on the other side, no longer dead but lush and green. There were people out there, tossing a ball back and forth in the sunshine.

He didn't know what he was seeing, if it was real or some kind of game House was playing with him, but he didn't care. He had to get to them.

"Help!" he yelled. "Help me!"

They didn't look up. He pulled on the sash with every bit of strength he had, but it wouldn't budge. "Help!" he screamed again, pounding with bloody fists on the glass.

Gavin looked around for something to break the window. A lamp lay on the floor, as still and lifeless as any other lamp. He reached for it and slammed the base into the glass. It shattered, and the House shook, agonizing and desperate screams sounding from somewhere deep inside it. He kicked at the broken shards, ignoring the way they tore at his pant legs. This was his last hope. He climbed to the ledge and looked back behind him. Darkness swirled there, pulsing. He held his breath and jumped.

When Gavin opened his eyes again, he wasn't outside.

He tried to feel whatever was in front of him but couldn't. Pain shot through the right half of his body, and he realized that something was holding his arms to his sides, wrapping around his chest and waist and all the way down to his feet. It was a crushing pressure that made it hard for him to breathe. Every centimeter of skin ached, throbbing and bruised. He could feel the solid weight of a wall at his back, but darkness swallowed everything. He saw only black, and the weight of it surrounded him, somehow both close and deep.

There were no more voices, only his own ragged breaths as he struggled to find enough air. He would have cried out, screamed, but something covered his mouth, pressing dusty and dank against his tongue. A cloth. A gag. The yard was huge and the fence seemed to insulate the house from even the closest neighbor. Nobody would be able to hear him scream anyway.

He could smell dirt again. He wasn't sure why, but the phrase "fresh grave" drifted through his head. He wondered where the smell came from, whether House had managed to tear itself open like a wound from the top of the roof straight down to the dirt beneath it. It smelled like rotten meat and worms, and he gagged, struggling to breathe in through his mouth again.

Gavin longed for the oblivion of only a year ago. He wanted his room and his warm bed. But more than that, he wanted Delilah. He wanted her safe. Gavin knew now that even if he somehow managed to get out, he would never escape. Whatever kindness had lived here and watched over him was gone, and only a monster was left in its place. It would follow him here or down the street, or down a hundred streets. It would hunt him down until he was brought back, and then he would be here, forever. Maybe House didn't know that he wouldn't stay the same, that if it killed him he wouldn't be baby Gavin again, or even the Gavin with the ice-cream cone that hung in the upstairs hall. Those Gavins were as good as dead too.

As if House could read his thoughts, he felt something slither around him, tightening. *"Shhh,"* it hissed. *"Shhh."*

Finally, for a minute—only a *minute*—because he was mourning and terrified and blind in the blackness, Gavin let himself cry. House hadn't killed him yet. It was waiting. And if they knew each other as well as he thought they did, he knew exactly what it was waiting for.

Delilah would be waiting at the bank at eleven just like they'd planned, and she would know he wasn't coming. House knew that. And then she'd come looking for him, hoping to *save* him. House knew that, too.

It hadn't killed him yet because now he was the bait.

CHAPTER TWENTY-NINE

HER

ONCE SHE REACHED THE PORCH, DELILAH realized there were about a million things she hadn't considered until she stood here, in almost total blackness. Namely, would the front door even be unlocked? Or would she need to break through a window? She eyed the ax in her hand with a mixture of relief and dread. Were the windows even made of glass, or were they some poltergeist-filled medium that wouldn't crack or snap or shatter?

A sound built from behind the heavy wood door, a deep groan, like wind coming up from underground, rattling the frame of the house, vibrating through the shingles outside, the shuttered windows. It knew she was here. She closed her eyes, taking a steadying breath.

This is it.

Delilah drew strength from every heroine she'd ever worshipped: Buffy standing with a fist curled around a stake.

Michonne wielding her gleaming katana. Kirsty Cotton against Pinhead, Ginny versus Jason. Clarice Starling as she faced Hannibal Lecter, Alice Johnson versus Freddy Krueger—*twice*.

This house expects you to fail.

But the knowledge that Gavin would have answered the door if he were able, that he *wasn't* able and was trapped in here—*alive, please let him be alive*—propelled her forward. She lifted her hand to the knob, biting back a terrified cry and jumping away as something pressed out from the wood grain of the door, impressions of screaming beasts with horrible tortured faces, teeth dripping blood and claws that could slice her in half. They took their shape in the wood, swirling in front of her and pressing and retreating, reaching for her, and all at once Delilah had a sickening thought: What if one of them breaks free?

From the sidewalk, Vani yelled, "You must go in, Delilah!"

She looked over her shoulder to see Dhaval and Vani sprint from the car and around the side of the house. With a deep, shaking breath, Delilah quickly reached through the gnashing demons, crying out when one slashed at her forearm. Teeth sank into her flesh, and she smacked at it with her free hand, grabbing the knob.

The door shook against her, but the knob turned easily and she stumbled inside, falling onto the wooden floor as the door slammed shut behind her. With a tight popping in her ears, all outdoor sound evaporated—sealing her in—and as she looked up at the decrepit house in front of her, she wondered in a fevered heartbeat if the opposite was true: Would anyone outside be able to hear her scream?

The house looked abandoned: The furniture was crumbling, the walls were sagging and water-stained. Cobwebs hung in thick, dusty tendrils from the ceilings and in every corner. Piles of charred wood tumbled from the fireplace, ash littering the floor like dirty snow. Whatever had kept this place looking new and cared for had vacated the downstairs entirely. Delilah had a flashing fantasy that she was in the wrong house. That Gavin had simply moved down the road, and the past four months in this monster had been nothing but a figment of her wild imagination.

But a droning creak from the floorboards overhead told her that everything was above her, lying in wait upstairs.

With Gavin.

Delilah shook from the cold. The cold bothered her more than the creaking, because at least the creaking came from some distance. The cold wasn't natural; it drifted down from the ceiling, frosty and thick, and spread all along her skin, icy fingers slipping under the collar of her shirt, sliding its hands down over her breasts, her ribs. She crossed her arms over her chest, gripping her elbows so tight she could feel the knobby, rigid shape of her bones. She called out in a shaking voice, "Gavin?"

The creaking stopped, and silence hollowed out her

thoughts. *So strange*, she thought, *that silence can feel so enormous, so consuming.*

In this sort of moment Delilah had always assumed she would be either brave or mute with terror, but she felt neither of those extremes. She was alert in her fear and listening more intently than she ever had before for any single human sound.

But the next sound that came wasn't human at all. It was a mad little growl that slid from beneath an unknown doorway to her left and felt cold when it reached her. Cold and broken and evil.

The sound of wood cracking, of plaster splitting, echoed in its wake.

Delilah swallowed a surge of panic, her heart throbbing, and pushed off the banister to keep moving. Her momentum propelled her toward the stairs, and she fought the terror of the emptiness, how no furniture was visible, as if it had all gathered in one room to ambush her.

"Gavin?" she called, jumping in surprise when the television flickered to life only feet from where she stood. How had she not seen it before? Had it slid into view so quietly?

"Gavin?" her own voice echoed from the dark box, a crackly, hollow copy of herself. *"Gavin, your house is going to kill me and there's nothing you can do about it."*

"No," Delilah said, stumbling forward and pressing her body flat to the hallway wall to shimmy past the television.

The ax clanged loudly against the plaster, startling her more. "Tell me where he is."

Her own voice laughed back at her, sickly sweet and mocking. *"You can dream, Delilah."*

As the television spoke, Delilah felt tiny, hysterical sobs form in her chest and begin to push up her throat and out into the air in front of her. The voice coming from the television warped from something recognizable to a high-pitched, terrifying squeal: *"Don't cry, don't cry, crybaby, don't cry, don't cry, crybaby, cry, baby, cry."*

She could get stuck here, terrified by the television come to life and inching toward her. She could be swallowed by this moment, heart beating so hard she worried she could die from it, the fear of what she would find upstairs making her sweat, making her throat tight, making tears stream wet down her cheeks.

Or, she thought with a deep breath, she could get her ass upstairs and put the ax to use.

Shaking herself into motion, Delilah pushed past, swinging her foot as hard as she could and cracking it against the side of the television, sending it sliding into the opposite wall. A crunch of glass sounded and filled the hall. Tendrils of wallpaper rolled down from above her, crinkling at her ears, tickling at her collar and growing sharper and more savage until they pierced at the flesh of her neck.

She shoved them away, ripping at them with her hands

and kicking the television hard again, as she lunged for the banister, propelling herself up the stairs.

The house will try to swallow you, she told herself. *It will try, but you are faster. You are smarter. Find him.*

Beneath the wind and the creaking, the mad little cackles and the freezing chill in the hall, Delilah could start to make out a faint, hollow noise. Something repeatedly hitting a wall, a

thunk, thunk,

thunk,

thunk . . . thunk, thunk.

The sound wasn't immediately threatening like everything else all around her. It had real weight, real effort. Delilah flushed, struck with understanding.

"Gavin!" she screamed, taking the slick stairs two at a time, tripping over the runner rug and the edges of wood that appeared beneath her shoes. She fell, cracking her kneecap on the table at the top of the stairs and shoving it violently away. "Gavin! *Gavin!*"

The sound stopped and then picked up again, rapid now, louder and more urgent. Rubber hit plaster over and over again, and then two sounds reverberated in tandem. His feet kicking a wall? Was he unable to *speak*? Terror clawed up her throat, cutting off her breath until she felt like she was choking, running down the hall. But what was once a short length with five rooms coming off it now stretched and loomed, growing and turning in front of her, as Delilah doubled back, lost in an unending maze of turns and dead ends. The carpet slid beneath her feet, pulling her back, and she kicked at it, running along the edge of the wood floor, ducking the paintings that fell, the doors that opened in her path.

She cracked her shoulder on the bathroom door and shoved it so hard it slammed closed and cracked. Dark, thick blood poured from the gash and slid down into the hall, lapping at her heels.

No matter how far Delilah ran, how many times she circled back in the hall and opened doors and ran deeper into the maze the house built all around her, the sound of Gavin kicking the wall never diminished. It always stayed just to her left. Delilah pulled up short, catching her breath and wiping the sweat from her face.

She closed her eyes, ignoring the rising tide of blood at her heels, the cackle so close to her ear she feared whatever made the sound could touch her.

The house could build whatever illusions it wanted, but Gavin hadn't moved.

The floor shook beneath her feet when she turned and faced the wall, the air growing violently frigid as walls seemed to close in on her.

"Go," the house hissed. *"Go."*

"It's not real," she gasped, reaching in her pocket for her flashlight. "He's right there, this whole time. It's not real, Delilah. It's not real."

When the blood failed to divert her attention, a trickle of insects teased at the edge of her boots and streamed from the baseboards up under her jeans, along her skin, inner thighs to hips. She could feel them swarming up her torso, pushing her back and away from the wall that separated her from Gavin.

"It's not real!" she screamed, pointing the flashlight at the wall ahead of her to gauge where she needed to bury her ax. The entire expanse was blank, starkly white. She shoved the flashlight back in her pocket and hefted the ax. Paintings rattled and flew at her from behind, cracking into her legs, her back, and barely missing her ducked head before falling dully to the floor.

Delilah could feel the spirits, the poltergeists—the *terrors*, whatever they were—swarming her, trying to find purchase on her clothing, her flesh. It felt like flashes of heat and cold, ineffectual fingertips tugging at her, and for the first time since she entered the house, Delilah was triumphant: They were weak, physically. If they remained in the house, they would have to collapse the structure to hurt her, and they'd hurt Gavin at the same time. But without the solid shape of the house, they were nothing but a haunting.

"Gavin, back up!" she cried. "I'm coming through for you!"

A muffled cry came in response, and Delilah's hatred for the house doubled, tripled, grew so enormous it became a hot, violent thing in her blood. He was gagged in there; muted and trapped by something he'd believed all his life had *loved* him.

"You *monster*." She pulled the ax back and swung as hard as she could, straight at the wall.

The house screamed, a thousand voices, as if in pain and wild anger, and wind whipped so violently down the hall that Delilah nearly fell over, but she widened her stance and narrowed her focus, hissing through her teeth as she swung again, wrenching her shoulder painfully as the blade cracked into plaster and wood. Blood poured from the walls and something thicker—an illusion of organs, of hearts and intestines slopped onto the floor.

With a strangled cry, Delilah jumped back and gave herself three seconds to get over it.

It wasn't real.

The insects crawled up her neck, over her face, but she closed her mouth and inhaled through her nose—*it's not real; it's not real*—and took a savage, determined chop at the wall.

Swinging the ax was so different from carrying it. It was top heavy and imbalanced with the enormous blade at the top, but the momentum she got with every slice chipped into the structure bit by bit until a stream of warm air blew into the freezing hallway.

Gavin's face appeared at the gash, his mouth tied and covered with fabric, and the part of his face visible was covered in dust and dried blood, cheeks, nose, and chin scraped in a hundred tiny places, but when his wild, terrified eyes met hers, Delilah choked out a sob, desperate to get to him.

"Back up, Gav. I'm almost there. Hold on. I'm coming. I'm coming."

He nodded, eyes pleading, and disappeared from her sight.

The gash in the wall grew with every swing until Delilah's arms felt like they might fall off and the space was just large enough for her to shove her way in—around stabbing boards and scraps of carpet wrapping around her legs, her feet, her arms. She tumbled in, headfirst, and landed on top of him.

Her first instinct was to kiss his face, all over, hands tugging away the gagging, rank cloth from over his mouth, frantically untying rope that was wrapped up and down his body.

Gavin cried out when he was free, stretching his arms and arching his back as if he'd been glued like this for hours—and maybe he had. His cry was a horrible sound—hoarse and low—more tortured than anything she'd heard on her way up to get to him. It was loss and anger and the deepest, most profound terror. Had he been tied up like this the entire time they'd been apart? He looked dehydrated and weak. He looked pale and *broken*.

"Lilah," he groaned. "We have to get out of here."

She nodded, turning to hack at the hole in the wall from this side, widening it and shoving away wet scraps of tissue, of unknown, sticky gore. She felt as though she were carving through a chest, through bone and cartilage, through muscle and organ. Her hands were covered in something dark and wet; what she'd thought was wood in the walls squelched under her blade.

"Gav, take my hand."

He reached for her, shaking and stunned, and she began to guide him back through the wall. The house rocked around them, storms of dust and debris clouding around their faces. Gavin pushed Delilah through first and then crawled through the hole after her, but an enormous tremor rocked the entire structure, and with a sickening crack, Gavin's arm snapped beneath a fallen wooden plank.

He yelled in pain, eyes squeezed shut and hands wildly shoving at the board. Delilah tripped over picture frames and torn carpet to get back to where he was trapped, helping him messily free an arm that hung all wrong, that had a sick, limp twist to it. His face had gone pale, eyes glassy.

"Gavin," she gasped. Fear created a nausea inside her so intense it folded her in half. Clutching her sides, she looked up at his face. "Gavin look at me." His eyes searched the area near her forehead, her cheeks, and then lit up when he caught her gaze. "We just have to get out, okay? We just have to get out of here, and then we can go, and it will be what we wanted. I'm not leaving you. You have to stand up and walk with me down the stairs, through the kitchen, and out to the backyard."

He nodded, mute and clearly in profound shock. She didn't know how long he would stand the pain—it had to be unfathomable, and from the way his face twisted in agony, she knew they had to move fast. Delilah had never had this sick, anxious feeling before, and the only thing she could think was that they needed to escape. The step after that didn't matter. They just had to get out before the house collapsed all around them. Delilah looked up at the cracked hallway ceiling, at the floor with a long, jagged crease all down the center. The house had been blocking their escape, but so far she'd managed it. She had no idea how they were going to actually get to the backyard.

When he stood, Gavin swayed against the wall, grunting in pain. His eyes screwed shut, and with his good hand, he reached for her, grappling for support. His right arm swung loosely at his side, as if the bone inside had simply turned to dust.

"Look what you did!" she screamed at the house as she tore her vest from her body and helped Gavin use it to wrap his arm. "*Look what you did to him!* He loved you! He needed you! You've trapped him and scared him *and broken him*!"

Dust settled and the walls ceased their groaning. On the floor, the carpet lay still, and it was so quiet, not the calm before the storm, but the calm after—when, at last, there's a comparison to make: the chaos before and the quiet that follows.

But Delilah didn't trust the silence that trailed behind them as she helped Gavin stand and they stumbled back down the hall. It was the same hall as always, leading to solid steps, which led to the foyer, to the dining room, to the kitchen.

Delilah could feel every one of the phantoms behind her, pressing into the air at her back as they walked through the cold, silent kitchen and out the door.

Just like that.

Except the quiet dissolved into a horrible, black storm above them when the spirits of the house noticed Dhaval, kneeling on the grass and beckoning to them with eyes so full of courage and confidence that Delilah let her legs give out, tumbling with Gavin onto the grass and wrapping her arms around his wildly jerking shoulders.

"Stay with me," she whispered into his ear. "Stay with me, okay?"

He nodded, wordless still, and pressed his face to the damp skin of her neck, taking these huge, gulping breaths. Delilah had no idea what happened now. The lawn was dead and brittle beneath their knees. The trees were cracking in the wind. There was no fruit, no sense of family here. And none of this might work in the end. Delilah, Vani, Dhaval, and Gavin could anger these specters, bring them all out here into a furious storm of evil in the yard, and still they could fail.

Looking at Gavin, Delilah knew it was likely for all of them to die out here.

It was such a profoundly calm thought: *We could die right now*. The phantoms seemed torn—did they stay near Gavin or go to Dhaval?—but they could easily uproot a tree, crash down the house, open up the lawn into a yawning, jagged chasm and swallow them all.

The ground shook beneath them, and inside the house was an unending series of crashes: walls falling, furniture hurling, windows shattering inward as the spirits left and pooled in the air outside.

It was impossible to focus on only one of the hundreds of blurry spots in the sky, the ripples of glassy heat. But she could *feel* them, not just swirling but churning, screaming above her in a terrifying roar.

Not twenty feet from where she bent over Gavin's huddled body, Vani and Dhaval kneeled, arms around each other as they yelled and pleaded for these spirits to be taken back.

It was impossibly loud. Their urgent prayers. The poltergeists screaming and drumming above them in trees. The crumbling frame of the house.

Movement caught her eye, behind the swarm of terrors around her and inside the house: arms frantic, hands slamming to glass, mouth open in a silent scream.

A woman. It was a woman standing at the window, screaming.

Delilah cried out, pushing up onto her knees. Beside her Gavin let out a low groan.

It was a trap.

It wasn't real.

But if it was

if it was

if it was

Gavin would never forgive himself for leaving without her.

Stumbling to her feet, Delilah laid Gavin down on the grass.

"Lilah," he gasped. "Don't go back in there—"

But she was already charging back inside, holding her arms in front of her face to block the assault of debris and dust and dark, rotting earth. The kitchen had begun to cave, and she leaped over a wide crack in the floor, barreling down the hall toward the foyer. The stairs were a crumbling, slanting mess, and Delilah had to use the ax to grip at the rubble. Wood and glass tore at her clothes, her skin, her hair, and once she reached the top of the pile, Delilah gulped down a huge lungful of chalky air to stave off the panic at having no idea where she was inside the house.

"Hilary! Call out to me!" she screamed.

A thud sounded from the back of the house, deep at the end of the hallway. It could have been someone throwing something against a wall. Or, from the looks of the deteriorating house, it could just as easily have been something falling from a wall or through the attic floor. It could have been a room falling to pieces. But only seconds later, Delilah heard a thin, terrified wail. Without listening for more, Delilah sprinted over shattered wood and plaster, slamming against a wall and pounding at it with the ax.

The walls were dry, splintery wood, and with a lurch in

her stomach, she registered she wasn't battling a house pos-sessed as much as an ancient house on the verge of crumbling beneath her feet.

Chopping through the wall with exhausted, rubbery arms, Delilah began to sob, feeling the leaded weight of insan-ity pushing in on her. She sucked in giant, gulping breaths, released shrill, hysterical wails. Was there even anyone there? Had she lost her mind? Would she die in this falling-down house after all?

But then she sliced through, creating a hole only inches wide, and her heart stopped beating.

A woman stood inside.

She was tiny. Withered. Her wild, dark hair had gone mostly gray; her back had grown bent and arms turned skinny and weak.

"Delilah."

Delilah's mouth opened, and her tear-soaked eyes went wide. "Hilary?"

"I'm awake," the woman croaked. "Get me out of here."

There wasn't time to think about how long she'd been here, how she knew Delilah's name, or whether she was even real at all. Delilah hacked at the wall savagely, making the hole big enough for Hilary to climb through, and grabbed her hand. She yanked her out, ignoring the sound of fabric ripping, the cry when something sharp stabbed into Hilary's leg. Delilah fell backward, pulling her out, and then stood, tripping down the hall with Gavin's mother in tow as the house fell to pieces in their wake: ceilings crumbling into dust, floors disintegrating, walls bursting into fire. They fell down the pile of stairs, and Delilah had to nearly carry the woman down the hall to the kitchen and out the back door as fire chased them and singed the back of Delilah's shirt, the bottom of her braid.

Delilah fell onto the grass beside Gavin, curling her body over his and sobbing harder as it all seemed to hit her: She could have died in there, and then who would have looked after Gavin?

Hilary collapsed beside them, and Gavin turned, staring in shock. He shook, quaking violently in Delilah's arms.

"Is that?"

"I think so."

He reached out with his good arm, taking Hilary's hand. She was unconscious, a tiny lump of dark clothing on the lawn.

The fire in the kitchen grew, crackling into a thunder, and Delilah knew with absolute certainly now was either when they triumphed or it all ended. Shadows dug into her clothes, cold fingers sliding across skin. Her ears rang with the tortured screeches of the wordless poltergeists, and for tiny flashes she could see their gaping mouths, rank and putrid, so close to her face until they dissolved back into shadow. Pulsing at her, storming around her. Closer and away on an endless loop, their breath smelled like a century of rot and despair; the lash of their shapeless bodies felt like ice slashing her cheeks.

She'd never known such sound, such terror. It was impossible to cover Gavin with her body, but she tried, her shoulders shaking under the strain as she curled over him, arms wrapped around his head as if to shield him.

He'd gone still. Completely motionless in her arms, and if she couldn't feel the tiny warmth of his exhales on her neck, she would have feared he'd stopped breathing. He could barely take another minute of it—she knew—and she couldn't begin to comprehend his grief and horror and loss. His cheeks were wet with tears, face pressed into her neck so tight she knew she would feel the imprint forever.

The wind whipped through her hair. A million points of pressure leaned in on her, on them from all sides, trying to peel her away from him. Delilah held on, screaming back at them in the dark-as-night sky.

Dhaval and Vani crawled over to them, wrapping their arms around Gavin and yelling reassurances over the chaotic screams:

"We won't let you have him."

"You can't have him."

After all of it, the cold and screeching, the sight of their terrible, mangled not-faces, a clarity hit Delilah like a warm gust: *They can't hurt me like this, not really.* Her scratches were from the things they hurled, not the terrors themselves. Without the house they were nothing.

The sky rippled and cleared, and with a slight pull in her

chest and a popping in her ears, the world trembled and then fell completely silent.

It was so silent, in fact, that it felt pressurized, as if they'd been sealed inside a jar. It pushed at her ears, pulling, pulling, pulling away until the world seemed to snap and the breeze returned, coursing through the brittle branches of the cherry tree. The smell of spring in the mud and grass beneath their knees mingled with the burned wood and crumbled concrete. Gavin looked up at the house, and her gaze followed his.

It was barely standing: nails hung loosely from shingles, paint curled in long strips, bowing to the ground. Windows were shattered, the porch nearly collapsed. It looked like it had been lifted in a tornado and dropped in the yard.

It looked completely lifeless.

And then he turned and stared at his mother, his face crumpling.

Delilah closed her eyes, collapsing into Gavin, and didn't open them again until the sun shone through a window and a gentle hand shook her awake.

CHAPTER THIRTY

HIM

S HE WAS SO BRAVE. HE COUNTED SEVENTEEN stitches on her face alone, but when she opened her eyes and saw him, it wasn't panic in her expression or fear. It was relief.

She sat up slowly, looking around, and finally took in his outfit: a cotton gown.

"We're in the hospital," he explained. "They brought us here after . . . well."

Although his memory of the past day and a half was a turbulent mix of images mostly fragmented by shock and horror, Gavin did remember it took a lot of calm, whispered assurances to separate him and Delilah last night after they'd put his mother in an ambulance and driven away. The way he clung to Delilah was one of the few things his mind pulled from the chaos of the flashing lights, the reporters, the madness of discovery.

He remembered begging the paramedic to let him stay with Delilah in the ambulance.

He remembered after an hour of confusion, of policemen and firemen and paramedics swarming the block, the woman—Gayle—brought there specifically for him, to handle him. It sank in for everyone around the same time: Gavin had always believed he'd been there alone. But he hadn't: His mother had been trapped there, kept barely alive in a secret room just beside his.

Gayle held him, promising him over and over that no one was taking Delilah away from him.

He might have felt a little mortified over his hysteria if he still didn't feel the tickle of it in his chest and all along his spine.

But eventually, with Gayle's gentle assurances and Delilah's parents standing shell-shocked and mute in the background, Gavin had let them tend to his shattered arm while they loaded an unconscious Delilah into a separate ambulance.

"After all *that*, I passed out?" she asked, looking horrified.

A small smile curved his mouth. "I'd say it was the best time to pass out. I'm actually going to thank you for not passing out sooner."

"Are you okay?" She reached for him, pulling him close, shaking violently as it seemed to come back to her. That jerking recollection had happened to him, too, this morning, waking under a haze of sedatives that weren't strong enough to make him forget. "Gavin, oh my God."

Her arms shook, and he knew she was sore and bruised from swinging the ax, from the fragments of House that rained down on her for God knows how long while she tried to get to him and, later, his mother.

Holding on to her, he told her what he could remember: that he thought police arrived only a minute or so after the strange silence hit. That they'd initially handcuffed Dhaval and Vani, questioned Gavin, but despite their skepticism, there wasn't much doubt that something truly supernatural had happened. The house was virtually crumbling. Furniture was embedded in walls, in trees outside. Fires had started in tiny discrete pockets. And, most horribly, there was his badly malnourished mother whom no one had seen in nearly seventeen years. Apparently, Gavin had been so terrified when he'd seen her under the police lights that he had been unable to stop screaming for several minutes.

The town, the state, and soon the entire world would know what had happened last night at the Patchwork House.

Gavin didn't think he had more tears, but he did after all. He had tears and bewildered words and more grief than he knew what to do with.

Delilah held him, careful not to jostle his casted arm, speaking quietly about their life together after this, the love she felt for him and what they'd managed to do together. He knew she was right: This was how it had to happen, if not yesterday than at some point in the future, because whatever was in House—whatever had raised him, loved him, sequestered him, and eventually tortured him—had also locked his mother up his entire life, simply so that it could keep Gavin all to itself.

But even now it was hard to forget a time when it wasn't so very terrible.

Gavin pressed his lips to her neck, screwing his eyes closed. The air felt completely empty, unburdened from the weight of the spirits that had tracked him his whole life. Past this moment of shock, and anguish, with her arms around his neck, he could truly breathe for the first time in what felt like forever.

Delilah curled into his side, running a warm hand over his ribs and up his neck, into his hair. Beneath them, the blankets bunched on the mats they'd put on the floor of the music room. They hardly ever had time alone lately, but here in their secret fortress, when the clock hovered between two and three in the morning, and where they were so close together Delilah's warm bare skin slid over his every time she breathed, he could forget the frenzy of the past two weeks.

"Puget Sound," she said, kissing his chin.

He looked down into her wide blue eyes. "Why there and not Northwestern? Or Harvard?"

They had their pick, after all. After the Silence, as Gavin and Delilah thought of it—or after the Falling of Patchwork House, as everyone else did—they were the darlings of the world's media. Even with the blistering attention of the press, there were some perks. Donations, for one. A full ride to any college, for another. And the new, warm concern of a million strangers. Gavin had gone from having no parents to having a planet full of them, including one birth mother who would be released from the hospital in a matter of days.

He saw her every day, spent hours sitting by her bed and reading her books, playing her music, telling stories of things he did when he'd left the house and she couldn't hear him moving around. The house had let her watch him sleep; let her listen when he practiced Piano. It had brought her out, in a trance, when it needed a signature, a parent to send away the school official, Social Services, and once, the police. But her memories were fragmented and—worse—her guilt was consuming. Gavin worked frantically to reassure her in his time with her that his life had been good.

He had been cherished, actually.

Every day she seemed to believe him a little more; she'd seen it with her own eyes, after all. Yesterday she'd even smiled.

At length, Delilah admitted, "I think I want to be near water."

It seemed to be such a specific request, but he could understand it. Nothing could be more different from the landlocked suburbia of Morton than an archipelago of islands and water going on forever.

"Okay."

"Just like that?"

He smiled, kissing her jaw. "Just like that."

"Will Hilary be able to come?"

He blinked away and shrugged. His mother was a mess physically, but emotionally, too, she was broken. "I know she'll be near us eventually. I don't know if she'll be able to right away." He knew Delilah heard the implied, unspoken message: *We'll bring her to us as soon as she's ready. I'm not staying in Morton a day longer than I have to.*

"Gavin?"

"Hmm?" He pulled back to look down at her, and his heart tripped a little inside his throat at the determined look in her eyes. Gavin didn't think it was possible to keep feeling more, but he did. More admiration and lust and gratitude and adoration. At least for now his world still felt tiny; other than his stranger-mother, Delilah was his only person, but she was such a consuming presence he only really wanted her near him while the shock ebbed and the reality of this new, odd life took shape.

"I love you," she said simply.

"I love you, too."

"We can do this, you know?" She ran a soft fingertip over a scratch on his cheek that had nearly healed and then slowly rubbed his lower lip, distracting him. "Eventually people will forget about us. Your mom will be better. She'll find a way to be okay. Maybe not for a while, but after we graduate, it's going to be what *we* wanted. College in a new town, just us. Living in an apartment together."

He bent, kissing her as he rolled her to her back, hovering above. Her legs slid up his sides, her hair spread out beneath her, and while he loved the image of the future she described, he couldn't deny how much he appreciated this view, too.

"You mean someday we'll do this on a real bed?" he asked, giving her the smile she liked, the hungry one that made her eyes go unfocused and her cheeks heat.

She nodded, dazed, but it was almost impossible for either of them to imagine, he knew. It wasn't easy to process all of this. Their lives would never be normal after what had happened.

He kissed her with his smiling mouth. He didn't need normal. He didn't even *know* normal, and she'd never seemed to want it anyway.